CW01313860

THE DEVIL'S SYMPHONY
VATICAN ARCHAEOLOGY THRILLERS
BOOK TWO

GARY MCAVOY

LITERATI
EDITIONS.

The Devil's Symphony

Vatican Archaeology Thrillers series - Book 2

Copyright © 2025 by Gary McAvoy

All rights reserved. No part of this publication may be reproduced, distributed, or transmitted in any form or by any means, including photocopying, recording, or other electronic or mechanical methods, without the prior written permission of the publisher, except in the case of brief quotations embodied in critical reviews and certain other noncommercial uses permitted under current copyright law. For permission requests, write to the publisher using the email or postal address below.

Hardcover ISBN: 978-1-954123-67-0
Paperback ISBN: 978-1-954123-68-7
eBook ISBN: 978-1-954123-66-3

Library of Congress Control Number: 2025903563

Published by:
Literati Editions
PO Box 5987
Bremerton WA 98312
Email: info@LiteratiEditions.com
Visit the author's website: GaryMcAvoy.com
R0525b

This is a work of fiction. Names, characters, businesses, places, long-standing institutions, agencies, public offices, events, locales, and incidents are either the products of the author's imagination or have been used in a fictitious manner. Apart from historical references, any resemblance to actual persons, living or dead, or actual events is purely coincidental.

All trademarks are property of their respective owners. Neither Gary McAvoy nor Literati Editions is associated with any product or vendor mentioned in this book.

This book contains original and copyrighted material that is not intended to be used for the purpose of training Artificial Intelligence (AI) systems. The author and publisher of this book prohibit the use of any part of this book for AI training, machine learning, or any other similar purpose without prior written permission.

The author and publisher do not endorse or authorize the use of this book for AI training, and shall not be liable for any damages arising from such unauthorized use. Any unauthorized use of this book for AI training is strictly prohibited and may violate applicable laws and regulations.

The author and publisher reserve all rights, including but not limited to, the right to seek damages and injunctive relief, against any person or entity that uses this book for AI training without prior written permission.

If you wish to use any part of this book for AI training, please contact the author and publisher to obtain written permission.

BOOKS BY GARY MCAVOY
FICTION

FICTION

The Devil's Symphony

The Hildegard Seeds

Covenant of the Iron Cross

The Apostle Conspiracy

The Celestial Guardian

The Confessions of Pope Joan

The Galileo Gambit

The Jerusalem Scrolls

The Avignon Affair

The Petrus Prophecy

The Opus Dictum

The Vivaldi Cipher

The Magdalene Veil

The Magdalene Reliquary

The Magdalene Deception

NONFICTION

And Every Word Is True

Supernatural: *adjective*

A manifestation or event attributed to some force beyond scientific understanding or the laws of nature.

PROLOGUE

APPENZELL, SWITZERLAND - 1775

A bitter winter storm raged outside the isolated château at the foot of the Alpstein mountains, its howling winds battering the ancient stone walls. Within, the air was heavy with the acrid scent of burning herbs and the pungent tang of molten metals. The room was dimly lit, its only illumination coming from dozens of black candles arranged in a wide circle, their flickering flames casting eerie, shifting shadows on the vaulted ceiling.

In the center of the room stood Vincenzo Malvagio, an elderly man of unearthly composure, his gaunt face framed by long, jet-black hair streaked with silver. A crimson robe hung from his shoulders, embroidered with arcane symbols that seemed to ripple in the candlelight. Around him knelt eleven figures, similarly robed, their heads bowed as they chanted in a guttural, unnatural tongue that resonated with the stones of the château itself.

Before Malvagio, on an intricately carved oak table, sat an object of unparalleled craftsmanship: a music box, unlike anything the world had ever seen. It was roughly the size of a small shoebox, though it seemed to swallow more air than it displaced. Its casing was forged from a curious alloy, the dark metal veined with gold and silver, and adorned with engraved sigils of unknown origin. The lid featured a mosaic of tiny gemstones arranged to depict a serpent devouring its own tail—the Ouroboros, a symbol of eternity and the cycle of creation and destruction.

Malvagio's thin hands moved deftly over the box as he whispered incantations, his voice barely audible over the chanting. Beside him, an iron brazier smoked, filled with a blend of rare herbs: dried belladonna, mandrake root, and wolfsbane. Their smoke coiled upward, merging with the fragrance of frankincense and myrrh, creating a cloying fog that thickened the very air.

The music box had taken Malvagio over forty years to create, each component meticulously crafted under conditions dictated by forbidden texts. The tiny gears and springs were alloyed with metals harvested during lunar eclipses, and the box's mechanisms were lubricated with oil infused with the essence of nightshade. The heart of the box uniquely employed crystals and jewels of specific sizes and characters to emanate sounds with clarity and precision. Below them, a spindle with a scrolled musical score awaited activation. A single piece of black onyx, its surface carved with a sigil said to bind infernal forces, served as the winding key to begin the movement of the spindle.

Tonight, the final step in its creation would take place.

Malvagio raised his hands, and the chanting ceased. The room plunged into a pregnant silence, broken only by the faint crackle of the brazier's embers. His voice rang out, clear and commanding, as he addressed the assembled cultists.

"Tonight, we summon the eternal power. Tonight, we defy the heavens and bring forth a melody that will resonate with the forces of creation and destruction."

He gestured to the music box. "Behold, the Vessel. Through it, we shall transcend the mortal plane and harness the song of the eternal. Prepare yourselves, for the symphony begins."

The cultists resumed their chant, louder and more fervently, their voices intertwining in a discordant harmony that made the very air itself vibrate. Malvagio retrieved a vial of thick, crimson liquid—blood from a freshly slaughtered black goat—and dipped his thumb in it. He smeared the viscous red liquid across his lower lips, symbolic of the sacrifices to come.

He wound the onyx key with deliberate precision, each turn accompanied by an almost imperceptible hum, as if the box were awakening. When the key reached its limit, he stepped back and reached for an ornate baton, then raised his arms high.

"Now, witness the birth of *The Purification Symphony!*"

With a sharp click, the music box began to play.

At first, the sound was faint, almost gentle: a single, haunting note that lingered in the air like a ghostly sigh. Then a second note joined it, and another, until a full melody emerged. The tune was unlike anything human ears had ever heard. It was achingly beautiful yet profoundly unsettling, a harmony of sweetness and malice, as if an angel and a demon were locked in a duet.

The effect on the room was immediate. The cultists, still chanting, faltered as their voices wavered. Some clutched their heads, as though the sound was burrowing into their minds. Others began to tremble, their chants dissolving into gasps and cries.

The candles' flames flickered wildly, casting the room into moments of near-darkness. Then, one by one, the flames extinguished, leaving only the glow emanating from the music box itself. The box pulsed with an unnatural light, shifting between hues of deep crimson and pallid green. The air grew heavier, charged with a dark energy that pressed down on everyone in the room.

A low, resonant hum filled the space, growing louder and deeper until it became a physical force. The walls of the château groaned as though under immense pressure, and cracks began to spiderweb across the stone floor.

One of the cultists, a young woman with fear etched into her features, let out a scream and fled toward the door. She barely made it three steps before an unseen force flung her backward, slamming her into the far wall. Her body crumpled to the ground, motionless.

Another cultist collapsed to his knees, tears streaming down his face as he muttered prayers in a desperate attempt to ward off the growing darkness. The others fared no better. Some clawed at their robes, as if trying to escape an invisible grasp; others fell unconscious, overcome by the oppressive energy.

Malvagio alone remained unaffected. He stood motionless, arms outstretched, baton held high, his eyes fixed on the music box, a twisted smile playing on his lips.

"Do you feel it?" he whispered, his voice barely audible over the cacophony of the melody. "The power of creation. The breath of destruction. It is *ours*."

As the melody neared a crescendo, the music box began to vibrate violently. The glow intensified, becoming blinding. The air was filled with an ear-splitting sound, a dissonant chord that seemed to tear at the fabric of reality itself.

One of the cultists, an older man with trembling hands, crawled toward Malvagio. His voice, weak and broken, carried a note of desperate pleading.

"You must destroy it," he croaked. "This... this is not purification. It is damnation."

Malvagio looked down at him, his expression devoid of sympathy. "You fear what you do not understand, Lucius. But I? I have seen the future. And it sings."

Then, with a deafening crack, the light from the box exploded outward, engulfing the room. For a brief moment, the music paused, everything was still. When the light faded, the room was left in utter darkness, save for the faint, residual glow of the box. Shadowed forms swirled in the gloom, ready, anxious, to burst forth into the world, as the music swelled once again and reached for its final climactic chords.

Malvagio's eyes widened, and he reached a trembling hand toward the miracle music box of his own creation, picked it up carefully, cradling it as one might a newborn child. He looked at his convulsing and crippled followers, at the demon shadows awaiting to enter at the final score's chords, his hand clutching the box, his mind grasping at a realization.

Moments later, outside, the storm continued to rage, its howling winds carrying the faintest echo of the melody—a sound that would linger in the world, waiting for the next time it would be played.

CHAPTER ONE

PRESENT DAY

The heavy oak door groaned on its ancient hinges as Marcus Russo stepped into the dimly lit chamber deep within the Vatican's Secret Archives. The subterranean room, sealed since the eighteenth century, carried an almost sacred stillness, its air thick with the scent of centuries-old parchment, decayed leather, and stone dust. The faint glow of Marcus's lantern cast long, flickering shadows on the walls, illuminating rows of untouched shelves laden with forgotten relics.

"Dr. Russo, are you sure about this?" Gideon Dandolo, a young archivist, asked nervously as he trailed behind Marcus. His voice wavered, and he clutched a clipboard to his chest like a shield.

Marcus didn't respond immediately. His attention was focused on the intricacies of the room. The architecture was unlike other parts of the Archives, with carved pillars featuring symbols and sigils he recognized as protective wards. The air felt heavier here, as if the room itself were holding its breath.

"This room hasn't been opened for over two hundred years," Marcus finally said, his voice low but steady. He pointed to the door's rusted iron mechanism. "Sealed by papal decree. It's rare to find something this well preserved."

Gideon nodded, though his wide eyes darted nervously to the dark corners of the room. "The records suggest this chamber was closed during the papacy of Pius VI. They described it as... dangerous."

Marcus's brow furrowed as he ran a gloved hand over the closest shelf. The layer of dust was thick, but the objects beneath it were intact. Marcus had been hired as the Chief Archaeologist for the Vatican, which had taken him to deserts and mountains and valleys throughout the world in search of Church artifacts. But he had recently realized that unearthing the myriad objects already secured, but unrecorded, in the Vatican Archives was just as intensive and enlightening as exploring caches in caves or digging for ruins in sand. Among the artifacts before him now were aged tomes with cracked spines, strange metal instruments, and ornate chests. The sigils on the walls confirmed his suspicions: this was a repository for items deemed heretical or too volatile for the outside world.

"Artifacts linked to heretical movements," Marcus murmured, mostly to himself. He brushed the dust from the cover of a leather-bound ledger. Its surface bore an embossed fleur-de-lis intertwined with an inverted cross. "The question is, why weren't these items destroyed instead of hidden?"

Gideon's voice dropped to a whisper. "Maybe they feared destroying them would unleash... something worse?"

Marcus didn't answer. He didn't have to. The thought had already crossed his mind.

He continued his exploration, his tall, broad-shouldered frame casting an imposing silhouette against the ancient walls. At fifty-three, his once jet-black hair had surrendered to distinguished silver at the temples, framing a face weathered by decades of fieldwork across five continents. Deep-set brown eyes, sharp and observant beneath thick brows, missed nothing as they scanned the chamber. His Roman ancestry was evident in his aquiline nose and strong jawline, though years of academic intensity had etched permanent lines around his eyes and mouth. Unlike many of his colleagues who preferred the comfort of university lecture halls, Marcus's sun-darkened skin and calloused hands spoke of an archaeologist who believed knowledge was found in dirt and stone, not just in books.

"Catalog everything carefully," he instructed. "Photographs, descriptions, the works. Nothing leaves this room until we've assessed it properly. Understood?"

Gideon nodded, setting down his clipboard and snapping on a pair of gloves. But as they worked in silence, Marcus couldn't shake the unease growing in the pit of his stomach. This was no ordinary chamber. It felt alive, as if it were watching them.

HOURS PASSED as Marcus and Gideon meticulously examined the artifacts. Most were what Marcus had expected: esoteric texts, forbidden relics, and alchemical tools. But as Gideon opened a small, unassuming chest tucked in the far corner of the room, he let out a sharp gasp.

"Dr. Russo," Gideon called, his voice tinged with awe and unease.

Marcus turned, his lantern casting light over the object Gideon held aloft. It was an ancient music box unlike any Marcus had ever seen. The dark metal casing gleamed faintly, etched with intricate Latin inscriptions that appeared to writhe in the flickering light. Interspersed with the inscriptions were occult symbols Marcus instantly recognized: sigils of binding and protection, alongside others whose meaning eluded him.

"Handle that gently," Marcus instructed, swiftly crossing the room. His tone startled Gideon, who froze mid-motion.

"It's beautiful," Gideon murmured, his fingers tracing the delicate carvings. "And these markings... they look like some kind of alchemical formula."

Marcus's unease deepened as he leaned closer. "Those markings aren't just alchemical. They're ceremonial. And this isn't just a music box—it's a vessel." Just then a call came to Marcus through his earpiece, which he pressed to his ear. The reception in the Archives for phone signals was poor at best.

In the meantime, Gideon's curiosity outpaced his caution. Before Marcus turned back and could stop him, the archivist twisted the onyx key embedded in the side of the box. An acute click echoed through the chamber, followed by the first notes of a melody.

It was unlike anything Marcus had ever heard. The music was hauntingly beautiful, each note achingly precise, yet there was an unsettling undercurrent to it, a discordant whisper that he felt crawl just beneath his skin. The melody filled the room, vibrating in the very air around them. By then the call on his earpiece had already cut out, and he turned to the archivist.

"Gideon, stop that... Now!" Marcus ordered, his voice rising. But Gideon didn't respond. He fixed his wide eyes on the box, his expression one of rapture and terror.

The melody grew louder, its resonance almost palpable. Marcus felt the hair on his arms stand on end, and an inexplicable chill swept through the chamber.

"Gideon!" Marcus shouted, shaking the young man's shoulder.

The archivist let out a strangled gasp and crumpled to the ground, and the music box slipped from his grasp and landed on the cold stone floor. As it struck the hard surface, the melody ceased abruptly, leaving a ringing silence in its wake. Surprisingly, it appeared unscathed, which Marcus couldn't say for his young helper.

He knelt beside Gideon, who was pale and trembling. His lips moved, mumbling incoherent phrases. Marcus leaned closer, catching fragments: "Shadows... watching... the melody... devours..."

A flicker of movement caught Marcus's eye. He looked up abruptly. The chamber, which had been still and silent moments before, now pulsed with an unnatural energy. The lantern's light flickered, casting shadows that danced and twisted across the walls. For an instant, Marcus could have sworn the shadows were reaching toward him.

The temperature in the room plummeted. A sudden gust of wind blew through the chamber, though there were no windows or openings. The sigils carved into the walls seemed to glow faintly, their protective power straining against the growing darkness.

His instincts screamed at him to leave—to get this cursed artifact as far from the Archives as possible. Grabbing the music box, Marcus wrapped it hastily in a cloth and shoved it into his satchel. He hauled Gideon to his feet, half-carrying the dazed archivist toward the chamber's exit.

As they stumbled into the main hall of the Archives, the oppressive energy lifted slightly, though Marcus's unease only deepened. He fumbled for his cell phone, not trusting his earpiece this time, dialing Secretary of State Cardinal Severino with trembling fingers, hoping he could get through quickly.

"Your Eminence, I'm calling on a matter of some urgency," Marcus said as soon as the call connected. "We've found something in the sealed chamber of the Archives. Something that may be dangerous."

The cardinal's voice was calm but firm. "What kind of something, Dr. Russo?"

Marcus glanced at the satchel slung over his shoulder, the faint weight of the music box pressing against him like a physical warning.

"A relic, possibly tied to occult practices," he replied. "It's already had... an effect on one of my team. I need your authorization to secure it immediately."

After Marcus ended the call, he turned to Gideon, who was still pale but more alert. The young man's eyes darted nervously around the room, and he whispered a single, chilling phrase: "The shadows are awake."

Marcus's grip on the satchel tightened. Whatever they had unearthed, it was far more than a relic. And he knew, deep in his gut, that this was only the beginning.

CHAPTER
TWO

The Vatican was a fortress of routine and tradition, a place where centuries of discipline had shaped its halls into an ordered sanctuary. But that serenity was shattered in the days following the discovery of the music box.

Marcus Russo noticed it first. As he made his way to the Archives early one morning, the air in the corridor felt unusually cold. The chill wasn't the type that came from poor insulation or an open window. It was deeper, pervasive, and clung to his skin like an unwelcome presence. Shivering, Marcus pulled his coat tighter around him as he passed a Swiss Guard on patrol.

"Cold today, isn't it?" he said, trying to sound casual.

The guard hesitated before nodding. "Yes, Dr. Russo. But... it's strange, isn't it? The temperature drops so suddenly in these halls lately."

Marcus offered a polite smile and moved on, but unease prickled at his spine. This wasn't the first time he had heard such a remark. Over the past two days, whispers had begun to circulate among the Vatican staff. Clerics and archivists spoke in hushed tones about odd occurrences: doors closing on their own, faint voices murmuring in empty rooms, and statues seeming to shift their expressions in the flickering candlelight.

That morning, as Marcus entered the Archives, he saw Gideon sitting stiffly at his desk, his face pale and drawn.

"Gideon," Marcus greeted him, setting down his satchel. "You look like you've seen a ghost."

Gideon's eyes darted around the room. "Maybe I have," he whispered. "Last night, I came in to finish cataloging the artifacts. I heard... something. A voice, I think. But no one was here. And then the lights—they flickered, like a storm was coming."

Marcus frowned. Gideon wasn't the type to scare easily, but the previous week's incident had left the young man uneasy ever since. "You should take the day off," he said. "Get some rest."

Gideon shook his head. "It's not just me, Dr. Russo. Everyone's talking about it. They're saying the chamber... the things we uncovered... they may be cursed."

Marcus dismissed him with a reassuring smile, though the knot in his stomach tightened. As he moved deeper into the Archives, he noticed the air growing colder the closer he came to where the music box had been secured. It was still wrapped in cloth and locked away in a reinforced cabinet, but its presence was undeniable, like a sleeping predator waiting to wake.

BY THE AFTERNOON, Marcus knew he couldn't investigate this alone. He needed someone who understood the Vatican's spiritual and historical complexities—someone who could approach the problem from angles beyond archaeology. That person was Father Michael Dominic.

Michael was already in his office at the Archives when Marcus called him. Dressed in his simple black cassock, he exuded an air of calm authority that immediately steadied Marcus's nerves. Michael, more than a decade younger than Marcus, was as enthused as he was about the discoveries that history could bring to light for the world. Michael's penchant for early morning runs and fresh food gave him the same athletic appearance as the archaeologist, and the two easily turned the heads of female colleagues and parishioners. Much to the chagrin of the women, however, Marcus's passions ran to the intellectual and Michael's to the spiritual.

"Marcus," Michael greeted, clasping his hand firmly. "You sounded urgent. What's going on?"

Marcus gestured for him to follow. "I need your expertise on an artifact we discovered in a sealed chamber in the underground Archives annex. It's unlike anything I've ever encountered. And... there have been unusual phenomena since it was uncovered."

Michael raised an eyebrow but said nothing, letting Marcus lead him to the secured cabinet. As Marcus unlocked it, he explained the artifact's context.

"As you know, the chamber was sealed in the eighteenth century," Marcus began. "It contained items linked to heretical movements. But this... this music box stood out."

Michael leaned forward as Marcus unwrapped the box. The dark metal gleamed in the low light, its intricate engravings catching Michael's eye. He reached out but stopped short of touching it.

"The craftsmanship is exquisite," Michael said. "These

symbols... they're not random. That's a binding sigil, and here..." He pointed to another engraving. "That's the mark of an alchemist's guild that operated in Appenzell, Switzerland during the 1700s. They were notorious for their experiments in combining music and mysticism."

Marcus nodded. "I've read about them. They believed certain melodies could alter the natural world—invoke storms, heal wounds, even summon spirits. But it was all theory. Superstition."

Michael's expression darkened. "Superstition or not, this box may be far from benign. You said there have been... phenomena?"

Marcus recounted the cold spots, the whispers, and Gideon's strange experiences.

Michael listened intently, his brow furrowing.

"These are classic signs of spiritual disturbance," he said. "If this artifact is tied to the Appenzell Guild, they may have created it for a specific ritual. One that could still be resonating through time."

Marcus crossed his arms, his skepticism warring with his growing unease. "You think the music box is still active? After all this time?"

Michael's gaze met his. "Though I'm generally skeptical of such things, I think we'd be foolish to dismiss the possibility out of hand."

THAT EVENING, Marcus and Michael met with Cardinal Severino in the cardinal's private study. The room was a stark contrast to the cold, shadowed Archives—warm light from a crackling fire bathed the richly paneled walls and rows of theological texts.

Severino listened intently as the two men presented

their findings. Marcus outlined the artifact's discovery and the disturbances that followed, while Michael explained its potential ties to the Appenzell Guild. Marcus ended their explanation by informing the cardinal that the young archivist helping him, the one who first played the music box, hadn't been the same since the incident, and finally had to be hospitalized.

When they finished, Severino leaned back in his chair, steepling his fingers. "This is troubling," he said. "Artifacts like these have the potential to undermine the Church's authority. We cannot allow word of this to spread."

Marcus bristled. "With all due respect, Your Eminence, this isn't just about preserving appearances. We already have one archivist sickened from contact with it. If this artifact is truly dangerous, we need to understand it."

Severino's gaze hardened, but Michael intervened before the tension could escalate. "Marcus is right, Eminence. We've already seen signs of its influence. Containment is only a temporary solution. If we can uncover its origins, we may be able to neutralize it completely."

The cardinal sighed, rubbing his temples. "Very well. But you must proceed discreetly. If this music box has ties to heretical practices, it is a stain the Church cannot afford."

Severino's attention shifted to Marcus. "Dr. Russo, your expertise in artifacts is invaluable, but you'll need additional support. Someone with the knowledge to decipher these symbols and their context."

Marcus nodded. "I already have someone in mind: Hana Sinclair. She's an investigative journalist with a background in historical symbolism. I've worked with her before—she's thorough and trustworthy."

Severino frowned.

Not long ago, former Pope Ignatius had opened the clergy to priestly marriage and soon after, Michael had announced his engagement to the attractive journalist. He realized that the cardinal, knowing this situation, was likely having reservations about the couple working closely together on this project.

Michael broke into the cardinal's thoughts with, "Your Eminence, Ms. Sinclair and I have, as you know, worked together on many other projects for the Vatican. Which is actually how we met. I assure you our efforts in this regard will be held to the same standards and decorum."

Severino smiled. "Of course, Father. I had no question on that. But a journalist..." He sighed."Yes, bring her in, then. But remember, this investigation must remain within the Vatican's control. No unauthorized disclosures."

As they left the cardinal's study, Marcus glanced at Michael. "What do you think?"

Michael's expression was thoughtful. "Of course I'll be pleased to see Hana. She's been on an assignment for *Le Monde*, so we haven't seen each other for a bit and I'm looking forward to it. But on a professional note, I think you're right to bring her on board. Her expertise could be invaluable. But Marcus... be careful. Artifacts like these have a way of revealing truths that are better left buried."

Marcus didn't respond immediately. His thoughts were already on the days ahead and the daunting task of uncovering the music box's secrets. For all his training and experience, he couldn't shake the feeling that he was stepping into something far darker than he had ever faced before.

CHAPTER THREE

The streets of Rome shimmered under the warm afternoon sun, the ancient city buzzing with its usual blend of history and chaos. Hana Sinclair stepped off the train at Termini Station, pulling her small suitcase behind her. Her keen eyes scanned the crowded platform, a mixture of curiosity and priority in her expression. Marcus's call had been uncharacteristically cryptic—he rarely reached out unless something extraordinary was at hand.

She was dressed in a light trench coat over a tailored blouse, her dark hair swept back into a loose braid. Although her recent inheritance of her grandfather's considerable financial empire could have affected her, Hana's passion for journalism and interest in history kept her grounded. In fact, she had just wrapped up an intense investigative series in Paris where she had long kept her own apartment, but Marcus's tone during their brief phone call had intrigued her. He had spoken of an artifact unearthed in the Vatican's Secret Archives, something with potentially dangerous implications. That alone was enough to draw her back to Rome. But the bonus of being able to see her fiancé, Father Michael Dominic, made her decision unquestionable.

Exiting the station, she spotted Marcus waiting near a taxi stand. His rugged features appeared slightly drawn, and tension edged his usually calm demeanor. He raised a hand in greeting, his smile faint but genuine.

"Hana," he said, striding forward to meet her. "It's good to see you."

"Likewise," she replied, letting him take her suitcase. "But you didn't call me for a social visit. What's going on?"

Marcus glanced around as if checking for eavesdroppers before gesturing her toward a waiting taxi. "Let's get to the Archives first. I'll explain everything there."

BY THE TIME they arrived at the Vatican, Hana's curiosity had morphed into full-blown anticipation. Marcus led her through the labyrinthine halls of the Secret Archives, their footsteps echoing softly on the polished stone floors. The air grew cooler as they descended into the deeper chambers, the impact of centuries of history pressing down on them.

"You've been busy," Hana said, glancing at the rows of meticulously cataloged artifacts lining the shelves. "What exactly did you find?"

Marcus stopped in front of a secure cabinet, unlocking it with a set of keys and a security code. He retrieved a small bundle wrapped in cloth and placed it on the nearest table. With careful hands, he unwrapped the object to reveal the music box.

Hana's breath caught.

The box was exquisite. Its mysterious metal casing gleamed faintly in the soft light, intricate carvings twisting across its surface in a language she didn't immediately recognize. The Latin inscriptions interspersed with alchemical symbols hinted at its arcane nature. Despite its size, it radiated a presence, as though it were alive.

"Where did you find this?" Hana asked, her voice barely above a whisper.

"In a chamber sealed since the eighteenth century," Marcus replied. "It was part of a collection tied to heretical movements. But this... this is different. It's been causing disturbances ever since it was uncovered."

Hana leaned closer, examining the box's carvings. "Disturbances?"

"Cold spots, flickering lights, strange sounds," Marcus said. "And the young archivist who found it... he's been muttering about shadows and a cursed melody ever since."

Hana's brow furrowed. "Let's see what we're dealing with."

She spread her notes and reference materials across the table, quickly falling into the meticulous rhythm of analysis she had honed over years of investigative journalism. Marcus watched as she sketched the symbols from the music box, cross-referencing them with alchemical charts and theological texts.

"This one here," she said, pointing to a sigil near the box's base. "It's a binding symbol, often used in rituals to contain spiritual forces. And this Latin phrase..." She traced her finger over the engraving. "*Vinculum Aeternum.*

An eternal bond. It suggests this artifact was designed to hold something—or some force—within it."

Marcus leaned over her shoulder. "And this symbol here? It looks like a variation of the Ouroboros."

Hana nodded. "Good eye. It's a modified version, incorporating elements of the Philosopher's Stone. Whoever made this box was deeply steeped in alchemical traditions. But it's not just alchemy. These markings... they're also tied to demonology."

Marcus stiffened. "Demonology? You're sure?"

"Positive," Hana replied. "This here is the Seal of Astaroth, a name that's been associated with knowledge and temptation. If someone created this artifact in the eighteenth century, it may have been part of a ritual by one of the alchemical guilds active in Appenzell at the time. They were notorious for pushing boundaries between science and mysticism."

Marcus exhaled slowly, the implications settling over him. "That would align with the other artifacts we found in the chamber. But why create something like this? What purpose could it serve?"

Hana shrugged, though her expression was grim. "If the guild believed they could control what they summoned, this box might have been designed as a vessel... or a trap. Either way, it's dangerous."

As she spoke, Marcus noticed a flicker of movement out of the corner of his eye. He turned abruptly, but the room was still. Just the light playing tricks on him, he thought.

LATER THAT EVENING, Marcus and Hana visited the infirmary where Gideon was being cared for. The young archivist lay pale and trembling in his bed, his eyes darting nervously to the shadows in the room.

"Gideon," Marcus said gently, pulling up a chair beside him. "How are you feeling?"

Gideon's gaze flickered to Marcus, then to Hana. His voice was hoarse, barely audible. "The melody... it's cursed. I can still hear it, even when it's silent. Didn't you hear it, Dr. Russo? How could you not?"

Marcus sat back, shrugging. Then it dawned on him. "I had my earpiece in and had just gotten a call. So yes, I heard it, but not as clearly as you did. But Gideon, the sound is gone now. What still has you so disturbed?"

"The shadows... they're waiting. Watching."

Hana exchanged a worried glance with Marcus. "What do you mean, shadows?"

Gideon's hands gripped the blanket tightly. "They came out of the music. They're alive. They move when you're not looking. They... they're coming for us all."

Marcus felt a chill creep up his spine. Gideon's words echoed the strange sensations he had experienced in the chamber: the flickering lights, the cold spots, the shifting shadows.

Hana placed a reassuring hand on Gideon's arm. "You're safe here," she said firmly. "We're going to figure this out."

But as they left the infirmary, her confidence faltered. "Marcus, this isn't just some historical curiosity. That box is still active. It's affecting him... and us."

Marcus nodded grimly. "I know. And the more we uncover, the clearer it becomes that we're dealing with something far beyond our understanding. I appreciate your insights into this. I assume you'll be able to stay for at least a bit to help?"

For just a moment, Hana's intense expression softened, and she half smiled. "After what I've already seen, it would be difficult to keep me away. As it so happens, my last assignment has been put to bed, and most of my grandfather's estate issues are being handled by others for the moment. So, I have the time, and I definitely have the interest." Her expression deepened again. "I only hope that I can be of help."

For a moment, neither spoke, the weight of the discovery settling over them like a shroud. The music box, with all its intricate beauty, was more than a relic. It was a harbinger of something dark—and it had only just begun to reveal its secrets.

CHAPTER
FOUR

Marcus sat in the softly illuminated study deep within the Vatican Archives the next day, a leather-bound diary open before him. The diary, discovered alongside the music box, was remarkably well-preserved. Its cover bore no title, but the initials "VM" were embossed in faded gold at the bottom right corner. The handwriting inside was elegant yet erratic, the ink smudged in places as though the author's hand had trembled while writing.

"Vincenzo Malvagio," Marcus murmured, running his fingers over the page. The name had surfaced in obscure accounts from the eighteenth century, often surrounded by whispers of heresy and madness.

Hana, seated across from him, leaned forward. "You've mentioned his name before. A composer, right? What's his connection to the box?"

Marcus tapped the diary. "According to this, Malvagio believed music was more than art. He saw it as a form of alchemy—a way to manipulate reality. He wrote about creating melodies capable of summoning forces beyond human understanding. The music box was likely his masterpiece."

Hana's brows knitted together. "Summoning forces? That sounds like more than artistic ambition."

"It wasn't just ambition," Marcus replied, his tone darkening. "It was obsession. This entry here..." He pointed to a passage written in hurried script. "'The melody will bridge the worlds. It shall be my symphony of creation, fulfilling my destiny to purge the world, purify it for all time.'"

Hana shivered. "Sounds more like a manifesto than a diary. Was he associated with any particular movement?"

"The Appenzell Guild," Marcus said. "A secretive group of alchemists and occultists. Malvagio was their prodigy, but his ideas became too extreme, even for them. He was excommunicated and disappeared shortly after."

Hana gestured to the music box resting on the table, its sinister beauty undeniable. "And you think this box is part of his so-called symphony?"

Marcus nodded. "If the diary is accurate, this box contains one of his melodies—one designed to contain... something. Or to summon it."

Hana's gaze lingered on the box. "Summoning forces. Bridging worlds. If this is what he left behind, I'd hate to imagine what he thought he could control. Thankfully, only Gideon was affected. And the cold and shadows are the only other manifestations."

"For now." Marcus closed the diary, a weight settling on his chest. "But even that begs the question of what else is waiting to get out."

. . .

THE DEVIL'S SYMPHONY

BUT THE FOLLOWING DAY, the disturbances in the Vatican grew impossible to ignore. Marcus's usual walk to the Archives was interrupted by hushed conversations among the clergy. Groups of priests stood clustered in the hallways, their faces pale and their voices anxious.

"What happened now?" Marcus asked a passing Swiss Guard.

The guard's expression was grim. "Statues in the reliquary room were found shattered this morning. No one entered the room, but... it's like something struck them."

Marcus's stomach tightened. He hurried to the reliquary room, where he found Father Michael already investigating. Shards of marble and plaster littered the floor, the once-pristine statues of saints reduced to ruin. The air was redolent with the scent of incense, as if someone had tried to cleanse the room.

"This is the third incident this week," Michael said without looking up. He was examining the base of a broken statue. "First, the flickering lights in the chapel. Then the voices near the confessional. And now this."

"And the clergy?" Marcus asked, glancing at the doorway where several priests lingered nervously.

Michael straightened, his expression grave. "Some of them claim to have seen shadowy figures in the halls at night. Others report hearing faint music... the same melody you described from the box."

Marcus felt a chill run down his spine. "It's spreading."

Michael nodded. "Whatever energy is tied to that artifact, it's sweeping through the Vatican. And it's getting stronger."

As they left the reliquary room, Marcus's thoughts raced. The music box wasn't just a relic; it was an active force. Whatever it had released in those first notes of a tune was growing more powerful with each passing day.

THAT EVENING, Michael summoned Marcus to his study. The soft glow of a desk lamp illuminated the room, with shadows cast over shelves lined with ancient texts. On the desk lay a stack of documents stamped with the Vatican's seal.

"I pulled these from the restricted archives," Michael said, gesturing for Marcus to sit. "They're records from Malvagio's time: letters, reports, and… confessions."

Marcus raised an eyebrow. "Confessions?"

Michael handed him a yellowed parchment. The handwriting was shaky but legible, the ink faded with age. It was a statement from a monk who had witnessed one of Malvagio's compositions.

"'The music was divine,'" Marcus read aloud. "'And yet, it carried the stench of damnation. When he played, the air grew thick, and shadows danced where there was no light. He claimed the melody was a pure gift, but we knew it was a curse.'"

Michael leaned back in his chair, his fingers steepled. "There are other accounts, all pointing to the same conclusion. Malvagio believed he had made a pact with a metaphysical force. He called it the Muse Eternal."

Marcus set the parchment down, a heaviness settling over him. "The Muse Eternal… you think that's what's tied to the box?"

Michael nodded slowly. "It's possible. If Malvagio's pact was real, the box might be a conduit. A way to channel that force."

Marcus frowned. "I'm not ready to jump to

conclusions. The language they're using is symbolic. They could be talking about unleashing chaos in a more metaphorical sense—mass hysteria, destabilizing governments..."

Michael cut him off. "This isn't just symbolism, Marcus. The Vatican has records going back centuries, depicting cults like this using rituals to summon forces beyond human understanding. You've seen the effects of the melody yourself. Are you really going to dismiss the possibility that it's connected to something supernatural? Something inherently evil?"

Marcus didn't respond immediately. "I don't know what to believe," he admitted.

His mind raced. If the melody could influence its surroundings so profoundly, what else was it capable of? And how far could its reach extend?

"There's more at stake than just the Vatican," he said. "If this melody's influence continues, it could spread beyond these walls."

Michael's features hardened. "Then we need to act quickly. The longer we wait, the greater the risk."

As the two men sat in silence, the faint sound of a melody hummed in the air, just beyond the edge of hearing. Marcus's hands clenched into fists. The music box wasn't just a relic of the past; it was a harbinger of what was to come.

CHAPTER
FIVE

The Vatican's Secret Archives were a maze of narrow corridors and towering shelves, the silence broken only by the occasional flicker of a lantern or the muted steps of Swiss Guards Karl Dengler and Lukas Bischoff as they made their rounds. The air was thick with the scent of old paper and varnished wood, a smell that clung to everything within these sacred halls. Tonight, however, the silence felt heavier, almost oppressive.

Karl adjusted his grip on his halberd, glancing at his partner. "Lukas, tell me I'm not imagining things," he said, his voice low. "Does it feel... colder in here to you?"

Lukas, the younger and more skeptical of the two, rolled his shoulders. "It's an old building, Karl. Drafts happen. You've been listening to too many rumors."

Karl frowned but didn't press the issue. The rumors Lukas referred to had been spreading among the Vatican staff for days. Whispers of unexplained phenomena: voices murmuring in empty rooms, objects shifting on their own, and—most troubling of all—the faint sound of music echoing through the halls at odd hours. Karl had dismissed it at first, chalking it up to the overactive imaginations of the archivists. But now, patrolling these corridors in near total darkness, he wasn't so sure.

As they turned a corner, Lukas's lantern flickered, the flame sputtering as though caught in an unseen breeze. He muttered a curse and shielded the lantern with his hand.

"See? Just drafts," Lukas said, though his voice lacked conviction.

Karl paused, his ears straining. "Do you hear that?"

Lukas stopped walking, the two of them standing in tense silence. At first, there was nothing. Then, faint and distant, came a sound that made Karl's blood run cold. It was a single note, soft and mournful, like the first pluck of a string instrument. It hung in the air for a moment before fading into the silence.

"It's probably just… someone playing music in their quarters," Lukas said, though his hand tightened on his halberd.

Karl shook his head. "Not in here. There's no one allowed this deep after hours."

The two guards exchanged uneasy glances before continuing their patrol, their steps quicker now, their lanterns creating jittery shadows that seemed to stretch and twist unnaturally.

The cry came suddenly, cutting through the oppressive silence like a knife. Karl and Lukas froze, ass the sound echoed through the corridors.

"That came from the eastern wing," Karl said, already moving toward the source.

Lukas followed close behind, their boots pounding against the stone floor. As they neared the eastern wing, the air grew colder, the lantern light dimmer. When they rounded the final corner, they found a junior archivist slumped against the wall, his face pale and his breathing shallow.

"Hey, are you all right?" Lukas knelt beside the young man, checking for injuries.

The archivist's eyes darted around wildly, his hands clutching at his chest. "It was... here," he whispered hoarsely. "In the shadows... watching me. Then it moved."

"What moved?" Karl demanded, scanning the corridor.

Before the archivist could answer, a movement caught Karl's eye. A shadow detached itself from the far wall, slipping into the next corridor with an unnatural fluidity. It was no trick of the light; it moved with intent.

"There!" Karl shouted, bolting after it.

Lukas hesitated for only a moment before following, leaving the archivist slumped against the wall. The two guards pursued the shadow through the labyrinthine corridors, their lanterns swinging wildly as they tried to keep up. The thing was fast, faster than anything human, vanishing and reappearing at will, always just out of reach.

They burst into a wide reading room, their breaths ragged. The shadow was nowhere to be seen, but the room bore signs of its passage. Books lay scattered on the floor, chairs were overturned, and the air crackled with an unnatural energy. The guards stood in silence, their senses on high alert.

"What was that?" Lukas finally asked, his voice no louder than a breath.

Karl didn't answer. He didn't know.

· · ·

THE NEXT MORNING, Marcus arrived at the Archives to find Karl waiting for him outside the eastern wing. The guard's usual stoic demeanor was gone, replaced by a tight-lipped anxiety.

"What happened?" Marcus asked as Karl led him to the scene of the attack.

"One of the junior archivists was... well, attacked, for lack of a better word," Karl said. "Lukas and I saw... something. A shadow. It moved like it was alive."

Marcus's jaw tightened, eyes narrowing, but he said nothing as they reached the corridor. The faint chill from the previous day had intensified, and Marcus could feel it sinking into his bones. The walls seemed darker, the air heavier.

He knelt where the archivist had been found, examining the floor and walls with a practiced eye. At first, there was nothing unusual. But as he moved closer to the corner, he noticed faint markings scratched into the stone.

"Bring me a lantern," Marcus said.

Karl obliged, holding the light steady as Marcus traced the markings with his fingers. They were Latin phrases, crudely etched but legible.

"*Cave melodiam*," Marcus read aloud. "Beware the melody."

He moved to the next phrase. "*Ira melodiae*. The melody's wrath."

Marcus sat back on his heels, his mind wrestling with implications. These warnings weren't recent; the scratches were old, their edges worn smooth over time. Whoever had carved them had known the dangers of the music box.

"This confirms it," Marcus said, rising to his feet. "The

box isn't just an artifact. It's a catalyst. Whatever force it's tied to… it's already affecting this place."

Karl's hand tightened on his halberd. "What do we do?"

Marcus looked down the darkened corridor, his thoughts heavy. "We need answers. And we need them fast."

But deep down, Marcus knew that answers alone might not be enough to stop what was coming.

CHAPTER SIX

The Vatican Archives were unsettlingly quiet at night. The vast, vaulted halls that hummed with scholarly activity during the day fell into an eerie stillness, disturbed only by the faint creak of settling stone or the distant drip of condensation. But this particular night was different. The air felt heavier, oppressive, as though the walls themselves were bracing for something unseen.

Deep within the Archives, in a room where the most restricted materials were kept, a faint vibration emanated from the music box. Encased in its protective glass cabinet, it sat undisturbed—or so it seemed. The box's dark metal exterior shimmered faintly in the low light, its engravings catching the occasional flicker of the emergency lanterns. Then, without warning, it began to glow. A pale, sickly green light pulsed from its seams, casting unnatural shadows on the walls.

At the same moment, the air in the room grew frigid. Frost crept along the edges of the glass, and the faint hum of the box became audible. A single note—clear, mournful, and resonant—escaped from the box, vibrating through the room like a ripple on still water. The sound was beautiful, yet deeply unsettling, as though it carried with it the depth of centuries.

The note faded, and silence returned... briefly.

Then slipstreams of darkness, like tendrils of black smoke, seeped from the edges of the music box, slid across the secured glass enclosure through invisible fissures, moved out into the room, under the door, and into the hallway of the Archives proper. There, the swirls of black coalesced. And they emerged.

Figures took shape. They were humanoid, but their forms were indistinct, as though they were made of smoke and darkness. Their movements were jerky, unnatural, and their presence exuded a malevolent energy. One of the figures drifted toward a nearby shelf, its shadowy hand brushing against the spines of ancient texts. As it moved, the books tumbled to the floor, the sound echoing like a thunderclap in the silent room.

The sudden noise roused a junior archivist who had been working late in the adjoining hall. He peered into the restricted section, his flashlight casting trembling light into the darkness. When his eyes fell on the shadowy figures, his breath caught in his throat.

"Who's there?" he called, though his voice wavered.

The figures turned toward him as one, their movements synchronized and deliberate. The archivist stumbled backward, his flashlight slipping from his grasp and shattering on the floor. In the brief flare of light, the figures appeared almost solid, their eyes—or what passed for eyes—glinting with a predatory gleam.

The archivist turned and ran, his screams echoing

through the corridors as the shadows surged forward, their forms melding into the darkness around them.

MARCUS ARRIVED at the Archives minutes after Karl's urgent call. Father Michael Dominic was close behind him, both men moving with purpose despite the late hour. The moment they stepped inside, the oppressive atmosphere hit them. The air was icy, and their breaths formed visible clouds as they hurried toward the restricted section.

"The guards reported figures moving in the shadows last night and found an archivist frightened at that time," Marcus said as they walked together. "But tonight was worse, and this archivist... he's in shock. Whatever happened here, it wasn't a trick of the light."

Michael nodded, his face grim. "If the music box is connected to this, its influence is expanding."

When they entered the restricted section, the sight that greeted them was chaotic. Books and scrolls lay scattered across the floor, several shelves had toppled over, and a thick layer of frost coated the surfaces. The glass cabinet containing the music box was intact, but Marcus noticed immediately that the box itself was vibrating faintly, as though alive. Its eerie green glow had subsided, but the sense of foreboding it radiated was unmistakable.

As Marcus approached the cabinet, a sudden gust of wind swept through the room. The light of their lanterns flickered violently, and several books flew off the shelves as though hurled by unseen hands. Marcus froze, his eyes scanning the room.

"Did you see that?" he asked.

Michael nodded, his hand tightening around the crucifix he wore. "We're not alone in here."

Another book shot across the room, narrowly missing Marcus's head as he ducked instinctively. Then he turned to see a shadowy figure emerging from the far corner. It was indistinct, but its presence was palpable, a void that nearly consumed the light around it.

"Michael," Marcus said, his voice low but urgent. "Do you have anything for… this?"

Michael stepped forward, raising his crucifix. "In the name of God, reveal yourself!"

The shadow hesitated, its form flickering, but it didn't retreat. Instead, it appeared to pulse with energy, as if mocking the attempt to banish it. The air grew colder, and a low, guttural sound filled the room—not quite a growl, but something far more unsettling.

"Marcus, get the box," Michael said. "We need to contain this before it gets worse."

Marcus hesitated, his eyes fixed on the shadow. It felt wrong to turn his back on it, but Michael's tone brooked no argument. Moving quickly, he unlocked the cabinet and carefully lifted the container holding the music box. The vibrations stopped the moment he touched it, and the room's temperature rose slightly. But the shadow didn't disappear.

Instead, it retreated into the far corner, merging with the darkness until it was no longer visible. The oppressive energy lingered, but the immediate threat had passed.

BACK IN THE warmer comfort of the main Archives office, Marcus placed the music box, still in its locked glass case, on the table. Its dark surface gleamed faintly, the intricate engravings seeming almost alive in the flickering lantern light. Hana arrived moments later, her expression a mixture of concern and curiosity.

"What happened?" she asked, taking in the disheveled state of Marcus and Michael.

Marcus ran a hand through his hair, his exhaustion evident. He explained what they saw tonight as well as what Karl told him of the night before. He concluded, "Those shadowy figures in the restricted section are tied to the box somehow. I... I don't know how to explain it, Hana. But this isn't just a relic. As I said before, I think it's a beacon."

Hana's gaze shifted to the box. "A beacon for what?"

"For whatever forces were tied to its creation," Marcus replied. "The melody... it's not just music, I think. It's a key. It's awakening something that's been dormant for centuries."

Michael crossed his arms, his face lined with worry. "If that's true, then we need to determine exactly what Malvagio intended when he created it. And we need to find a way to stop it."

Hana nodded, but her unease was tangible. "We've already seen what this thing can do. And if Marcus is right, it's only going to get worse. Are we sure we're equipped to handle this?"

For a moment, no one answered. The heft of the situation hung heavy in the room, the flickering lanterns throwing shadows that stretched and twisted unnaturally.

Finally, Marcus spoke. "We don't have a choice. If we don't stop this, no one else will."

Hana met his gaze, her expression resolute despite her fear. "Then we'd better figure out how."

CHAPTER
SEVEN

Hana flipped through the brittle pages of a centuries-old ledger, her face mired in concentration. The Vatican Archives—with their endless volumes of forgotten lore—were a labyrinth of secrets, but Hana's investigative instincts had already led her to a promising trail. Beside her, Marcus sat with a stack of documents, his fingers tracing faded ink across yellowed parchment.

"Look at this," Hana said, sliding a journal toward Marcus. Her finger tapped an entry dated 1728. "This ledger details commissions for religious music, but there's a curious note about a 'Vincenzo Malvagio.' Apparently, his work was... controversial."

Marcus skimmed the entry, his interest piqued. "'Controversial' might be putting it lightly. According to this, Malvagio claimed his compositions were divinely inspired... and sometimes infernally so. He wrote that he could hear melodies that others couldn't, as though they were whispers from another realm."

Hana raised an eyebrow. "Divinely influenced? Infernal inspiration? That sounds like the kind of ego a composer would have."

Marcus shrugged. "It's true that ego was a common denominator of composers in that era. Beethoven and Mozart are fine examples of those who lived in his time."

Marcus shook his head, setting the journal aside. "But there's more to it than ego. Malvagio's music was reputed to have strange effects on those who heard it. Reports of sudden trances, uncontrollable weeping, even... hallucinations."

Hana leaned back in her chair, chewing on the end of her pen. "That would explain why his name keeps coming up in connection with occult practices. What else do we know about him?"

"I found out he met the German physician Franz Mesmer in the Jesuit University of Dillingen in 1754. Franz was a young and eager student; Malvagio was older, still deeply involved in writing compositions, even though discredited by the Church long before that. Malvagio was doing research at the university, and they apparently met and ended up fast friends for a while, with both interested in how things outside of the body, like sound, can affect the mind. Mesmer went on to study medicine and established a treatment he called 'animal magnetism,' but which others referred to as 'mesmerizing.' In fact, that was the beginning of hypnotism, which, in itself, is a form of mind control."

"You said Malvagio was discredited by the Church?"

"Yes," Marcus admitted, "Malvagio's works were banned by the Church, and most records of his life were destroyed. Which is why I could find little else about him.

This..." He gestured to the journal. "This might be one of the few surviving references."

Hana reached for another volume. "If the Church wanted his memory erased, it must have been because his work posed a real threat. Let's see what else we can find."

Michael entered the reading room, a stack of freshly retrieved documents under his arm. His face was grim as he joined Marcus and Hana at the table.

"I think I found something you'll want to see," Michael said, setting the documents down. He opened one to reveal an ornate manuscript, its edges gilded and its pages filled with intricate illustrations. "This is a transcript of a hearing held by the Vatican in 1730. Malvagio's name is mentioned extensively."

Marcus leaned forward. "A hearing? Was he accused of heresy?"

Michael nodded. "Worse. The transcript details an investigation into a secretive group operating in northern Italy during that time. The group, known as the 'Consonants of Eternity,' claimed to explore the boundaries between divine and infernal music. Malvagio was one of their leaders."

Hana's pen hovered over her notebook. "And the Church's response?"

Michael flipped a page, his finger tracing a section of dense Latin text. "The group was denounced, their gatherings disbanded. Several members were excommunicated, and Malvagio..." He paused, his expression darkening. "Malvagio was granted protection by Cardinal Antonio Bellari. Bellari argued that Malvagio's music could be used to reveal the divine will, even if it skirted dangerous territory."

THE DEVIL'S SYMPHONY

"A cardinal defending a heretical composer?" Marcus said, incredulous. "That's unexpected."

Michael leaned back, his fingers steepled. "Bellari was an influential figure in his time, known for pushing the boundaries of acceptable theology. But his association with Malvagio tarnished his reputation. There are rumors that Bellari believed the composer had uncovered a universal truth hidden within music—a truth Malvagio intended to use to reshape the Church."

Hana scribbled furiously in her notebook. "And how does this tie back to the music box?"

Michael gestured toward the manuscript. "The Consonants of Eternity believed that certain melodies could open a conduit between the material and spiritual worlds. If the music box is one of Malvagio's creations, it's likely a vessel for such a melody."

Marcus's gaze drifted to the music box resting on the nearby table, its dark surface gleaming faintly in the dim light. "If that's true," he said quietly, "then this isn't just a historical artifact. It's a door to something we may not want to open."

LATER THAT EVENING, Marcus, Hana, and Michael sat across from Cardinal Severino in his private study. The room was warm and inviting, the fire casting dancing shadows on the richly paneled walls. But the atmosphere was tense, the toll of their findings pressing down on the group like a physical presence.

Severino's expression was unreadable as Michael finished recounting their discoveries. When the priest fell silent, the cardinal steepled his fingers and regarded them thoughtfully.

"What you've uncovered is both fascinating and dangerous," Severino said at last. "Vincenzo Malvagio is a name the Church has tried to erase for good reason. His work represents a dark chapter in our history, one that could undermine the faith of countless believers if exposed. It was for good reason that Cardinal Bellari was 'retired' early from his posting. And, with Malvagio denounced and no longer in the public eye, the matter was closed. As it should be."

"With respect, Your Eminence," Marcus interjected, "we're not talking about just undermining faith. We're talking about a tangible threat. If the music box is what we think it is, then its existence could have consequences far beyond the Church."

Severino turned to Marcus. "I understand your concerns, Dr. Russo. But you must also understand the position of the Church. If this artifact were to be linked to Malvagio, it would raise questions about the Church's complicity in his work. After all, it was a cardinal who protected him."

Michael spoke up, his tone measured. "Eminence, hiding the truth won't make this problem disappear. We need to investigate further, to understand what we're dealing with before it escalates."

Severino's gaze shifted to Michael, his expression softening slightly. "I do not disagree, Father Dominic. But we must proceed with the utmost caution. If word of this gets out, the damage to the Church's reputation could be scandalous."

Hana, who had been silent until now, leaned forward. "Your Eminence, if the Church's reputation is at stake, then it's all the more reason to grasp its significance, in order to dispute its power."

The cardinal sighed, rubbing his temples. "You are all correct, of course. But discretion is paramount. I will allow your continued investigation, but you must keep your findings strictly confidential. And Dr. Russo..." He turned to Marcus. "You are to ensure that the music box remains under lock and key at all times. Am I clear?"

Marcus nodded. "Crystal clear, Your Eminence."

Severino stood, signaling the end of the meeting. "May God guide you in this endeavor. And may He protect us all from what you might uncover."

As the group left the cardinal's study, Marcus felt the weight of Severino's warning settle heavily on his shoulders. Whatever truths lay hidden in Malvagio's legacy, they were as dangerous as they were tantalizing. And the deeper they delved, the more Marcus feared they were unearthing something that should have remained buried.

CHAPTER
EIGHT

The study was eerily quiet as Hana carefully examined the music box. Its engraved metal surface shimmered faintly under the desk lamp, the intricate carvings of Latin inscriptions and alchemy symbols etched like whispers of the past. Marcus and Michael sat across from her, their expressions a mix of anticipation and concern.

"Are you sure no one has tampered with this?" Hana asked, glancing up at Marcus.

"Positive," Marcus replied. "It's been under lock and key since we recovered it. If there's more to it, we haven't found it yet."

Hana nodded, her fingers tracing the grooves along the box's edges. Something about its craftsmanship felt deliberately cryptic, as though it had been designed to conceal more than it revealed. Her thumb caught on a small, irregular bump along the side.

"Wait," she said, leaning in closer. She pressed against the bump, feeling a faint give beneath her fingers. With a soft click, a hidden compartment slid open from the base of the box. The air in the room seemed to still as she carefully pulled out a folded piece of parchment, its edges brittle with age.

"What is that?" Michael asked, leaning forward.

Hana unfolded the parchment with delicate precision, revealing a dense array of symbols, charts, and notations written in an elegant, almost otherworldly hand. The script was unlike anything she had seen before, blending Latin, ancient Greek, and symbols from alchemical traditions. At its center was what appeared to be a musical score, incomplete but strikingly intricate.

"It's either a formula of sorts or an encrypted manuscript," Hana said, her voice hovering just above a whisper.

"Wait..." Michael motioned back to the opening. Just above where the folded manuscript had lain was a rolled piece of parchment placed around a metal rod or spindle. He carefully pulled out the roll, gently unfurled it, and saw what appeared to be a musical score, strikingly intricate, but with the bottom edge torn off.

"But this..." Hana pointed to the roll Michael held. "This looks like a musical score. Or part of one anyway."

Marcus stood and leaned over her shoulder, his breath catching as he examined the parchment and roll. "This might be the key," he said, "the missing piece to understanding what Malvagio was trying to achieve."

Michael crossed himself. "Let's hope understanding it doesn't come at too high a cost."

MARCUS SPENT the next day safeguarding the music box as he transitioned it from the Secret Archives to the technical engineering laboratory dedicated to Vatican projects. The technician assigned to examine the music box was a young woman whose piercing blue eyes flicked to Marcus—just long enough to register him, to measure him—before returning with quiet intensity to the object between them. Her focus was clinical, reverent, and wholly unbothered by his presence, yet something in that brief glance suggested not indifference, but a shared fluency in solitude and discipline, as though she already knew him without needing to say a word.

Marcus recognized in her the consummate professional, like him, with passions that ran more to her career than social interests. He had only briefly been married in his early years and found, after a mutually agreed-upon divorce, that single life suited him. He guessed that might end up the case for this young woman as well, as she bent to her work.

Her slender fingers used precision tools, the best that technology had to offer, penetrating the ornate box with spectrograms, X-rays, and other instruments for electromagnetic scanning to examine its inner workings without impinging on its integrity. It took hours before everything was laid out before Marcus and her in a private room in the lab. Images of the X-rayed contents and reference materials filled a whiteboard before them as she finally began to voice her assessment. Marcus had been patient, but every step in the process had been agonizingly slowed by his standards.

"Dr. Russo," she began, "let me explain that what we have here is, to say the least, amazing, and I feel honored that the Vatican has allowed me to assist you with this task." She turned to the object and glanced at it once more, now with not so much an analyst's eye as with reverence.

Then she looked back at the board and began her explanation.

"What we have here is a unique structure intended to create sounds. Of course, you are aware of that. However, its mechanics are not just unique but also without precedent. Have you ever heard of a 'glass armonica'?"

Marcus nodded. "Music that involves wine glasses?" His musical expertise wasn't extensive, but he did recall seeing such a demonstration at one point. How could this relate to his discovery?

"Yes and no." She nodded eagerly. "The glass harp is what you refer to. Those have been documented in Persia since the fourteenth century. It was discovered early on that glassware could be filled to various levels, and then a careful manipulation or touch around the rim with a wet finger could create a resonance or a sound. Street musicians became a popular attraction in the 1700s as they lined up glasses with various levels of water and rubbed their fingers on the rims to create haunting tunes, making money for their street music.

"The American statesman Benjamin Franklin, in one of his trips to Paris, witnessed this, and his creative mind latched onto it. In 1761, Franklin created what became known as a 'glass armonica,' a large structure of about eighteen kilograms and sixty centimeters in length that consisted of a metal tube on which thirty-seven hand-blown glass rings of various thicknesses and circumferences were threaded. These graduated glass rings then vibrated against the metal when a moist finger glazed over them and created sounds. The instrument was highly sophisticated compared to liquid-filled wine glasses. But this"—she turned and motioned to the music box—"this takes that concept beyond anything Franklin ever conceived of."

The woman's eyes flitted across the whiteboard as she continued to point and explain the mechanism. The craftsman had employed natural crystals and gemstones instead of glass to create sounds. According to her instruments, these included diamonds, rubies, and sapphires. She could only guess at the exact method, but it was clear enough: stimulated in some way by the score turning on the spindle, the gems could release the musical tones.

"The result would be a frequency and sound unlike anything produced by any man-made piece of glass. Something, if I dare say so, otherworldly." The young woman looked up at Marcus, her eyes now wide with anticipation. "Dr. Russo, it would be an honor if I could hear—"

"Sorry, that won't be possible," he cut her off. She blinked, taken aback by his sudden response.

"But just a few notes, possibly? I only meant to—"

"Again, sorry," he said with finality, already placing the music box back in the locked case he had used to transport it. He noticed her crestfallen expression. "I thank you for your analysis, but your observation is also correct. To say it is 'otherworldly' is all too close to the truth. It may have been built in this world, but the nature of the sounds it creates is something we can't afford to have brought into this world. Even a few notes."

As he left, he thought of the damage already done and wondered how much more was yet to come from his discovery of this instrument with its otherworldly intentions.

. . .

THE manuscript and roll of musical score had been placed under glass for preservation, but their mysteries continued to unravel as Marcus, Hana, and Michael worked late into the night. The analysis Marcus had shared with them from the lab technician only deepened their need to understand the purpose of the musical score that would be played on this delicate instrument. Hana cross-referenced the symbols from the manuscript with the Archive's database, her laptop screen glowing in the darkened room.

"This symbol here," she said, pointing to a circular sigil with an intricate geometric pattern at its center, "I've seen it before. It's on a relic stored in the eastern wing of the Archives—a chalice confiscated during the eighteenth century. The notes called it a tool for 'spiritual transmutation.'"

Marcus frowned. "And this one," he said, pointing to a triangle encased in a serpent's coils. "It's carved into the base of a statue we found in the same chamber as the music box. The label identified the statue as belonging to an occult sect from the Appenzell region."

Michael leaned back in his chair, his expression grave. "This isn't a coincidence. These symbols—they're part of a larger network. Malvagio's work wasn't isolated. He was connected to a broader movement."

Hana nodded. "An occult network operating across Europe. If these artifacts share the same symbology, they might have been created for a unified purpose. The music box could be the centerpiece of whatever they were trying to achieve."

"But why music?" Marcus asked, his tone tinged with frustration. "Why use something so ephemeral?"

"Because music isn't just sound," Hana replied. "It's vibration, frequency, resonance. It affects people on a subconscious level. If Malvagio's goal was to manipulate reality—or summon forces—music might have been the perfect medium."

She continued to explain, "The theory that music can control the mind has been around for thousands of years, and not without basis. In tribal days, the use of rhythmic drums could put participants into frenzies and states of mind beyond our understanding. Everything from Buddhist mantras to Gregorian chants can serve the same purpose of opening the mind. There's something about certain rhythmic patterns of music that echo the heartbeat and pair with bodily systems that can produce altered states of emotions, memory, and even motor control. It has been used for various conditions, from anxiety and depression to physical rehabilitation, and even to trigger memories that have been lost to the conscious mind. When it comes to crossing into other realms, I'd say I'm a skeptic on that. But, who's to say?"

Michael's gaze turned to the parchment. "Whatever his intentions, this network must have known the risks. These symbols… they're not just tools. They appear to be warnings."

WHILE THE TEAM worked in seclusion, reports of strange occurrences began to filter in from beyond the Vatican walls. At first, they were scattered and isolated: a priest in Naples dreaming of shadowy figures whispering in an unfamiliar language, a nun in Vienna waking to find her crucifix inexplicably bent into a circle. But as the days passed, the phenomenon grew more frequent—and more violent.

Hana sat at her laptop, reading the latest report aloud.

"A monastery in Germany reported an outbreak of violent outbursts among the clergy. One monk attacked another during evening prayers, claiming he was trying to 'silence the shadows.'"

Marcus looked up from his notes, his face pale. "This is escalating. These can't just be coincidences."

Michael nodded solemnly. "If the melody's influence is spreading beyond the Vatican, it's affecting anyone attuned to spiritual practices. Clergy, monks, nuns... they seem to be more sensitive to its resonance."

Hana closed her laptop and rubbed her temples. "If this is from your archivist, playing only a few notes of the incomplete melody, what happens when someone tries to play the full thing?"

The room fell silent, the enormity of her question sinking in. Marcus's gaze drifted to the music box, its dark metal surface gleaming ominously under the lamplight.

"We can't let that happen," he said firmly. "We need to find the rest of the melody and figure out how to neutralize it. Otherwise, this... whatever it is... could spiral out of control."

Michael stood, his expression resolute. "Then we keep digging. If Malvagio's work is the key, we need to uncover every piece of it before someone else does."

Hana nodded, though unease lingered in her eyes. "We're dealing with forces we barely understand. Let's hope we're not too late to contain what has already been set loose."

CHAPTER NINE

Marcus sat in the softly lit reading room of the Vatican Archives, maps and reports scattered across the large oak table. Hana and Father Michael sat on either side of him, their expressions grim as they reviewed the latest accounts. Reports from various European cities were piling up, each one more unsettling than the last.

"Here," Marcus said, pointing to a red pin on the map marking Vienna. "Three days ago, a cathedral choir rehearsal was interrupted by what witnesses described as an 'invisible presence' shaking the pews and making the stained-glass windows vibrate."

Hana added a note to her tablet. "And in Munich, a group of nuns reported hearing faint music coming from the chapel—a melody that no one could place." She glanced up. "The reports are too similar to ignore. These events are all tied to sacred spaces, and they've all occurred within the past week."

Michael sighed, resettling himself in his chair. "Sacred

spaces make sense if the melody's origins are tied to Malvagio and his work. If his compositions were meant to challenge divine authority, then it stands to reason they would have the strongest effect in places of worship."

"But how is it spreading?" Hana asked. "The music box hasn't left the Archives."

Marcus rubbed his temples, his thoughts whirling like leaves in a storm. "It's not the box itself. It's the melody. Music is vibration, frequency. If the melody is somehow imprinted onto the ether—like a ripple in water—then it doesn't need the box to spread. It just needs to be heard."

Michael's eyes darkened. "So, exactly how would it spread?"

Marcus hesitated before answering. "If anyone who hears it hums or plays even fragments of the melody, they could be perpetuating its influence. Which means"—his brow crinkled as he figured the path—"Gideon could have hummed it to anyone in the clinic or hospital, just to explain what he'd heard. It's then imprinted on the minds of those hearing it. If they then travel to another of the Church's facilities, like our traveling nurses often do, it travels with them. I don't know. I mean, maybe even thinking about the tune can release its effect."

Hana's fingers hovered over her tablet. "That means we're not just dealing with an artifact. We're dealing with a contagion."

THE HEART of the Vatican was in turmoil. Earlier that morning, St. Peter's Basilica had become the epicenter of an event that left both pilgrims and clergy shaken. Word spread quickly, and by the time Marcus, Hana, and

Michael arrived, the basilica's grand nave was abuzz with anxious whispers.

"What exactly happened?" Marcus asked as they approached a cluster of Swiss Guards near the entrance.

One of the guards, visibly pale, straightened at their arrival. "A group of pilgrims was praying near the Altar of the Chair when they saw... something. They described it as a man dressed in eighteenth-century clothing. He appeared for only a moment, standing near the altar, and then vanished. But before he disappeared, he... smiled."

Marcus exchanged a tense look with Hana. "Show us where this happened."

The guard led them to the altar, where a faint chill lingered in the air despite the warmth of the sun streaming through the basilica's massive windows. A small group of pilgrims knelt nearby, praying fervently and casting nervous glances at the altar.

Marcus inspected the area, his trained eye scanning for any signs of tampering or trickery. But there was nothing unusual—no hidden devices, no footprints, nothing to suggest the event had been staged.

Hana approached one of the pilgrims, an elderly woman clutching a rosary. "Excuse me," she said gently. "I'm trying to understand what you saw. Could you describe it?"

The woman's hands trembled as she spoke. "He was standing right there," she said, pointing to a spot near the altar. "Tall, with dark hair and distinct features. He was dressed in strange clothes, like something from a painting. And his smile... it wasn't kind. It was... knowing."

Michael's expression grew even more somber. "Maybe it wasn't just a vision, but a manifestation. I suspect

Malvagio's work is no longer confined to the past. It's bleeding into the present."

BACK IN THE ARCHIVES, Marcus paced the room, his mind racing with possibilities. The apparition in the basilica wasn't just an isolated incident; it was a warning. The melody's influence was growing, and with each new report, the scope of its reach became clearer.

"The melody isn't just spreading," Marcus said, breaking the tense silence. "It's growing stronger. Every time it's played, heard, or remembered, it's as if it's feeding on the energy of its surroundings."

Hana leaned against the table, her arms crossed. "But why now? The music box was sealed for centuries. What changed?"

Michael spoke up, his voice steady but grave. "It was sealed, but more than that. It was suppressed. The rituals and wards placed on the box were meant to contain its influence. When young Gideon turned the key to start the music, that broke those seals. Now the melody is free to resonate again."

Hana frowned. "Then every second we wait, it gets worse."

Marcus stopped pacing, his eyes locked on the music box resting on the table. "We need to find a way to stop it. The only way to do that is to understand its purpose."

Michael nodded. "Then we focus on the manuscript we found with the music box and the diary that was nearby. Also, if Malvagio's work was tied to a larger network, there might be clues in the suppressed records within the Vatican or elsewhere as well. But whatever we do, we must act quickly."

Hana's eyes rested on the music box, her unease conspicuous. "Let's just hope we're not already too late."

CHAPTER TEN

Hana Sinclair strode briskly through the cobbled streets of Rome, the faint aroma of espresso and baking bread wafting from nearby cafés. Her destination was a small antiquarian bookshop nestled between two unassuming buildings. It was one of the few places outside the Vatican that might hold supplementary records about Vincenzo Malvagio. Marcus had suggested she follow this lead while he and Michael dug deeper into the Vatican's restricted archives.

As Hana pushed open the heavy wooden door, a small bell jingled, announcing her arrival. The shop's interior was veiled in dusky light, the air thick with the scent of old paper and leather bindings. Shelves lined the walls from floor to ceiling, crammed with tomes that looked as though they had been undisturbed for decades.

"Good morning," the shopkeeper greeted her from behind a cluttered desk. "Can I help you find something?"

"I'm looking for records or journals about an

eighteenth-century composer named Vincenzo Malvagio," Hana said, scanning the shelves.

The shopkeeper frowned. "Malvagio? That's an unusual name. I don't recall anything specific, but you're welcome to search."

Hana thanked him and began browsing, her fingers trailing over the spines of the books. After several minutes, she pulled down a volume titled *Unseen Masters: Forgotten Composers of the Baroque Era*. As she flipped through the pages, a voice interrupted her.

"Looking into Malvagio, are we?"

Hana turned, startled by the sudden intrusion. A tall man with silver-streaked hair and piercing blue eyes stood a couple of meters away, his demeanor exuding both charm and authority. He held a leather-bound notebook, its corners worn but its spine pristine, and wore an immaculate gray suit that contrasted sharply with the dusty surroundings. The way he carried himself—confident, almost theatrical—immediately put her on edge.

"I'm sorry, do I know you?" Hana asked, her tone cautious as she tucked the book she was holding against her side.

The man smiled faintly, an expression that didn't quite reach his eyes. "Dr. Adrian Baumann, historian and specialist in occult traditions. I couldn't help but overhear. Malvagio is a fascinating figure, isn't he?"

Hana's instincts flared. There was something too rehearsed about his introduction. "Fascinating and dangerous, from what I've read," she replied, keeping her tone neutral. "What's your interest in him?"

Baumann's smile widened, and he took a deliberate step closer, his movements fluid and unhurried. "The same as yours, I presume. Understanding his work, his influence. There's a certain allure to the mysteries he left behind, wouldn't you agree? The interplay between genius and madness, the thin line between divine inspiration and something... darker."

Hana stiffened slightly, shifting her weight as she considered her next words. "I'm not sure I'd call it alluring. Malvagio's work seems more like a cautionary tale than a mystery worth unraveling."

Baumann tilted his head, his smile never wavering. "Cautionary tales often hold the greatest truths. Don't you think? Malvagio's melodies didn't just push boundaries—they obliterated them. His compositions bridged worlds, or so the legends say. Surely someone like you would want to explore the origins of such profound artistry."

"Someone like me?" Hana's tone had a slight edge. "You seem to know a lot about me already, Dr. Baumann."

Baumann's expression softened, though his eyes remained calculating. "It's my job to know. Investigative journalists like yourself tend to leave trails. Your work on historical artifacts is rather impressive. I suspect you're here for the same reason I am: to uncover the truths that others have tried to bury."

Hana's grip tightened on the book in her hands. "I didn't realize I was so predictable."

Baumann chuckled lightly, the sound devoid of true humor. "Not predictable, Ms. Sinclair. Just... thorough. And perhaps a bit idealistic. But that's what makes you effective, isn't it?"

Hana didn't reply immediately, her mind sifting through possibilities in assessing the situation. Baumann's interest in Malvagio was too pointed to be coincidental, and his knowledge of her work suggested that he had been watching her for some time. Whatever his intentions were, they weren't entirely academic.

"If you'll excuse me, Dr. Baumann," Hana said, stepping back toward the counter. "I have work to do."

Baumann didn't try to stop her. Instead, he inclined his head, his smile lingering. "Of course. But do tread carefully, Ms. Sinclair. Malvagio's legacy is… volatile. The more you uncover, the closer you come to the edge. And some edges aren't meant to be approached…"

Hana turned and left the shop without another word, her pulse quickening as she stepped back into the bustling streets of Rome. Baumann's presence felt like a shadow clinging to her thoughts, and she couldn't get past the feeling that he knew far more than he had revealed.

LATER THAT DAY, Hana returned to the Vatican to relay her encounter to Marcus at his office. His reaction was immediate and predictable: suspicion.

"Baumann's name has come up before among my colleagues in archaeological circles," Marcus said, pacing the length of the room. "He's known for pushing boundaries, often dabbling in subjects the academic community considers taboo. If he's interested in Malvagio, it's not for idle curiosity."

Before Hana could respond, there was a knock at the door. A Swiss Guard stepped in, announcing that Dr. Adrian Baumann had arrived and was requesting an audience. Marcus and Hana exchanged a tense glance. Marcus held up his hand to hold the guard in place momentarily. He pulled out a red damask cloth from a desk drawer and, after setting it in place behind him, nodded to the guard.

"Send him in," Marcus said, his voice steady but edged with wariness as he stood up.

Baumann entered the room with the same self-assured air Hana had observed earlier. He nodded politely to both of them, his gaze taking in the surroundings.

"Dr. Russo, Ms. Sinclair," he began, his tone pleasant. "Thank you for seeing me. I understand my presence here might raise questions, but I assure you, my intentions are purely academic."

Marcus folded his arms. "Then let's dispense with pleasantries. What do you know about Malvagio and the music box?"

Baumann's composure faltered almost imperceptibly, a momentary tightening around his eyes that lasted only a fraction of a second before his practiced smile returned. But Hana had caught it—that brief flash of genuine surprise that disrupted his carefully cultivated façade.

"Music box?" Baumann repeated, his voice maintaining its smooth cadence despite the subtle shift in his demeanor. He moved toward one of the ancient wooden chairs in the room and, without invitation, lowered himself into it with deliberate grace.

"Now that's... unexpected," he began. "I've spent decades tracking Malvagio's legacy through fragmentary references and obscure journals. The music box has always been the most elusive element—a theoretical cornerstone in his harmonic system that most scholars dismiss as apocryphal."

Marcus remained standing, his posture rigid. "You seem well-informed about something most people have never heard of."

Baumann's smile faltered for a moment before he recovered. "I know quite a bit about it, actually. Malvagio's work has long fascinated me, particularly his belief in music as a bridge between worlds. As for the elusive music box... well, let's just say I've been following its legendary trail for years."

Hana's eyes narrowed. "Following its trail? Why?"

Baumann leaned forward slightly, his voice dropping to a conspiratorial tone. "Because it's part of something larger. Malvagio wasn't working in isolation. He was part of a network—a cult, if you will—that sought to harness the power of sound to alter reality. The music box is one of their creations, a key to unlocking their ultimate goal."

Marcus's jaw tightened. "And what is that goal?"

Baumann's gaze turned cold. "That, Dr. Russo, is what I intend to find out. But I need your help. The Vatican's resources are unparalleled, and I believe our interests align more than you'd like to admit."

"I suggest you consider the idea of us working in tandem," he continued, "Now I'll take my leave so you can consider that. Thank you for seeing me on such short notice. Until we meet again."

After Baumann left, the room was charged with tension. Marcus and Hana sat in silence for a moment, processing the encounter.

"He's hiding something," Marcus said finally, his voice low. "That much is obvious."

Hana nodded slowly, tapping her pen against the edge of her notebook. "Agreed. But he's also right about one thing. The music box is part of a larger puzzle. If there's a network tied to Malvagio, Baumann might know more than he's letting on."

Marcus sighed, running a hand through his hair. "Which makes him either an invaluable ally or a dangerous adversary."

Hana leaned forward, her expression resolute. "Then we find out which one he is. But Marcus, we need to be careful. Baumann's too calculated to make a move without an agenda."

Marcus turned, his gaze shifting to the music box resting on the table behind him, concealed beneath the red damask cloth. Removing the cloth, its dark surface gleamed faintly under the dim light of the desk lamp, as though it were listening. "Agreed. But if Baumann's involvement brings us closer to understanding this thing... we can't afford to ignore him."

Hana tilted her head thoughtfully, her gaze locked on the now silent artifact. "It's possible he's trying to get us to trust him just enough to gain access to whatever we find. Did you notice how carefully he chose his words? He was probing us, testing what we knew without giving away anything concrete."

Marcus's expression hardened. "I noticed. And I don't trust him. But he knows something about the cult he mentioned. If that group is still active, they're a bigger threat than Baumann himself."

Hana leaned back, crossing her arms. "Then we use him as much as he's trying to use us. If he's connected to this cult, he might lead us to them... or expose their next move."

Marcus frowned, his mind clearly running through potential outcomes. "You think he's actively working with them? Or is he just an opportunist chasing the same leads?"

"Either way, he's dangerous," Hana replied. "Even if he's not directly involved, his obsession with Malvagio makes him unpredictable. His way of describing the music box showed more than mere curiosity. There was reverence. That's what worries me."

Marcus let out a heavy breath, the burden of their predicament pressing down on him. "We'll keep him at arm's length for now. If he tries anything, we'll cut him off. But until we know more about this cult and their intentions, we need every piece of information we can get."

Hana nodded, though her unease was perceptible. "I just hope we're not making a mistake by letting him get this close." She began to put her notes away. "I'm meeting Michael for dinner in a little bit. I can help you get everything here secured if you want to join us."

"No, you two enjoy yourselves. I know your careers usually keep you apart, so take advantage of a little alone time." He smiled. "I want to work a bit longer on this before I secure it all."

As Marcus resumed work, the shadows in the room appeared to stretch longer, their edges sharper against the walls. The music box remained silent, yet its presence pressed at the edge of his awareness, impossible to ignore. For a fleeting moment, he thought he saw a shimmer along its surface—like the ghost of a smirk. He shook off the thought, but the unease clung to him like dust.

Baumann's motives might remain a mystery for now, but one thing was certain: his path would cross theirs again, and when it did, the stakes would be higher than ever.

CHAPTER
ELEVEN

The next day, Father Michael Dominic and Marcus Russo sat in a secluded alcove of the Vatican Archives, surrounded by stacks of parchment and bound manuscripts. The air hung heavy with the scent of aged vellum, and the faint flicker of candlelight added to the solemnity of their work. Before them lay a series of letters, their ink faded but legible, written in a bold, flowing hand. The name Vincenzo Malvagio appeared repeatedly in the headers, alongside dates spanning the late 1720s.

Michael picked up one of the letters, his brow furrowing as he translated the Latin text aloud. "'To my most trusted confidant, the melody is nearly complete. It came to me in fragments, as though whispered by unseen voices. They have shown me the way… a perfect harmony that shall bind the material and the divine.'"

Marcus leaned closer, his eyes scanning the words. "'Whispered by unseen voices'… that's not just poetic language. He's talking about some kind of external influence."

HANA SINCLAIR SAT IN THE ARCHIVES' adjoining study, her laptop open beside a pile of historical records. The room was softly lit, but her focus was razor-sharp as she cross-referenced Malvagio's letters with documented events from the eighteenth century. Her fingers danced over the keyboard, compiling a timeline of disasters and unexplained phenomena.

"Hana, what have you found?" Marcus's voice broke her concentration as he and Michael entered the study, taking a break to stretch their backs and legs. She looked up, her face pale but resolute.

"A pattern," she said, turning the laptop toward them. A map of Europe was on the screen, dotted with markers and annotations. "During the years Malvagio was active, there were reports of mass hysteria, unexplained deaths, and even structural collapses in towns where his music was performed."

Michael's brow creased. "You're saying his compositions caused these events?"

"Not directly," Hana replied. "But there's a correlation. Look at this: in 1729, a cathedral in Naples collapsed during a recital of Malvagio's work. Witnesses described a 'wailing sound' that seemed to come from nowhere just before the structure gave way. And in 1731, a town in northern Italy reported a sudden outbreak of mass hysteria after a performance of one of his cantatas. People claimed they saw shadowy figures lurking in the streets."

Marcus leaned over her shoulder, studying the map.

"Malvagio's music, if connected to those events, was more than just art. It was a weapon."

Hana nodded. "A weapon, or a ritual. Either way, it's clear he wasn't just composing for human ears. And he didn't mind the cost of it in the lives and sanity of anyone who came into contact with his work."

The trio gathered around the table where the letters were laid out, their collective unease growing with every revelation. Marcus picked up one of the documents, his fingers tracing the elegant script.

"There's something else here," he said, his voice thoughtful. "These phrases he uses… 'whispered by unseen voices,' 'shown the way,' 'demand a price.' They're consistent with historical descriptions of possession or channeling. What if his imagination wasn't the only thing at play?"

Hana tilted her head. "You think he was actually in contact with… something?"

Marcus nodded slowly. "If we're to take these letters at face value, Malvagio wasn't working alone. He believed he was a conduit for something greater. And the results—the disasters, the hysteria—suggest that whatever influenced him wasn't human."

A shadow crossed Michael's face. "If that's true, then the melody isn't just dangerous because of its composition. It's dangerous because of its source."

Hana's eyes narrowed as she leaned closer to the letters. "Look at how he describes the music's effects… 'it moves not only the spirit but the fabric of reality itself.' That's not just artistic ambition. He's describing something… elemental."

Marcus began pacing, his thoughts racing. "What if the

melody is more than a creation? What if it's a message? Or worse, a key?"

Hana turned to him, her brow furrowing. "A key to what?"

Marcus stopped and gestured toward the music box. "To whatever is on the other side of these whispers. If Malvagio was receiving guidance—or commands—from some entity, then the melody could be designed to open an even more direct path to it."

Michael crossed his arms, his tone grave. "Which means every note, every chord, was crafted with intent. This went beyond a man simply experimenting with sound. He was building something precise."

Hana kept her eyes on the music box, her unease growing. "And if he was building a key, then completing the melody might unlock something that can't be controlled."

Marcus nodded, his expression grim. "Exactly. And whatever Malvagio was in contact with… it doesn't sound like it had humanity's best interests at heart."

Michael picked up one of the letters and read aloud: "'They have promised me eternity, but they have shown me glimpses of a world that is both beautiful and terrible. A world where their music reigns supreme, and our own becomes silence.'"

The room fell quiet as the implications sank in. The trio exchanged uneasy glances, each of them grappling with the magnitude of what they had uncovered.

Hana finally broke the tension. "We need to find out more. First, the rolled score in the music box has the final chords torn off. Why? And, if we find that piece, and the melody is completed, then what? Whoever—or whatever

—was guiding him might still be waiting for it to be played."

Marcus nodded, his gaze hardening. "Then we'll start with the records tied to his performances. Somewhere in all this, there's a clue to what he was trying to achieve."

Michael's voice was steady but laced with caution. "And we must tread carefully. If we're right about the nature of this melody, then uncovering its secrets might come at a greater cost than we're prepared to pay."

CHAPTER
TWELVE

Marcus and Hana sat in a quiet corner of the Vatican Archives, their faces illuminated by the glow of Hana's laptop screen. The faint hum of the room's lighting fixtures heightened the tension as they scoured a trove of digital records Marcus had uncovered in a restricted database. Each entry brought new revelations, their implications more disturbing than the last.

"Look at this," Marcus said, pointing to a file labeled *Ordo Musicae*. The document contained photos of modern gatherings, their participants clad in robes reminiscent of eighteenth-century attire. At the center of each group was a symbol they had come to recognize: the coiled serpent encircling a triangle, the emblem Malvagio had used in his manuscripts.

Hana zoomed in on one image, her brow furrowing. "These people are treating Malvagio like some kind of prophet."

"Not just a prophet," Marcus replied. "A messiah. They believe his work holds the key to... something."

Hana's fingers flew across the keyboard as she navigated to a series of intercepted messages attached to the file. "Listen to this," she said, reading aloud. "'The melody will restore balance to a corrupted world. Only through its perfection can we achieve the cleansing.'"

Marcus's expression turned dark and unyielding. "Cleansing. That's never a good word when it comes to cults."

Hana nodded, her gaze fixed on the screen. "They're not just worshipping Malvagio—they're actively trying to complete his work. And judging by these dates, they've been searching for the music box for years."

Marcus leaned back, raking a hand through his hair. "We need to figure out how far they've gotten. If they have access to any part of the melody, it could already be causing damage."

THE SUN WAS SETTING over Rome as Marcus and Hana met Michael in a secluded office within the Vatican. Spread across the table were documents, photos, and correspondence—pieces of a puzzle they were racing to assemble. The atmosphere was dense with tension as they shared what they had uncovered.

"There's more," Hana said, sliding a photograph across the table. It showed Adrian Baumann standing in a softly lit room, his silver-streaked hair unmistakable. Robed figures surrounded him, his hand raised as if leading a ceremony.

Michael's eyes widened. "Baumann's involved?"

Marcus nodded grimly. "Not just involved. He's leading them."

Michael picked up the photo, his jaw tightening. "This explains his interest in the music box. He's been playing us from the start."

Hana added, "The cult views Malvagio as a prophet, but they see Baumann as the modern voice of that prophecy. He's using the melody as a tool to summon... something."

Michael's gaze darkened. "What exactly are they trying to summon?"

Hana hesitated, then opened a file containing excerpts from intercepted communications. "They call it the Cleansing Flame. According to their doctrine, the melody will act as a gateway, allowing a powerful entity to cross into our world. They believe this entity will purify humanity by eradicating its corruption."

Marcus's gaze fixed on the music box resting on a nearby shelf. "Regardless of what they believe," he admitted, "Baumann's involvement means this cult is more organized—and more dangerous—than we thought."

As NIGHT FELL, the trio delved deeper into the cult's intercepted communications. The Vatican's intelligence network had provided access to a treasure trove of encrypted messages, and Hana was working tirelessly to decode them. Each revelation added a new layer of importance to their mission.

"Here's something," she said, her voice breaking the silence. "A sermon Baumann gave to his followers. 'The melody is the voice of the Cleansing Flame. Through its notes, we will summon the agent of renewal, and the corrupted world will burn away.'"

Michael's jaw clenched. "They're preparing for an apocalyptic event."

Hana glanced up, her skepticism at such far-reaching assertions evident in her scowl.

Michael leaned forward, his tone firm but measured. "I understand your skepticism, Hana. But the Vatican's archives are full of accounts that defy logic. Take the possessions in Loudun, France, or the exorcisms of Anneliese Michel. These weren't just psychological phenomena. They were battles against forces we couldn't fully comprehend."

Hana frowned, her fingers tightening around her pen. "Those cases could still have scientific explanations. Mental illness, mass delusions... people are susceptible to fear and suggestion."

Michael interrupted gently. "Perhaps. But consider this: every culture, across every era, has accounts of entities beyond human comprehension. They're described differently—as demons, spirits, gods—but the patterns are consistent. Are you willing to dismiss all of them as coincidence?"

Hana's shoulders sagged slightly, the import of his argument settling over her. "I don't know," she admitted. "But what if this cult is just using those patterns to manipulate people? Baumann's smart enough to exploit mythology for his own gain."

Marcus, who had been silent, spoke up. "Either way, the result is the same. Suppose they succeed in discovering and playing the melody. In that case, whether it's supernatural or feeds off the psychological belief of its power, the consequences will be catastrophic: it could trigger insanity either way. We need to stop them before they reach that point."

Michael nodded. "Agreed. The question is, how do we disrupt a group this well-organized?"

Hana tapped her pen against the table, her mind sorting through the chaos, eliminating the improbable. "We start by finding their next move. If Baumann is planning a ritual, he'll need specific conditions: a location, the right timing, and the tools required for composing and playing the melody. We need to intercept them before they do that."

Marcus stood, his determination evident. "Then let's get to work. If Baumann wants to use the melody to destroy the world, we'll ensure he never gets the chance."

CHAPTER
THIRTEEN

The Vatican Archives was a fortress of knowledge, its vast halls and chambers designed to protect the Church's secrets from time and prying eyes. Yet on this night, as Marcus Russo locked the door to his study, an unsettling stillness hung in the air. The encrypted manuscript rested inside a reinforced case on his desk, its delicate parchment illuminated by a single lamp.

Marcus lingered for a moment, his instincts prickling. The manuscript they had found within the music box—a treasure trove of Malvagio's cryptic notations—rested with the rolled parchment score inside a reinforced case on his desk, its delicate parchment illuminated by a single lamp. The music box, likewise, was nestled in the velvet cushion of another locked security box. Reassured of their safety, and with a final glance at the room, he turned off the light, locked the door, and left to meet Father Michael and Hana in a nearby chamber.

Moments later, as he walked down a hall, the lights flickered. The hum of electricity faltered, plunging the

Archives into near darkness. Emergency lanterns activated, casting eerie shadows across the walls. The sudden power outage set alarms buzzing in Marcus's mind.

"What's going on?" Hana asked, entering the hallway with Michael close behind.

Marcus shook his head, already moving back toward his study. "Stay here," he instructed.

As he neared the door, a faint creak echoed down the corridor. His heart pounded as he unlocked the study and stepped inside. The room was in disarray. Books lay scattered across the floor, and the glass case that had held the manuscript was shattered. The manuscript itself was gone—and so was the case for the music box

Marcus cursed under his breath, scanning the room for clues. His gaze landed on a window left ajar. A cold gust blew in, carrying with it the distant sound of footsteps fading into the night.

"Adrian Baumann," Marcus said, his voice tight with anger. He had rejoined Hana and Michael in the Archives' main chamber, explaining the break-in. "This has his fingerprints all over it."

Hana nodded grimly. "He's been circling us for days. This outage was no coincidence."

Michael frowned. "If Baumann has the manuscript and the music box, he's one step closer to completing the melody. We can't let him succeed."

Marcus pulled out his phone, scrolling through the Vatican's internal security feed. One camera near the eastern gate captured a figure in a gray coat slipping out of the compound.

"That's him," Marcus said, holding the screen up for Hana and Michael to see. "He's heading into the city."

The trio rushed to the Archives' exit—Michael calling the Swiss Guards to ready a Vatican car, Marcus patching through to the security office. As they navigated the narrow streets of Rome, guided by input from the surveillance cameras fed to them by the security sector, Marcus used the city's public access CCTV network to track Baumann's movements. The dim glow of streetlights flickered across Hana's face as she monitored intercepted communications on her laptop.

"Got him," Hana said suddenly, her voice alert with necessity. She pointed to a grainy image showing Baumann entering an old warehouse near Trastevere. "That's where he's gone."

The car screeched to a halt outside the warehouse, a crumbling structure with faded graffiti and rusted metal doors. The surrounding streets were eerily quiet, the silence cut through by the distant hum of traffic. Marcus stepped out first, scanning the area before gesturing for Hana and Michael to follow.

Inside, the air was damp and heavy, the faint scent of mildew mingling with something metallic. Their flashlights cut through the gloom, illuminating stacks of broken crates and scattered debris. Every sound—the creak of wood, the drip of water—was amplified in the oppressive stillness.

"This place looks abandoned," Michael whispered, his voice barely audible. "Why would Baumann come here?"

"It's secluded," Marcus replied. "The perfect spot to buy time and study the manuscript. Stay close."

They moved cautiously through the maze of debris, their footsteps muffled by the grime-covered floor. In the far corner of the warehouse, a faint light glimmered beneath a heavy metal door. Marcus signaled for Hana and

Michael to hold back as he approached, his hand resting on the doorknob. With a nod to his companions, he pushed the door open.

The scene inside was both startling and enraging. Adrian Baumann stood at a makeshift table, the stolen parchment score unrolled before him, the music box and manuscript resting beside it. A single lamp illuminated his face, casting shadows that accentuated his calm yet defiant expression. He looked up, his piercing blue eyes locking onto Marcus with an almost casual acknowledgment.

"You're persistent, I'll give you that," Baumann said, his tone laced with mock admiration. "But you're too late."

Marcus stepped forward, his voice taut with anger. "Hand it all over, Baumann. This ends now."

Baumann's smirk deepened. "Stop this? You can't. The melody is inevitable—it's already in motion. You must have triggered part of it when you uncovered it, yes? We heard the rumors, the manifestations... They were our signal. Proof that the awakening had begun. And now"—he gestured toward the stolen items—"we have everything we need."

Hana moved to flank Marcus, her eyes scanning the table. "You don't understand what you're playing with," she said, her tone intense. "This isn't about power or prophecy. It's destruction."

Baumann chuckled, his demeanor unshaken. "Destruction? No, Ms. Sinclair. This is renewal. Humanity has rotted from within, and the melody will cleanse it. You should be thanking me."

Before they could respond, Baumann's hand darted toward a small device on the table. He pressed a button, and the room was instantly filled with thick, acrid smoke. Marcus lunged forward, but Baumann was already moving, slipping through a hidden door at the back of the room.

"After him!" Marcus shouted, coughing as he waved the smoke away.

The trio gave chase, their flashlights bouncing wildly as they navigated the labyrinthine corridors of the warehouse. Baumann's footsteps echoed ahead, always just out of reach. At one point, they emerged into a loading bay, only to find it empty. The sound of an engine roared in the distance as Baumann's silhouette disappeared into the night.

"Damn it!" Marcus slammed his fist against the wall, frustration etched across his face. "He's gone."

Hana caught her breath, leaning against a nearby pillar. "But he didn't get everything." She held up several pages of notes she had swept up from the table before giving chase behind the other two. "These might be enough to piece together his next move."

Marcus nodded, his resolve hardening. "Then let's not waste any time. Baumann may have escaped, but we're not letting him finish this."

BACK AT THE VATICAN, the team regrouped in a conference room. Hana spread out what they had recovered from Baumann's hideout: maps and notes he had made. Together, they pieced together his plan.

"He's heading to a monastery outside the city," Hana said, pointing to a map marked with a red circle. "Santa Lucia. From what I've read here, it's secluded, abandoned for decades, and historically tied to Malvagio's network."

The light in Michael's eyes dimmed. "If he's planning a ritual, that's the perfect place for it."

Marcus nodded. "He's trying to perform the melody. Only we know that the ending of the score is torn off and missing, so we have some time in our favor. But if he succeeds in completing the score and performs it, the consequences could be catastrophic."

Michael added, "Or he could play it as it is—incomplete. Who knows what result that could have?"

Hana's skepticism surfaced. "We're still talking about a melody. A piece of music. How much damage can it really do?"

Michael turned to her, his voice steady but firm. "You've seen the effects of the melody so far. The hysteria, the visions, the chaos. Imagine that amplified a hundredfold. If this ritual opens a gateway to… whatever Baumann believes it will, we'll be facing more than just music."

Hana didn't reply, but the tension in her posture betrayed her unease. She glanced at Marcus, who was already gathering his gear.

"We don't have time to debate," Marcus said. "We need to get to Santa Lucia before Baumann can finish what he started."

As they prepared to leave, the magnitude of their mission weighed heavily on all of them. The stolen manuscript had given Baumann a dangerous advantage to finishing the torn score, and the stakes had never been higher. Outside, the city lights glimmered against the night sky, but the darkness beyond them felt ominous, as if the melody's reach was already spreading. The clock was ticking, and the battle for Malvagio's legacy had only just begun.

CHAPTER
FOURTEEN

The night was thick with mist as Marcus and Father Michael approached the crumbling remains of the Santa Lucia Monastery. Its towering walls, weathered by centuries of neglect, loomed ominously against the pale moonlight. The air carried an unnatural chill, as though the monastery itself resisted their presence.

Marcus crouched behind a cluster of overgrown shrubs, his eyes scanning the shadowy courtyard. Beside him, Michael adjusted his clerical collar, his jaw tight with resolve. They both knew the risks of confronting the cult head-on, but there was no alternative.

"Hana," Marcus whispered into his earpiece, "we're in position. Any movement on your end?"

Hana's voice crackled through the comms. "Negative. The perimeter's clear, but I'll keep monitoring. Be careful in there."

"Always," Marcus replied, his tone laced with grim determination.

Michael glanced at him. "Do you think Baumann has started the ritual yet?"

"If he hasn't, he's close. He'd planned the theft carefully, and I wouldn't be surprised if he had his cultists already assembled in anticipation of this," Marcus said, nodding toward a faint flicker of light spilling from one of the monastery's broken windows. "Let's move."

The two men crept toward the monastery's main entrance, their footsteps muffled by the damp earth. The heavy wooden doors were ajar, a sign that the cult had no reason to fear intruders. Marcus pushed the door open slowly, its rusty hinges groaning in protest. The scent of burning incense and something metallic, possibly blood, permeated the space inside.

They entered a long corridor, its stone walls lined with decayed tapestries. The flickering light they had seen from outside grew brighter as they neared the main chapel. Marcus held up a hand, signaling Michael to stop.

Voices echoed from the chapel, low and rhythmic, chanting in a language Marcus couldn't recognize.

"We're close," he whispered. "Stay behind me."

Michael nodded, his hand tightening around his pectoral cross to silence its jangling. Together, they pressed forward, their senses heightened as the ritual's ominous energy grew stronger.

The chapel was a grotesque mockery of its former sanctity. Rows of robed cultists knelt in a semicircle around a raised altar, where Adrian Baumann stood with the stolen manuscript spread before him. The air hummed with an unnatural vibration as Baumann chanted, his voice rising and falling in a hypnotic rhythm. Behind him, a massive iron candelabrum cast jagged shadows across the walls, its flames dancing in time with the chant.

THE DEVIL'S SYMPHONY

Marcus and Michael hid behind a collapsed pillar, observing the scene. The cultists' movements were unnervingly synchronized, their heads bowing and rising as if pulled by invisible strings. On the altar, the music box—its surface glowing faintly—emitted a haunting melody that seemed to bypass the ears and resonate directly in the mind.

Michael's face was pale. "Do you hear that?"

Marcus nodded, his jaw clenched. "It's the melody. It's not complete, but it's enough to do... this." He gestured to the cultists, many of whom were visibly trembling, their movements jerky and erratic.

The melody's effect was perceivable, its dissonant notes weaving through the air like an invasive force. One by one, the synchronization began to falter, replaced by an unsettling chaos. Some cultists clutched their heads, as though trying to block out the sound. Others rocked back and forth, their bodies wracked with tremors. Whispers filled the air, soft at first, then growing louder, overlapping in an incomprehensible cacophony. The cultists looked around in confusion, their eyes darting toward unseen figures lurking in the shadows.

"It's affecting them," Michael said, his voice barely audible over the growing din. "The melody's driving them mad." His brow crinkled in question as he asked, "But why aren't we—"

"The earpieces," Marcus answered. "There is something about them interrupting the sounds enough, I'm guessing." There was no more time to speculate, as suddenly one of the cultists let out a bloodcurdling scream and collapsed to the ground, his body convulsing violently. Another began clawing at her face, her nails leaving bloody streaks across her skin. The chaos spread like a contagion, infecting the once-unified group. Some cultists began to sob uncontrollably, their wails echoing through the chapel. Others turned on each other, their hands grasping at robes and throats in blind panic.

Marcus watched in horror as one cultist stumbled toward the altar, his face contorted with fear. "The shadows," he cried, his voice cracking. "They're everywhere!" He collapsed before reaching Baumann, his body twitching as though struck by an unseen force.

Baumann's voice cut through the chaos, intense and commanding. "Hold your places! The melody is not yet complete! Focus, or all will be lost!"

But the cultists' obedience was crumbling. A woman near the back of the room shrieked and bolted for the exit, only to be intercepted by another member who tackled her to the ground. Their struggle devolved into a brutal fight, their screams piercing the heavy air. Meanwhile, a group of cultists near the altar began tearing at their robes, their eyes wide with terror as they mumbled incoherently.

Marcus turned to Michael, his expression grim. "This is what happens when you try to play God," he muttered. "We have to stop this."

Michael nodded, his grip tightening on his crucifix. "Agreed. But look at them, Marcus. They're already breaking. The melody's incomplete, and it's tearing them apart."

Near the altar, Baumann's frustration was evident. He raised his arms, his voice booming over the chaos. "Do not falter! We are on the brink of salvation! The Cleansing Flame awaits us!"

The melody's intensity surged, its dissonant notes colliding in a way that made the very air seem to shudder. The flames in the candelabrum flared wildly, casting grotesque shapes onto the chapel walls. Some cultists began to wail, their voices blending with the melody in a grotesque harmony. Others fell to their knees, their hands clasped in fervent prayer as tears streamed down their faces.

The oppressive atmosphere closed in, the strains of the melody pressing against Marcus's chest. He pressed his earpiece tighter into his one ear, hoping to keep the debilitating effects of the sounds at bay. But even though the full effects were broken by his one-sided hearing of it, he could feel it clawing at his mind, an invasive presence that sought to unravel his thoughts. Beside him, Michael's expression was strained, but his resolve remained unbroken.

"We have to move now," Marcus said, his voice hoarse. "Before it's too late."

Michael nodded, his eyes fixed on the altar where Baumann stood, a figure of twisted conviction amid the chaos. The cultists were unraveling, their humanity stripped away by the very force they had sought to wield. And yet, despite the mounting destruction, the melody played on, its haunting notes promising not salvation, but ruin.

Marcus and Michael moved swiftly, using the chaos to their advantage. They slipped between rows of fallen cultists, their eyes fixed on the altar where Baumann remained steadfast, his hands raised as he chanted. The music box's glow intensified, casting eerie patterns across the chapel walls.

Marcus reached the base of the altar and ducked behind a column, motioning for Michael to follow. "You distract him," he whispered. "I'll grab the music box."

Michael hesitated for a moment, then nodded. He

stepped out from behind the column, his voice ringing out with authority. "Adrian Baumann! Stop this madness!"

Baumann turned, his expression shifting from surprise to disdain. "Father Dominic," he said, his voice dripping with mockery. "I wondered when you'd show up. Tell me, are you here to save your flock? Or to beg for a glimpse of the truth?"

"This isn't truth," Michael said, stepping closer. "It's destruction. You're tearing these people apart, and for what? To summon a force you can't control?"

Baumann laughed, a hollow sound that echoed through the chapel, a counterpoint to the music. "You speak of control as if it's necessary. The Cleansing Flame will burn away the corruption of this world, and in its place, we will find purity. You should embrace it, Father."

As Baumann spoke, Marcus had crept toward the altar, keeping low to avoid drawing attention. His heart pounded as he reached the table and saw the manuscript, its pages filled with Malvagio's intricate notations, and the music box beside it, its sounds hauntingly echoing in the air, building toward the uncompleted chord, ready to unleash who knew what additional horrors. Without hesitation, he grabbed for them.

Baumann reacted just as quickly and snatched at Marcus's hands. The two struggled, the manuscript fluttering to the floor as the music box teetered on the altar between them. Marcus swung his arm up to twist away as Baumann leaned in to gain leverage. Baumann's elbow caught the music box, which clattered to the floor, its drawer at the bottom flying open. Instantly, the music stopped, and cultists around them collapsed. Baumann and Marcus saw the rolled score thrown off the slender rod that had been in the drawer, and they both lunged for the fallen objects.

The fingers of Marcus's right hand snatched the scroll even as his left reached for the music box, but Baumann's elbow smacked into his face, and Marcus fell to the side. He kicked out with both feet, connecting with Baumann's neck with one foot and chest with the other. The man fell sprawling backward, grabbing at his neck, gagging as he hit the ground.

Marcus looked up. Several cultists stood ready to jump him, eyes blazing with fury, and he scrambled to his feet.

"You dare interfere?" Baumann gasped from where he lay. "You don't understand what you're meddling with!"

"I understand enough to know this needs to stop."

Michael had rushed to Marcus's side, his hand gripping his crucifix. "We need to get out of here," he said urgently. "This place isn't stable." A wave of energy rippled through the chapel, and the floor began shaking beneath them all.

Marcus nodded, his gaze lingering on the music box behind, where two of the cultists had already advanced on them.

"Leave it," Michael said. "We'll deal with it later."

They turned and ran toward the exit, the melody's incomplete performance lingering in their minds like a haunting memory. As Marcus and Michael emerged into the cool night air, they found Hana waiting, her expression a mix of relief and worry.

"Did you get it?" she asked.

Marcus held up the score. "Got the brain behind it. But Baumann still has the music box and the manuscript. He's not done yet."

Hana glanced back at the monastery, where the glow of the ritual still flickered faintly. "Then neither are we."

CHAPTER
FIFTEEN

The Vatican, a stronghold of faith and history, had always seemed impervious to the darker forces of the world. But tonight, as shadows deepened in the corridors and whispers carried on a windless air, the sense of sanctity felt disturbingly fragile. Karl Dengler, a veteran of the Swiss Guard, stood near the entrance to the Apostolic Palace, his hand resting on the hilt of his ceremonial sword. His keen eyes scanned the softly illuminated hallway for anything out of place.

Beside him, his partner, Lukas Bischoff, a younger but no less dedicated guard, shifted uneasily. "Do you feel that?" he asked, his voice low. The question hung in the air, heavy with dread.

Karl nodded, his expression grim. "The temperature dropped as soon as we entered this wing. Something is wrong. Stay alert."

As they moved deeper into the palace, the atmosphere grew more oppressive. Paintings on the walls—depicting scenes of saintly triumphs and divine miracles—shimmered unnaturally in the flickering candlelight. Lukas paused near a display case holding a relic—a fragment of the True Cross. The air around it seemed to ripple, as though reality itself were bending.

A sudden crash shattered the silence. The sound echoed through the corridors, followed by a guttural growl that made the hairs on the back of Karl's neck stand on end. Drawing his sword, he gestured for Lukas to follow.

The source of the noise was in the Chapel of St. Sebastian. As they entered, they saw overturned pews and shattered candlesticks scattered across the marble floor. The golden tabernacle had been knocked from its pedestal, its doors flung open. Above it, a shadow writhed on the wall, amorphous and menacing. It moved like smoke but pulsed with a malevolent energy that felt almost alive.

Lukas gasped. "What is that?"

Karl's grip on his sword tightened. "Something that shouldn't be here."

The shadow surged forward, its form stretching unnaturally toward them. Karl stepped in front of Lukas, raising his sword. "In the name of Christ, be gone!" he commanded, his voice steady despite the fear gripping him.

The shadow hesitated, as if recoiling from the authority in Karl's words. But it didn't retreat. Instead, it let out a bone-chilling shriek that pierced through the very fabric of the chapel. Lukas stumbled backward, clutching his ears.

Karl advanced, his sword gleaming in the faint light. With each step, he recited the Lord's Prayer, his voice growing louder and more resolute. The shadow began to waver, its edges fraying as if dissolving under the weight of his words. Finally, with a last, anguished scream, it dissipated, leaving the chapel eerily silent.

Lukas rose shakily to his feet. "That... that wasn't human."

"No," Karl said, sheathing his sword. "And something tells me that won't be the last of it."

LATER THAT NIGHT, Karl and Lukas gathered in the security control room, where a bank of monitors displayed live feeds from across the Vatican. The atmosphere was tense as they reviewed footage of unexplained phenomena: flickering lights, objects moving on their own, and strange, shadowy figures that appeared and disappeared in an instant.

"This isn't random," Lukas said, leaning closer to the screen. "These things are targeting specific locations."

Karl nodded. "Relics. They're drawn to anything sacred."

Lukas frowned, his brow furrowing in thought. "If they're attacking holy objects, maybe there's a way to repel them."

He pulled a small prayer book from his pocket and began flipping through its pages. "There are hymns and prayers specifically meant to combat evil. Maybe..."

Before Karl could respond, the room grew cold, and the lights dimmed. A low, guttural growl filled the air, sending a shiver down their spines. Lukas stood abruptly, holding up the prayer book. He began to sing a hymn he had learned as a boy, his voice steady despite the fear in his eyes.

"Christus vincit, Christus regnat, Christus imperat..."

The growling intensified, and a shadow began to

coalesce in the corner of the room. But as Lukas continued the Latin hymn, the shadow faltered, its form flickering like a dying flame. By the time he reached the final line, it had vanished entirely.

Karl stared at Lukas, his expression a mix of awe and relief. "It worked."

Lukas nodded, his hands trembling slightly. "The words have power. Maybe we can use this."

Over the next several hours, the two guards tested their theory. Armed with prayer books and hymnals, they patrolled the Vatican, reciting prayers and singing hymns whenever they encountered a manifestation. Each time, the entities retreated, their presence unable to withstand the force of sacred words.

By dawn, the Vatican was quiet once more, though the guards knew the peace was temporary. They had discovered a way to defend against the entities, but the source of the disturbances remained.

IN THE EARLY MORNING, Karl and Lukas joined Marcus, Michael, and Hana in a secure briefing room. The group looked haggard, their faces lined with exhaustion and concern.

"What's the status?" Marcus asked, his voice clipped.

Karl leaned forward, resting his hands on the table. "We've been dealing with manifestations all night. Shadows, growls, objects moving… it's like the whole Vatican is under siege."

Lukas spoke up. "We discovered that specific prayers and hymns repel the entities. It's not a permanent solution, but it's effective."

Hana looked skeptical. "Prayers? Hymns? These things

sound more like poltergeists than demons. Maybe it's some kind of energy reacting to the relics."

Marcus shook his head. "No, it's more than that. These manifestations started after the melody was played."

Michael frowned. "The melody?"

"Think about it," Marcus said. "The melody isn't just music. It's a frequency, a resonance. If it's incomplete, it's unstable. That instability could be creating a kind of... beacon."

Hana raised an eyebrow. "A beacon for what?"

Marcus's features hardened. "For whatever these entities are. They're drawn to the melody's unholy resonance. It's like it's calling out to them."

Michael nodded slowly. "And the relics?"

"They're symbols of faith and sanctity," Marcus said. "The entities are attacking them because they're the only thing standing in the way of the melody's full influence."

Michael nodded gravely. "That makes sense. Considering their attacks are centered on the Vatican, the most sacred of sites, that confirms the demonic nature of these forces we're facing."

The room fell silent as the weight of his words sank in. Hana broke the silence. "If the melody is the cause, then we must prevent it from happening again. Especially stopping any full playing of that melody."

Marcus nodded. "Agreed. But until we can, we need to fortify the Vatican against what has already been released. Karl, Lukas—keep using the prayers and hymns. We'll work on finding a way to neutralize the melody once and for all. You two have the night shift for now, right?"

Lukas nodded.

"Good. But spread the word to the guards on any shift

as well, that if they encounter anything unusual, they should do the same."

The group dispersed, each carrying the heavy burden of their task. As Karl and Lukas returned to their patrol, they couldn't shake the feeling that the worst was yet to come. The melody's power was growing, and with it, the darkness threatening to consume the Vatican.

CHAPTER
SIXTEEN

The Vatican Library was unusually quiet as Marcus and Hana sat across from each other at a long oak table. Between them lay a scattering of reports, intercepted communications, and hastily scribbled notes. The dim light from an overhead chandelier cast long shadows, amplifying the sense of unease that hung in the air.

Hana pushed a sheet of paper toward Marcus, her brows knitted tightly together. "It's happening faster than we thought," she said. "Baumann's cult is imploding."

Marcus picked up the report, scanning the highlighted sections. "Loyalists are digging in," he muttered, his tone grim. "They're claiming the melody's failure at Santa Lucia is a test of faith. And blaming us for their failure. Meanwhile, others are calling Adrian Baumann a fraud, and some are renouncing the group and leaving."

Hana leaned back in her chair, running a hand through her hair. "This kind of fracture is dangerous. The ones who stay will be more fanatical than ever. They'll feel like they have something to prove."

Marcus nodded, his gaze still fixed on the paper. "And the ones who leave?"

"Potential allies," Hana replied. "Or casualties. If Baumann sees them as a threat, he won't hesitate to silence them."

Marcus sighed, setting the paper down. He studied the chaotic notes spread before them. Each line told a story of desperation: intercepted whispers of betrayal, glimpses of violence as old alliances crumbled. The cult had once operated with chilling precision, united by Baumann's vision. Now it was fragmented, its members scattered like shards of broken glass.

"This is what happens when faith meets failure," Marcus whispered. "They're lost without the promises Baumann gave them. Some are angry, some are terrified. But all of them are dangerous."

Hana tapped her pen against the table, her thoughts racing. "We have to use this. If they're fractured, we can exploit that. Reach the ones who've left and find out what they know."

"It's a gamble," Marcus replied. "The loyalists will double down. The more isolated Baumann becomes, the more desperate he'll get. That's when he'll be at his most dangerous."

Hana's lips thinned in quiet resolve. "Desperate leaders make mistakes. We need to make sure we're ready when he does."

A sudden knock at the library door startled them both. Father Michael entered, his face pale but composed. He carried a thin folder in one hand, his expression serious.

"I've just come from Cardinal Severino," he said.

"We've received confirmation that several defectors have reached out to independent contacts in Rome. They're looking for protection."

Hana's eyes lit up with determination. "Do we know who they are?"

Michael nodded. "One name has come up repeatedly: Luciana Mancini. She was part of Baumann's inner circle. If anyone knows his plans, it's her."

Marcus straightened in his seat. "Where is she now?"

"In hiding," Michael replied. "She's reached out to a contact near Aventine Hill. She's scared but willing to talk."

Hana immediately grabbed her bag, her focus shifting. "Then we don't have time to waste. If Baumann finds her first..."

Michael placed a calming hand on her shoulder. "We'll handle it. But we need to proceed carefully. Baumann's people will be watching for any sign of defectors."

"Then let's make sure we find her before they do," Marcus said, his voice resolute. "She's our best chance at understanding what Baumann's planning next."

THE NARROW STREETS of Trastevere were alive with activity as Hana made her way to a small café tucked into a quiet corner of the neighborhood. The late afternoon sun cast a warm glow over the cobblestones, but Hana's mind was far from the idyllic scene. She dwelled on the secure message received only hours before—a cryptic plea from someone claiming to be a former member of Baumann's cult.

The café was nearly empty when he arrived, save for a few locals sipping espresso at outdoor tables. Hana stepped inside, the aroma of freshly brewed coffee mingling with the faint scent of aged wood.

A young man behind the counter glanced up and gave a polite nod.

"Signorina Sinclair?" he asked, his voice low.

Hana nodded. "That's me."

The man gestured toward a corner table, where a folded newspaper lay atop a small envelope. "For you. The sender said you'd understand."

Hana crossed the room, her steps measured. She picked up the newspaper and the envelope, her fingers brushing against the worn paper. Sliding into the seat, she unfolded the note inside. The handwriting was hurried, almost frantic:

> I'm ready to talk. I can't do this anymore. Meet me at the old cloister near Aventine Hill, tonight at midnight. Come alone.

Hana read the note twice before slipping it into her pocket. She glanced around the café, her instincts on high alert. If this defector was genuine, the meeting could provide critical information about Baumann's next move. But if it were a trap, she would need to be prepared.

As she stood to leave, her phone buzzed in her bag. It was a message from Marcus: "**Got confirmation on the lead. Cloister at midnight. Be careful.**"

Hana replied with a single word: "**Understood.**"

Back in her apartment, Hana prepared for the meeting with meticulous care. She packed a small recorder and a flashlight. She reviewed the details of Luciana's background, piecing together a portrait of a woman from being a troubled child to a conflicted adult—the perfect candidate for being drawn into a cult. She became fiercely loyal to Baumann but had now turned against him. Could Hana trust her?

The hours dragged on as she waited for nightfall. When the time came, Hana slipped into the dark streets of Rome, her heart pounding with anticipation. The cloister near Aventine Hill loomed ahead, its ancient walls bathed in the pale glow of moonlight. The silence was oppressive, broken only by the faint rustle of leaves in the breeze.

MOONLIGHT BATHED the ancient cloister near Aventine Hill; its stone arches threw dark shadows across the overgrown courtyard. Hana arrived first, her heart pounding as she scanned the area. She had insisted on coming despite Marcus's warnings about the risks. This lead was too important to ignore.

A figure emerged from the shadows, their movements hesitant. It was a woman, her face partially obscured by a hood. She paused at the edge of the courtyard, her posture wary. Hana stepped forward, keeping her hands visible. "You're safe here," she whispered. "I'm Hana. You reached out to us."

The woman hesitated, then lowered her hood. Her face was pale, her eyes darting nervously. "My name is Luciana," she said, her words little more than a whisper. "I was part of Adrian Baumann's inner circle. But I can't do it anymore. Not after what I've seen. What I felt. It was…" She shuddered as if reliving the horrors unleashed in even that partial playing of the Devil's Symphony. "I just had to escape."

Hana nodded, her expression encouraging. "You're doing the right thing, Luciana. Tell me what you know."

THE DEVIL'S SYMPHONY

The clearly frightened woman glanced over her shoulder as if expecting someone or something to appear. "Baumann... he's not done," she said. "I know your people stole the score from the music box, but Baumann had already unrolled it and taken photos of it. He plans to set up the ritual again very soon. But he needs something else, too: artifacts tied to Malvagio. He thinks they'll give him the power to finish what the melody alone couldn't. Then he'll conduct the final *Purification Symphony*."

Hana's stomach tightened. "What kind of artifacts?"

Luciana shook her head, her eyes wide with fear. "I don't know all of them. But I've heard him talk about another manuscript... something that was hidden centuries ago. Something Malvagio himself used. He thinks it's here in Rome."

Hana's mind raced as she processed the information. If Adrian Baumann was searching for additional artifacts, their work was far from over. She reached out, placing a reassuring hand on Luciana's arm. "We'll stop him," she said firmly. "But we need your help. Can you tell us anything else?"

Luciana hesitated, then nodded. "There's a location... a villa outside the city. Baumann's been using it as a base. I can show you where it is."

Before Hana could respond, a distant noise broke the stillness—the sound of footsteps approaching. Luciana's eyes widened in panic. "He's found me," she whispered, her voice trembling. "You have to go."

Hana's grip tightened on Luciana's arm. "Not without you."

But before she could say more, Marcus emerged from the shadows, his expression urgent. "Hana, we have to move. Now."

The three of them slipped into the darkness, the depth of Luciana's revelations pressing heavily on their minds. Baumann still had the music box, and now they knew he also had a copy of the incomplete score. Between that and the fractured cult, the new artifacts, and Baumann's relentless ambition, the battle was far from over.

CHAPTER
SEVENTEEN

As dawn broke over Rome, the team gathered in Marcus's study, poring over maps, manuscripts, and intercepted communications from Adrian Baumann's cult. The clearly traumatized Luciana Mancini had revealed that the next place that Adrian planned to play the composition was in San Lorenzo Monastery, yet another abandoned place of worship, but this one a bit unique in its acoustics. Not trusting her fully, the team had worked diligently to confirm her assertion. Now they had concluded this was, in fact, Adrian's most likely next destination. And the clock was ticking. The atmosphere was electric with urgency.

"Baumann's next move is clear," Marcus said, pointing to a marked location on the map. "They're heading to the ruins of San Lorenzo Monastery. It's isolated, defensible, and, again, historically tied to Malvagio."

Hana scanned the map. "And if they get there first?"

Michael's voice was steady. "Then they'll play the melody, and the world will feel the consequences."

"San Lorenzo makes sense," Marcus continued, spreading out additional documents. "It's mentioned in some of Malvagio's earlier correspondence as a place where he conducted his more... experimental work. The site is tied to rituals involving the resonance of specific spaces."

Hana frowned. "Ritual acoustics?"

"Exactly," Marcus said. "The monastery's design amplifies sound in a way that would enhance the melody's impact. If Baumann's cult understands this, they'll use it to their advantage."

Lukas, standing near the doorway, spoke up. "We've fortified the Vatican as much as possible. But if these entities are drawn to the melody's resonance, they'll only grow stronger the longer this continues."

Karl nodded in agreement. "The longer we wait, the more dangerous this becomes."

Marcus's jaw tightened as he looked at his companions. "Then we don't wait. We head to San Lorenzo and stop Baumann before it's too late."

The group dispersed to prepare, each carrying the heavy burden of their mission. Hana packed her notes with deliberate care, her thoughts sharpened with both anticipation and dread. She glanced at Michael, who was deep in thought, his fingers brushing over the worn cover of a prayer book.

"Do you think we'll make it in time?" she asked.

Michael's gaze met hers, his expression resolute. "We have to. Failure isn't an option."

As the group reconvened near the entrance, the first rays of sunlight pierced the misty streets of Rome, casting ragged shadows that echoed the substance of their task.

With their plans set, they departed, each silently praying that their actions would be enough to counter the growing darkness. The melody's power loomed over them like a storm cloud, its unholy resonance promising devastation if left unchecked.

CHAPTER
EIGHTEEN

The ruins of San Lorenzo Monastery stood like a sentinel in the pre-dawn light, its jagged silhouette framed by the thick mist clinging to the hills. Marcus and Michael approached cautiously, their breaths visible in the chilled air. Behind them, in their vehicle hidden in the trees, sat Hana with Luciana Mancini. The village nearby had been served for centuries by this monastery, but time had relegated it to one more shadowed structure of the past. The monastery's eerie stillness was disturbed only by faint, otherworldly echoes that emanated from within, growing louder as they neared.

"Do you hear that?" Marcus asked, his voice just a thread of sound. He paused, tilting his head toward the building, even as he pressed his earpiece in tighter to avoid the effects of the musical echoes.

Michael nodded, his brow furrowed. "The melody. It's different now. Deeper, fuller. As if the monastery itself is amplifying it."

"Acoustics," Marcus murmured, scanning the surroundings. "Malvagio must have chosen this place for the resonance here... it's designed to carry sound to every corner."

The rhythmic chant of Adrian Baumann's cult grew louder, intertwined with the haunting tune of the music box already playing. It reverberated through the stone walls, creating a dissonance that sent shivers down their spines. The melody seemed alive, shifting and writhing as if feeding on the very air around them.

Marcus crouched near the entrance, his gaze scanning the broken doorway. "We have to move fast. The acoustics in this place could amplify the melody to dangerous levels."

Michael gripped his crucifix tightly. "If they complete the melody here, with this resonance... the consequences could be disastrous."

They exchanged a look of grim determination before stepping inside, the melody's haunting pull leading them into the heart of the monastery.

The main hall of San Lorenzo Monastery was vast and cavernous, its high arched ceilings and stone walls creating an acoustic chamber unlike any other. The melody emanating from the cursed music box filled the space, its haunting tune bouncing off the walls and converging in a pulsating wave of sound that permeated the very fabric of the room.

Dozens of robed cultists stood in concentric circles around an ornate altar, their chants blending seamlessly with the music. Adrian Baumann stood at the center, the music box before him on the altar. His arms were raised, conducting the cacophony with an almost ecstatic fervor.

"The melody is a bridge!" Baumann proclaimed, his

voice booming over the chants. "It will connect the realms and cleanse this world of its corruption!"

Marcus and Michael pressed themselves against a pillar at the edge of the room, their expressions tense as they took in the scene. The air hummed with the melody's resonance, a palpable force that vibrated through their bodies.

"It's not just sound," Michael whispered, his voice strained. "It's something more. It's alive."

Marcus's jaw tightened. "And it's getting stronger. We need to stop this now."

As they moved closer, the effects of the melody became more apparent. Cultists at the edges of the circle began to sway erratically, their movements jerky and unnatural. Some clutched their heads, as if trying to block out a sound only they could hear. The resonance in the room seemed to warp reality itself, distorting the space around the altar.

Michael clutched his crucifix tightly and stepped forward. "Adrian Baumann!" he shouted, his voice cutting through the cacophony. "Stop this madness! You don't understand what you're unleashing!"

Baumann turned slowly, his expression one of serene confidence. "Ah, Father Dominic. You're just in time to witness the culmination of Malvagio's masterpiece. Isn't it beautiful?"

"It's destruction," Michael said firmly, his voice steady despite the oppressive force of the melody. Although his earpiece dampened the effects, still the dark power of it pounded against his senses. "You're tampering with powers beyond your comprehension."

Baumann laughed, a hollow sound that echoed unnaturally in the chamber. "You think I don't understand? I have seen the truth! This melody will burn away the rot of this world and pave the way for purity."

Marcus used the distraction to edge closer to the altar, his eyes locked on the music box. The melody's intensity was almost unbearable now, its vibrations threatening to overwhelm his senses.

Suddenly, Baumann raised his arms, and the melody shifted, its tone deepening into a guttural resonance that shook the very foundation of the monastery. The cultists cried out in unison, their voices a mixture of ecstasy and agony.

"He's completing it," Michael said, his voice urgent. "We're out of time!"

Marcus surged forward, using the chaos to his advantage. He reached the base of the altar, his heart pounding as the melody's resonance intensified. The air around the music box shimmered with a malevolent energy, its surface glowing faintly as if alive.

"Stop him!" Baumann shouted, his voice commanding. Several cultists broke from their trance-like states and lunged at Marcus. He dodged the first and used his momentum to knock another to the ground. Michael stepped in, his crucifix raised as he recited the Lord's Prayer with unwavering conviction.

"In the name of Christ, I command you to cease!" Michael's voice reverberated through the hall, momentarily disrupting the melody. The cultists hesitated, their movements faltering as if restrained by an unseen force.

Marcus seized the opportunity and reached for the music box. The moment his fingers touched it, a shockwave of energy rippled through the room, throwing him backward as he seized the music box tightly to his chest, snatching the onyx key out from its hole. The melody sputtered and faltered, its dissonant notes clashing in a chaotic burst.

Baumann's face twisted in fury. "You don't know what you've done!" he shouted, his voice distorted by the melody's collapse. The resonance in the room began to destabilize, the air crackling with electricity.

Michael rushed to Marcus's side, helping him to his feet. "We have to get out of here. This place is coming apart."

As they made their way toward the exit, some cultists began to take chase, stumbling over others who still clung to their throbbing heads.

Baumann's voice rang out behind them. "You can't stop the effects of melody! It has already begun!"

The two men ran under the broken doorway and through the foyer. The floor beneath them trembled as the monastery's acoustics turned against itself, the remaining resonance spiraling into chaos behind them. The keystone to the doorway shifted, then fell, the stones of the arch tumbling down, blocking their pursuers. By the time they reached the courtyard, the melody had ceased, leaving an oppressive silence in its wake.

Hana's voice crackled through their earpieces. "What happened? Did you stop it?"

Michael answered, his voice weary but resolute. "For now. We recovered the box. The monastery... it's no longer a threat. But Baumann and his followers still are."

As they made it to the car, Marcus glanced back at the crumbling structure, its once menacing presence diminished in the dawn light. "We bought ourselves time," he said. "But Baumann won't stop. We need to prepare for what's coming."

Michael placed a reassuring hand on Marcus's shoulder. "Then we'll be ready."

The battle against Baumann's cult was far from over, but for the first time, they felt the faintest glimmer of hope.

CHAPTER NINETEEN

The Vatican Library was quiet, its vast halls illuminated by the soft glow of antique lamps. Hana sat hunched over a table scattered with notes from the original diary discovered with the music box. Her laptop was open, displaying an array of ancient symbols alongside notes and translations she had compiled over the past hours. The cryptic text of Vincenzo Malvagio's diary alongside the score had begun to unravel under her meticulous scrutiny.

"It's not just music," she muttered, her voice suffused with both fascination and dread. "This sequence... it's mathematical. Rhythmic. But it's also encoded with references to ancient hymns."

Marcus Russo leaned over her shoulder, his eyes scanning the screen. "What kind of hymns?"

Hana tapped a section of the manuscript. "This passage here references a hymn from the fourth century. It's a Gregorian chant, one that was reportedly used during exorcisms."

"Used to drive out demons?" Marcus asked.

"Well, yes, according to this, anyway. But it's more than that," Hana replied. She turned the laptop toward him, displaying a diagram. "The Malvagio melody's final chord, the part torn away, isn't intended to be just music. The diary explains it as a harmonic convergence of several sequences, all linked to these hymns."

Michael, seated across the table, studied the notes intently. "If the final chord is tied to hymns used for exorcisms, it's possible that it was designed as a counterforce. But a counterforce to what?"

"Exactly," Hana said, her voice quickening as her thoughts unraveled. "Look at this." She pulled up another section of the manuscript, annotated with notes on resonance and frequency. "Malvagio wrote about 'unlocking a bridge between worlds.' He believed this final chord would open a gateway—to what, I'm not entirely sure yet."

"Or it could be the key to amplifying the melody's power," she continued. "If someone with the right knowledge performs it, it might not just attract entities—it could summon something far worse."

Michael leaned back in his chair. "The descriptions here align with what the Church has documented in other cases —rituals that required specific incantations to invoke, or repel, supernatural forces. If this chord really can 'bridge worlds,' then the final chord needs to be carefully constructed to either open or close the doors to dark forces."

Hana sighed, her fingers running through her hair. "The manuscripts make it clear: this involves more than music. It's about power—power that Baumann's cult would wield without understanding the consequences."

She leaned forward, her voice overlaid with insistence. "The cult's already tried to perform it, even in its incomplete form. If we don't act, they'll finish what they started. We may have the music box, but Luciana said Adrian has copies of the score. As soon as he can find an instrument to play it, I'm sure he will."

"And if we act too quickly, we risk triggering something we can't control," Marcus countered. "This is more than just preventing disaster. It's about making sure we don't cause it ourselves."

Michael leaned forward. "Hana, focus on deciphering the rest of this sequence. Marcus and I will start planning our next move."

CHAPTER TWENTY

Back in the Vatican, the tension was distinct as Marcus, Hana, and Michael convened in a secluded chamber deep within the Apostolic Palace. The room was washed in a pale, anemic glow, its heavy drapes drawn tightly to block out the world beyond. The music box had again been secured in the restricted area. Spread across the long oak table were copies they had of Malvagio's manuscript and the diary. Beside them lay the recovered pages from Baumann's cult and Hana's meticulously organized notes. They felt as if they had all the pieces of the puzzle, but the puzzle wasn't coming together. Not yet.

Marcus leaned forward, his elbows resting on the table as he scrutinized a particularly intricate diagram. "The melody isn't just a sequence of notes," he said, his voice imbued with both awe and frustration. "It's a structure—a framework designed to resonate on multiple levels. Harmonic, spiritual, even metaphysical."

Seated across from him, Hana nodded as she adjusted

her reading glasses. "It's layered," she said. "Every chord, every interval, it's all interconnected. Malvagio didn't just compose music; he engineered a kind of sonic ritual."

Michael stood nearby, his arms crossed as he listened intently. "And that final chord?" he asked. "Have you been able to decipher what it *should* be?"

Hana gestured to a series of symbols she had transcribed onto her laptop. "I think so. It's a harmonic convergence of three distinct frequencies, each corresponding to a specific hymn from the past. When combined, they create a resonance that... well, it's hard to explain, but it's almost like it opens a door."

"A door to what?" Michael pressed, his voice heavy with concern.

Hana hesitated before responding. "That's the part I'm still trying to understand. Malvagio's notes suggest it's a gateway between realms. But whether that's literal or metaphorical, I don't know. And, as we discussed before, does that open our world to dark forces coming in or help keep them away from us?" She sat back, her gaze wandering across the table. "Remember how I explained those hymns in the final chord had been originally used for exorcisms? I'm thinking the key is to complete the score but also apply the principle of active noise cancellation. It's used to create a sound wave that is inverse to the unwanted sound. Both the sounds play, yes, but they block each other out for our ears. Doing that could fulfill the music being played but block out the effects of the final chords that pull in the dark forces."

Marcus exhaled deeply, his hand sweeping through his hair, leaving it tousled in irritation. "Maybe. Baumann was trying to play it to open that other world using Malvagio's original chords. If he succeeds, the consequences could be..." He trailed off, unable to find the words to describe the looming catastrophe.

Michael placed a hand on Marcus's shoulder, his gaze steady. "Then we can't let him succeed. I think Hana's idea might work. It both plays the symphony, opening the bridge, but prevents the crossing over. In essence, cutting off those forces that have already come across from their power source."

Hana glanced at the clock on the wall, her expression resolute. "We have the notes. We have the hymns. I know how to write the active noise cancellation notes. All that's left is to put it together."

A knock at the door interrupted the team's focus. Cardinal Severino entered, his presence commanding despite the weariness etched into his features. He surveyed the room, taking in the scattered manuscripts and the somber expressions of those present.

"I see you've made progress," Severino said, his tone measured. "But I must speak plainly. What you're attempting... it carries insurmountable risks."

Michael stepped forward, his expression calm but firm. "Your Eminence, if we don't act, Baumann's cult will complete the melody, come up with a way to play it, and the consequences will be far worse. We understand the stakes."

Severino's gaze hardened. "Do you? The Vatican's position in the world is already precarious. A public failure —or worse, a catastrophic event linked to this ritual— could devastate the Church's credibility. And let us not forget the spiritual toll. If this melody truly bridges realms, as you've suggested, the consequences could extend far beyond this world."

Hana stood, her voice steady but deferential. "With all

due respect, Your Eminence, we don't have the luxury of inaction. Baumann's already made significant progress. If we don't intervene, the Vatican's position will be the least of our concerns."

Severino's contemplation shifted to Hana, his expression unreadable. "You speak with conviction, Miss Sinclair. But conviction alone isn't enough. What you're dealing with is unprecedented. There is no roadmap for this."

Unable to contain his frustration, Marcus interjected. "That's exactly why we have to act now. If we wait for certainty, it'll be too late."

Severino's face softened slightly, but his tone remained stern. "You're right that we can't wait. But understand this: if you fail, it will not only be your burden to bear. The repercussions will fall on all of us—the Church, the faithful, and perhaps humanity itself."

Michael inclined his head. "We understand, Eminence. And we won't fail."

The cardinal studied them for a long moment, his gaze lingering on each face as if searching for reassurance. Finally, he sighed and folded his hands. "Then proceed. But remember, the results of your actions cannot be undone."

As Severino turned to leave, the room fell into a heavy silence. The door closed softly behind him, leaving the team to confront the enormity of their mission.

Marcus broke the silence, his voice tinged with sarcasm. "No pressure or anything."

Hana offered a faint smile, but her eyes betrayed her unease. "We've faced worse odds before," she said, her tone more confident than she felt.

Michael stepped forward, his expression resolute. "Then let's finish what we started."

LATER THAT EVENING, the team gathered in a small, ornate chapel within the Vatican. The space exuded a serene, almost otherworldly calm, its marble walls adorned with intricate frescoes and golden filigree. But the atmosphere among the group was anything but tranquil. The stakes of their mission weighed heavily on them as they prepared for the last confrontation.

Hana spread a map of St. Peter's Basilica across the altar, marking key points with a red pen. "If we're going to neutralize the melody's power, we need to conduct the ceremony here." She pointed to the basilica's central dome. "The acoustics will amplify my recorded sound cancellation notes, counteracting the melody's resonance."

Michael nodded, studying the map closely. "The dome is the heart of the basilica's design. If the hymns can reach their full resonance there, it might be enough to disrupt the melody permanently."

"And if Baumann shows up?" Marcus asked, his voice edged with tension.

Hana exchanged a look with Michael before responding. "Then we'll be ready. But we can't let him interfere. The ceremony has to proceed uninterrupted, no matter what."

Marcus crossed his arms, his expression grim. "Easier said than done. He'll expect us to act, especially now that we've disrupted his last attempt."

Michael's gaze was steady. "That's why we need the Swiss Guards. I've secured the exclusive use of the basilica dome through Cardinal Severino, and he sent word to the

Swiss Guard command to provide whatever security we need. They can secure the basilica and keep Baumann's cult at bay while we perform the ceremony."

Hana nodded. "I've already spoken with Karl. He and Lukas are assembling a team to manage security. They'll create a perimeter around the central dome and monitor all entrances."

Marcus glanced at the map again, his mind churning. "And the melody itself? How do we ensure your noise-cancelling chords will counteract it?"

Hana gestured to her notes, spread out on the table. "I've overlaid these notes with the harmonic frequencies in Malvagio's notes. When performed together, they should neutralize each other."

Michael's voice was calm but firm. "Remember, this isn't just a battle of sound. It's a battle of conviction. Malvagio's melody was designed to manipulate the spiritual realm. To counter it, we need to draw on the strength of our beliefs as well. Not just recorded counter notes."

Hana placed a reassuring hand on Marcus's arm. "We can do this. But we have to move quickly. Baumann won't wait for us to make the first move."

Marcus nodded, his resolve hardening. "Then let's make this count."

As the group finalized their plans, the onus of their mission hung heavily on their shoulders. The fate of more than just the Vatican hung in the balance. Failure wasn't an option, and as they prepared to face the unknown, they clung to the hope that their faith and determination would see them through.

CHAPTER
TWENTY-ONE

The Vatican Library was silent, save for the tapping of keys as Hana's fingers flew over the keyboard. Beside her, Michael rendered the notes she called out from the original hymns onto a roll of parchment to add to the final score for the music box.

In the meantime, Marcus had been scouring the diary and manuscript for explanations on how to set up the stage for playing Malvagio's symphony. "Oh," he murmured, his finger tracing a series of intricate Latin passages. "This isn't good."

Hana looked up from her work, leaned in, her glasses catching the light as she squinted at the faded text. "What does it say?"

Michael put down his pen, his voice low but steady. "Translate it, Marcus. We need to know exactly what we're dealing with."

Marcus nodded, his voice tight with concentration. "It says the completion of the melody requires a 'participant to offer up their connection to the divine.' The music acts as a bridge between realms, but in doing so, it demands a cost... a sacrifice."

Hana looked up, her expression a mixture of disbelief and dread. "'Offer up their connection'? What does that even mean?"

Marcus exhaled deeply, his shoulders tense. "It's more than just a symbolic act. Malvagio's notes describe it as an irreversible exchange. The person's soul becomes bound to the melody. They become... an intermediary of sorts. A vessel."

Michael's jaw tightened. "A vessel for what?"

Marcus hesitated, his voice dropping to a whisper. "For the forces that the melody summons."

The heaviness of his words hung in the air like a thundercloud. Michael gripped the edge of the table, his knuckles white. "If that's true, then completing the melody isn't just dangerous for those within earshot. It's damnation to the player."

"Does that mean," Marcus asked, "that it applies to whoever plays it to the end—even if the contrary tones we plan to use disrupt it?"

Hana's eyes darted between the two men. "But if we don't complete it, Baumann will as soon as he can. And he won't hesitate to pay any price. He'll unleash whatever this melody was designed to summon."

Marcus carefully set aside the manuscript, his expression grim. "Then we have a choice to make. Who plays the melody? And who is willing to pay the price?"

THE GROUP RELOCATED to a smaller chamber within the Vatican, its walls adorned with frescoes of saints and martyrs. The solemn imagery felt almost mocking in the face of the decision before them. Hana paced near the window, her hands clasped tightly in front of her. Marcus sat on a nearby bench, his head in his hands, while Michael stood in silent contemplation by the altar.

Finally, Hana broke the silence. "I'll do it."

Both men turned to her, their expressions a mixture of shock and alarm.

"No," Michael said immediately, rising to his feet. "Absolutely not."

Hana's gaze was resolute. "Why not? I'm not a priest. I don't have the same connection to the divine that you do. I'm not even employed by the Vatican like you, Marcus. If someone has to make this sacrifice, it should be me."

Michael stepped forward, his voice firm but gentle as he embraced her. "Hana, you don't understand what you're offering. This isn't simply about giving something up. It's eternal separation from God. From grace. It's a fate worse than death."

"And what about you?" Hana shot back, her eyes blazing. "You think I'm going to let you do this? You're a priest, Michael. Your connection to the divine is what gives you purpose. If you sever that…" She trailed off, her voice breaking. "I can't let you do that."

Marcus stepped between them, his expression a mixture of frustration and desperation. "Nobody is doing this! There has to be another way. We haven't exhausted all our options yet."

"We don't have time," Hana countered. "Baumann's likely already moving. If we wait, he'll complete the melody, and it won't matter who makes the sacrifice."

Michael placed a hand on her shoulder, his voice soft

but unyielding. "Hana, I swore an oath to serve others. If anyone is going to bear this burden, it has to be me."

She shook her head, tears brimming in her eyes. "No, Michael. There has to be another way."

In a rare moment of intimacy within the Vatican walls, Michael pressed his fiancée to his chest, caressing her head, holding her in his heart. They had been through so much in earlier adventures, facing capture and death. They had always found both sanctuary and success by working together. Once the papacy allowed priests to marry, it was a natural culmination of their love for each other to become engaged. But now, facing this abomination, both were willing to sacrifice for the other, yet all the while knowing neither could live a fulfilled life without the other by their side.

Marcus paced back and forth, allowing the couple their moment, yet all the while shaken. Finally, his hands gesturing wildly, he spoke. "We're talking about irreversible consequences here. We can't just rush into this decision."

The tension in the room was almost suffocating as Hana pulled back from Michael.

The group resumed their heated discussion. Hana crossed her arms, her expression defiant. "And what's the alternative? Sit back and let Baumann win? That's not an option."

Michael's manner was calm, but commanding. "Enough. Both of you. This means more than just strategy. It's about morality. If we're going to make this sacrifice, it has to be done with full understanding of what it means. And it has to be the right person."

Marcus turned to him, his voice flushed with

desperation. "And who decides that, Michael? Who has the right to make that call?"

"I do," Michael said firmly. "As a priest, it's my responsibility to spiritually protect others. If someone has to make this sacrifice, it's going to be me."

Hana stepped forward, her voice trembling with emotion. "You're not the only one who can protect others, Michael. I'm just as capable of making this choice as you are."

"This isn't about capability," Michael replied, his tone gentle but resolute. "It's about vocation. My life has always been dedicated to serving a higher purpose. If that means giving it up to save others, then so be it."

The room fell silent, the impact of his words sinking in. Marcus finally spoke, his voice quieter now. "And what about the rest of us? Do we just stand by and let you do this?"

Michael met his gaze, his expression unwavering. "If it means stopping Baumann and saving countless lives, then yes. That's exactly what you do."

Hana turned away, her hands clenched into fists. "I can't accept that. I won't. Is there any chance you misinterpreted it?"

Marcus placed a hand on her arm, his voice steady. "I don't believe so. None of us wants this, Hana. And I have no idea if playing the cancelling notes at the same time will negate this. But Michael's right. If this is what it takes to stop Baumann, then we have to let him do it."

Hana turned back to face them, her expression a mixture of anger and sorrow. "Then we'd better make damn sure it works."

The group fell into a heavy silence, the enormity of

their decision hanging over them like a storm cloud. They had taken a step closer to stopping Baumann, but at a cost none of them were prepared to face. The path ahead was uncertain, and the shadow of their choices would follow them long after the melody's final note was played.

CHAPTER
TWENTY-TWO

St. Peter's Basilica stood silent in the pre-dawn hours, its interior grandeur gilded by flickering candlelight. The cavernous space, usually bustling with pilgrims and tourists, now held an air of sacred stillness. Every sound, from the faint echo of footsteps to the rustle of clothing, felt magnified in the vast emptiness. Marcus, Michael, and Hana moved purposefully through the nave, their expressions etched with a mixture of determination and trepidation.

They rested the music box on the central altar, its ornate carvings catching the flickering light. Even in its inert state, the box looked as if it pulsed with an unspoken power, as though aware of the role it was about to play. Surrounding the altar, Swiss Guards stood at attention, their hands resting on ceremonial weapons. Their presence was both a shield and a stark reminder of the dangers that could descend at any moment.

Marcus adjusted the stand that held the box, his every movement precise. He stepped back and scrutinized his work, ensuring it was perfectly aligned according to Malvagio's diary. "This is the moment," he said quietly, his voice steady but shaded with apprehension. "Everything we've worked for comes down to this."

Hana stood beside him, her arms crossed tightly over her chest. Her eyes darted between the music box and the towering columns of the basilica, as though expecting Baumann and his cultists to emerge from the shadows. "We've reconstructed the counter melody, accounted for the acoustics, and secured the basilica," she said. Her voice was firm, but there was a tremor beneath it. "But I still can't shake the feeling that something unexpected will happen."

Marcus gave her a brief, reassuring look. "That's why they're here," he said with a nod toward the guards stationed at the main entrances. "Baumann and his cult won't get past them. And even if they try, we'll be ready."

Father Michael approached the altar with deliberate steps, his expression calm but resolute. In his hands, he held a small prayer book, its leather cover worn from years of use. He paused beside the music box, his gaze lingering on its intricate design. "The counter melody will do what it's meant to do," he said softly. "All we can do is trust in our faith and in each other."

Hana turned to him, her concern evident in her eyes. "Are you ready for this?" she asked. "You're the one who has to play it. If something goes wrong..." She didn't finish the sentence.

Michael's gaze didn't waver. "I've spent my life preparing for moments like this," he replied. "If this is my role, so be it."

The strain of his words settled over them, deepening the already charged atmosphere. Marcus cleared his throat and stepped forward, holding a diagram that detailed the basilica's acoustics. "The sound will carry perfectly from here," he said, pointing to the central dome on the schematic. "The architecture will amplify the melody, ensuring its resonance reaches every corner of the basilica."

"And Baumann?" Hana asked, her voice edged with unease.

"If he's coming, he'll have to get through the guards first," Marcus replied. "Lukas and Karl have positioned their teams strategically. We'll know the moment anything happens."

Michael nodded, his expression contemplative. "There's more at stake than just physical security," he said. "We're dealing with forces beyond what we can see. Prayer will be our strongest defense."

Hana glanced at the music box. "And if the counter melody doesn't work the way we think it will?"

Michael placed a reassuring hand on her shoulder. "Then we adapt. But we have to believe that this is the right path."

The three exchanged a solemn nod, their unspoken fears momentarily eclipsed by their shared resolve. Marcus returned to his preparations, ensuring every detail was in place. He adjusted the position of the candles surrounding the altar, their flames casting elongated shadows that flickered against the basilica's ornate walls.

Hana checked her laptop, which displayed a digital transcription of the noise cancellation melody. "Everything's aligned," she said, her tone a mixture of relief and tension. "The melody should play simultaneously with the score from the music box.

Michael stepped forward, his hands gently resting on

the music box. He closed his eyes for a moment, whispering a silent prayer. When he opened them, his expression was one of quiet determination. "It's time," he said.

The basilica seemed to hold its breath as they took their positions. Marcus and Hana stood a few steps back, their eyes fixed on Michael as he began to wind the black onyx key on the music box. The soft clicking of the mechanism was the only sound, a prelude to the melody that would decide their fate.

As Michael continued turning the key, a hauntingly beautiful melody filled the air, its notes resonating through the vast expanse of the basilica. This time, the sound was unlike anything they had heard before—simultaneously ethereal and otherworldly. The air bristled with energy, and the soft glow of the altar candles grew brighter, casting dancing shadows on the ancient walls.

Marcus and Hana stood nearby, their eyes fixed on the scene unfolding before them. "Do you feel that? It's like the music is feeding off the atmosphere surrounding it," Hana whispered, her voice trembling. "The air… it's alive."

Marcus nodded, his hands clenched into fists. "It's the resonance. The basilica's acoustics are amplifying it, just as we planned. But it's stronger than I anticipated, different from before, as if the holy setting itself is embracing the sound."

As the melody reached its crescendo, Hana's recording of the cancelling notes coincided with the hymnal chords and suddenly, the sound ceased and a blinding light erupted from the music box, filling the basilica with an almost unbearable brilliance. The guards stationed at the doors shielded their eyes, some dropping to their knees as the ground beneath them began to tremble violently. Marble statues quivered, and the great dome above echoed the melody, its vast space reverberating with the sound.

Michael's hands remained steady on the music box, his expression unwavering even as the tremors grew more intense. He recited a prayer under his breath, his voice firm despite the surrounding chaos as a haunting, guttural harmonic vibration reached into the very soul of the basilica.

Suddenly, dark shapes emerged from the shadows, their forms writhing and amorphous. The melody drew the entities that Baumann's cult had unleashed earlier; their unholy presence clashed with the sacred energy radiating from the music box. The air grew colder, and a low, inhuman wail echoed through the space.

"Michael!" Hana shouted, her voice cutting through the noise. "They're coming for you!"

Michael didn't flinch. "They won't succeed," he said firmly, his voice carrying an unshakable conviction. "The counter melody will purge them. It has to."

The light intensified, its brilliance now almost blinding. The entities writhed and screamed, their forms disintegrating as the ending of the symphony, unheard but felt in the very bones of all present, reached its peak. The tremors grew so violent that cracks began to form in the marble floors, but the music box remained untouched, its glowing symbols pulsating as if in harmony with the cancelled melody.

Hana saw it on her digital readout as the last note of the melody played, and the blinding light abruptly vanished, leaving behind a deafening silence. The tremors ceased, and the air grew still, heavy with the presence of what had just occurred.

Michael staggered back from the altar, his hands trembling. The music box, now dull and lifeless, sat motionless on the stand.

Hana rushed to Michael's side, her hands gripping his shoulders. "Are you okay?" she asked, her voice thick with loving concern.

Michael nodded slowly, his breathing uneven. "I'm fine," he said, though his voice was hoarse. "It's over."

The three stood in silence. The melody had been neutralized, and the immediate threat was gone. But they all sensed that their battle was only part of a larger, ongoing struggle.

As the first rays of sunlight filtered through the stained glass windows, illuminating the basilica in a kaleidoscope of colors, the group exchanged weary but determined glances. They had succeeded in their mission, but the cost —and the implications of what they had uncovered— would stay with them forever.

"This isn't the end," Marcus said quietly, his voice firm. "Not by a long shot."

Michael placed a hand on his shoulder, his expression solemn but resolute. "Then we'll be ready for whatever comes next."

CHAPTER
TWENTY-THREE

The vast expanse of St. Peter's Basilica was eerily quiet, the kind of silence that felt tangible, as though the air itself had stilled in reverence or fear. The vibrant life that had once pulsed through the sacred halls felt drained, leaving behind an emptiness that unsettled even the most stoic of hearts. The candles lining the nave flickered weakly, their flames struggling against an invisible force, casting faint, wavering shadows on the marble floors.

Marcus Russo stood near the altar, his breathing shallow as he surveyed the scene. The music box with its ornate carvings that had once held such sinister beauty now stood as merely a delicately crafted artifact of the past. Even the faint glow that had emanated from the box during its final moments had dissipated, leaving only a dim, lingering aura in the sacred space.

The basilica, usually bathed in light that symbolized divine presence, was now cloaked in a shroud of unease. The grand dome above, once an awe-inspiring reminder of human devotion and ingenuity, appeared darker, as if the very stones had absorbed the ritual's grim energy. The frescoes on the walls, depicting the triumphs of saints and martyrs, seemed to peer down with solemn disapproval.

The Swiss Guards, still stationed at the entrances, exchanged uneasy glances. Some clutched their weapons tighter, their disciplined stances betraying the fear that lingered in the air. One of them, a younger guard with wide eyes, whispered a prayer under his breath, his attention fixed on the cracks that had formed in the marble floors. The tremors from the melody's peak had left their mark, the fissures radiating outward from the altar like jagged veins.

Marcus's voice broke the silence, low and hesitant. "It doesn't feel right," he said, turning to Hana, who stood a few steps away. His voice carried a rare vulnerability. "The melody… it's gone, but it's like something's been left behind. Something tangible, not just cracks in the floor."

Hana nodded, her expression troubled. "The energy in this place… it's changed. It's not the same." She glanced at the dome above them. "Whatever that melody did, it's left a mark."

She stepped closer to the altar, her boots clicking softly against the marble. Her gaze lingered on the music box and her hand brushed against it, the faint chill of the material sending a shiver up her spine. "Even spent of its power," she said quietly, "it still feels wrong. Like it's waiting for something."

Marcus folded his arms, his facial features set in thought. "Whatever it was designed to do, it's finished now. But that doesn't mean we're free of its consequences."

The two fell silent again, their unease growing as the consequence of the moment pressed down on them. The basilica, once a beacon of faith and sanctity, now felt hollow, its sacred energy diminished by the ritual's toll.

Father Michael sat on the steps of the altar, his shoulders slumped and his hands clasped tightly around his prayer book. His face was pale, the lines of exhaustion etched deeply into his features. Beads of sweat clung to his forehead, and his breathing was slow, labored. He looked smaller somehow, as if the melody's completion had drained not just his strength but some intangible part of his spirit.

Marcus approached him cautiously, his footsteps echoing in the stillness. "Michael?" he said softly, kneeling beside him. "How are you holding up?"

Michael lifted his gaze, his eyes heavy with weariness but still carrying a spark of resolve. "The melody's power… it's gone," he said, his voice so soft it barely stirred the air. "But I can still feel its weight. Like an echo lingering in my soul."

Marcus frowned, his concern evident. "You've taken on more than anyone should have to. Are you sure you're okay?"

Michael managed a faint smile, though it didn't reach his eyes. "I'm still standing, Marcus. That's enough for now." He lowered his head, his fingers trembling as he opened the prayer book. In the silence that followed, his voice rose in a soft, steady cadence, reciting a prayer of penance.

"*Domine, miserere mei,*" he began, his words carrying the toll of his plea and gratitude. "Have mercy on me, O Lord, for I have borne what was not mine to bear."

The prayer unfolded like a balm, the Latin words weaving through the oppressive atmosphere of the basilica. Each line lifted a fraction of the heavy tension, though Michael's voice remained tinged with sorrow. As he continued, Marcus couldn't help but notice how each word seemed to ground the priest, reconnecting him to the faith that had carried him through so much.

When the prayer ended, Michael closed the book and exhaled deeply. He looked at Marcus, his expression resolute. Both men stood. "We did what we had to do. But the cost... it's not something I'll ever forget."

Marcus hesitated before speaking, his voice low. "You don't have to carry it alone. Whatever burden you're feeling, we're here too."

Michael placed a hand on Marcus's shoulder, his grip firm despite his weakened state. "Thank you," he said simply, the gratitude in his voice unspoken but deeply felt.

The two men stood in silence for a moment, the enormity of what they had experienced hanging between them. Above them, the dome's cracked surface caught the dim candlelight, a reminder that even the strongest structures could bear scars. Yet within that silence, there was a sense of resilience—a determination to move forward, no matter how heavy the burden.

HANA MOVED to her fiancé's side, gently taking his hand as her eyes searched his. "Michael... I need you to be okay. Tell me what you're feeling."

Michael's gaze lingered on the music box, his expression contemplative. "The melody was more than sound. It was a force, something ancient and powerful. I felt my prayers holding me in check from its power, but..." He met her gaze, his voice steady but imbued with caution. "You're right. The melody may be gone, but its legacy isn't. What we faced here is only part of something larger."

Marcus exhaled deeply, his shoulders tense. "So what do we do now? Just wait for the next crisis to find us?"

Hana's lips pressed into a thin line. "No. We study this. We learn from it. And we make sure nothing like this ever happens again."

The three stood in silence. Above them, the first rays of dawn filtered through the stained-glass windows, painting the floor in a kaleidoscope of light. And with the light, the basilica, though scarred, seemed to breathe again, its sacred energy slowly being restored.

They turned to leave. Behind them, the remnants of the melody and its mysteries remained, a testament to the power they had faced and the strength it had taken to overcome it.

CHAPTER
TWENTY-FOUR

The air inside St. Peter's Basilica was cool and heavy with incense, the faint scent mingling with the reverberations of an angelic choir rehearsal as the structure's normal activities began again a few days later. Voices rose and fell in practiced unison, the choir's harmonies soaring toward the grand dome above. The organist's fingers danced across the keys, weaving a majestic accompaniment that filled the sacred space with vibrant sound.

Michael Dominic stood in the shadows near the nave, observing the rehearsal with a rare moment of peace. The music reminded him of the basilica's enduring sanctity, a refuge against the chaos that had threatened its walls for centuries. He closed his eyes, allowing himself to absorb the beauty of the moment. For the first time in days, he felt a glimmer of hope.

Then, it happened.

A dissonant note rang out, piercing the harmony like a blade. The choir faltered, their voices stumbling over the sudden intrusion. The organist's hands froze above the keys, his expression twisting in confusion. For a moment, all was silent, the interruption hanging in the air like a blasphemous stain.

From somewhere high in the basilica, a haunting melody began to play. It was faint at first, a whisper of sound that drifted through the air. But as it grew louder, the familiarity of the notes sent a chill down Michael's spine. His breath caught in his throat as he recognized the tune. It was the same melody that had emanated from the music box—a melody they had destroyed.

The choir members exchanged uneasy glances, their whispers filling the silence. "What is that?" one of them murmured, clutching her sheet music tightly. Another backed away, her wide eyes scanning the basilica's towering columns as if expecting the source of the sound to materialize.

The organist stood abruptly, his chair scraping against the marble floor. "This is... impossible," he muttered, his voice trembling. "Where is it coming from?"

Michael stepped forward, his heart pounding. "Enough," he called, his voice firm but calm. "Everyone, please step outside. Now."

The choir hesitated, their confusion evident, but the authority in Michael's tone left no room for argument. Slowly, they began to gather their belongings, their murmurs growing louder as they filed out of the basilica. Michael remained behind, his eyes riveted to the upper reaches of the nave where the sound appeared to originate.

The melody swirled around him, its haunting notes reverberating through the sacred space. It was as though the walls themselves were alive with the sound, amplifying its eerie beauty. Michael's hands clenched into fists as he turned toward the altar. "What have we done?" he whispered, his voice barely audible.

BY THE END of that week, Marcus Russo had spread a series of diagrams and charts across the table in his Vatican office, the overhead lamp casting a harsh light on his intense expression. Each document represented a fragment of his ongoing investigation into the melody and its lingering effects. Despite the melody's destruction, the tune had infiltrated the very walls of the basilica, bringing a cessation of all planned uses of this most sacred of the Church's structures. Marcus's mind raced to make sense of it.

Hana sat across from him, her laptop open as she sifted through historical records. "So let me get this straight," she said, her tone skeptical but curious. "You think the melody left behind is... what? An echo?"

Marcus nodded as he tapped a pencil against one of the charts. "Not just an echo. It's more like residual energy. Think of it as a frequency that's still resonating in the environment. The music box may not be playing, but the sound it created... that kind of energy doesn't just vanish."

Hana leaned back in her chair, folding her arms. "And you think that's what the choir heard?"

"It makes sense," Marcus replied, his tone growing more animated. "The melody was engineered to interact with its surroundings on a profound level. The basilica's acoustics amplified it, embedding its frequency into the very fabric of the space."

Hana frowned, her pen tapping against the table as she mulled over his words. "If that's true, then again, we're dealing with something unprecedented. This is about more than just sound. It's about how that sound interacts with... everything."

"Exactly," Marcus said, his voice firm with resolution. "And if these echoes are strong enough to manifest as music, who knows what else they could trigger?"

Hana's expression grew sharp, like a blade unsheathed. "We need to figure out how to neutralize it. If the melody's energy is still active, it's only a matter of time before something worse happens."

Marcus nodded, his jaw set as he flipped through a stack of papers. "I'll start running tests on the basilica's acoustics. Maybe there's a way to counteract the frequency. But we're going to need more data."

"And fast," Hana added, her voice firm. "Because if Baumann's cult gets wind of this, they'll use it to their advantage."

Marcus's face grew grim. "They're already fractured. But if they see this as a sign, it could rally them back together. We can't let that happen."

The two exchanged a determined look, the impact of the situation settling heavily over them. They had stopped the music box, but the melody's legacy was far from over.

FATHER MICHAEL KNELT in the dimly lit chapel, his hands clasped tightly in prayer. The faint glow of a single candle illuminated his face, casting shadows that mirrored the turmoil in his heart. He had spent hours here, seeking guidance, but the silence was deafening.

The events of the day replayed in his mind with relentless clarity. The ghostly melody, the fear in the choir members' eyes, the lingering sense of dread that permeated the basilica—it was all too much. Michael's faith, unshakable through countless trials, felt fragile in the face of what they had unleashed.

"Lord," he whispered, his voice trembling, "I don't know what to do. The melody... it's not gone. Its essence is here, within these walls. Have we brought something unholy into this sacred place?"

As if in response, a faint sound echoed through the chapel. It was barely audible, but Michael recognized it instantly: the melody. Its notes were softer now, almost mournful, as though it too carried the yoke of regret. *Regret?* Michael's eyes snapped open, his breath catching in his throat.

He rose to his feet, his gaze sweeping the room. The candle's flame flickered wildly, casting erratic shadows on the walls. The sound grew louder, filling the chapel with its haunting beauty. Michael's heart pounded as he stepped toward the altar, his every instinct urging him to flee but his faith compelling him to stay.

"This cannot continue," he murmured, his voice firm despite the fear coursing through him. "If the melody has attached itself to this place, we must find a way to cleanse it. The basilica is a house of God, and I will not allow it to become anything else."

He turned and walked toward the door, his resolve hardening with every step. The echoes of the melody followed him, a haunting reminder of the task that lay ahead. Whatever had been left behind, it was his responsibility to confront it. The basilica's sanctity depended on it, and so did his faith.

CHAPTER
TWENTY-FIVE

Marcus sat hunched over a sprawling map of St. Peter's Basilica, its intricate lines and faded annotations illuminated by the warm glow of his desk lamp. He hoped to find something in the structure itself to help them in removing the echo of Malvagio's work. Instead, he found something even more useful. Or so he hoped.

The map, unearthed from a rarely accessed section of the Vatican Archives, depicted more than the basilica's grand structure; it hinted at secrets buried beneath its marble floors. His fingers traced a series of faint lines near the nave, his mind racing as he pieced together the clues.

"Look at this," Marcus said, beckoning Hana over. She crossed the room, her curiosity piqued by the gravity in his tone.

She crossed the room, her curiosity piqued by the gravity in his tone. She leaned over the map, surveying the centuries-old parchment. "What am I looking at?" she asked, brushing a stray lock of hair from her face.

"This here." Marcus pointed to a shaded area beneath the basilica's foundation. "It's a chamber... at least, that's what it looks like. The annotations here suggest it was constructed in the late eighteenth century, around the time Vincenzo Malvagio was active. That chamber was the brainchild of Cardinal Antonio Bellari, the same cardinal who stood up to save Malvagio from punishment when his work was denounced. It's not marked on any modern plans."

Hana studied the faint lines. "Why would they build something down there? And why hide it?"

Marcus leaned back in his chair, his gaze thoughtful. "It could have been a storage area, a secret meeting place, or even a vault for relics. But given Malvagio's ties to Bellari, it's not a stretch to think it was connected to his work."

Hana straightened, a faint chill running down her spine. "If that's true, then whatever's down there could be dangerous. This melody has already proven how much damage it can cause."

Before Marcus could respond, Lukas entered the room, his Swiss Guard uniform pristine despite the late hour. "What's going on?" he asked, his tone magnified with suspicion and curiosity. Marcus had called him earlier and asked if he could join them after his shift.

Marcus gestured to the map, his excitement barely contained. "We think there's a hidden chamber beneath the basilica. I'm going to need your help to access it."

Lukas raised an eyebrow, his posture rigid. "You're asking me to help you sneak around the most secure religious site in the world? Are you sure about this?"

Hana smirked, her confidence in clear contrast to Lukas's cautious demeanor. "It's not sneaking if you're with us."

THE DEVIL'S SYMPHONY

"But I gather this assignment hasn't been taken through channels?"

Marcus shrugged. "Well, that's true, but we know Cardinal Severino would approve, right? Besides, don't you want to know what's down there?"

Lukas hesitated, his hand resting on the hilt of his ceremonial sword. Finally, he sighed. "Fine. But if this gets us in trouble, I'm blaming both of you."

Marcus grinned, his eyes gleaming with determination. "Let's get started."

THE BASILICA WAS QUIET, its vast halls shrouded in shadows as the trio made their way toward the designated access point. Marcus carried a small satchel containing tools and a flashlight, while Hana clutched a notebook and Lukas kept a watchful eye on their surroundings.

They approached an ornately brocaded panel near the central nave. Hana looked at her notebook and shook her head. "This shows a staircase here, but I don't see one," she said.

Marcus walked up to the panel and gently moved it aside. The wall behind it had a seam going up and across the shape of a door panel. He worked quickly, using a crowbar to pry the panel loose. It gave way with a soft groan, revealing a narrow staircase spiraling downward into darkness.

"This is it," Marcus whispered, his voice reflecting both excitement and apprehension.

Hana peered into the darkness. "Do we know how far down it goes?"

"No idea," he admitted. "But there's only one way to find out."

Lukas drew a flashlight from his belt, its beam cutting through the gloom. "I'll go first. If there's anything waiting for us, I'd rather be the one to meet it."

The descent was slow and cautious, the air growing colder with each step. The narrow staircase eventually opened into a cavernous chamber, its walls lined with shelves that held dust-covered relics. The space was oppressive, the impact of centuries pressing down on them like a physical force.

Hana's breath caught as she took in the sight. "This... this is incredible," she murmured, her eyes scanning the rows of forgotten artifacts.

Marcus's flashlight swept across the room, illuminating faded tapestries, broken statues, and ancient manuscripts. But it was the table at the center of the chamber that caught his attention. Upon it lay a bundle of sheet music, the pages yellowed with age but still legible. His flashlight settled over the pages as he read them.

"This expands on Malvagio's work," he said, his voice filled with awe. "These notes... they're variations on the original melody. But there's more. It looks like he was working on an entire symphony."

He carefully lifted the sheet music and placed it into his satchel, his expression resolute. "This changes everything. Malvagio had written more than the singular symphony we found in the music box. His legacy is far more extensive than we realized. And if Baumann is searching for other melodies he wrote..."

"Then we're running out of time," Lukas finished grimly.

Marcus nodded and scooped up his satchel.

As they began their ascent, the oppressive atmosphere

of the chamber clung to them, a silent reminder of the secrets they had unearthed. The lingering echoes of their discovery would reverberate far beyond the basilica, setting them on a path they couldn't yet fully comprehend.

CHAPTER
TWENTY-SIX

The Vatican Archives felt unusually oppressive as Marcus and Hana pored over the newly discovered sheet music. Spread across a large mahogany table, the faded parchment revealed a labyrinth of notes, annotations, and cryptic symbols. Despite its age, the music's detail was astonishing, each stroke of the pen seemingly deliberate, as if imbued with intention beyond mere composition.

"This is no ordinary symphony," Marcus murmured, his finger tracing a sequence of notes. "Look at these annotations."

Hana leaned closer, her eyes narrowing. "'*Hymnus Atrum*,'" she read aloud, her voice tinged with unease. "Latin for the 'Black Hymnal.'"

Marcus nodded, his expression shifting from curiosity to gravity. "The Black Hymnal is one of those things you hear about in whispers. Even among historians, it's considered more of a legend than a reality. Supposedly, it's a codex of compositions so powerful that their performance could alter the human mind, compelling people to act against their will."

"Alter the mind? You mean like brainwashing?"

Marcus's jaw tightened as he carefully adjusted the magnifying glass he held. "Not quite. Brainwashing is crude, forceful. The Black Hymnal's compositions were said to be more... insidious. The music wouldn't just compel you—it would make you believe that what you were doing was your own choice. Imagine hearing a melody so beautiful, so intricately crafted, that you felt a deep, unshakable desire to follow its call, no matter the consequences."

Hana leaned back. "If it's that dangerous, how is it that we've never seen solid evidence of its existence?"

Marcus set the magnifying glass down, his gaze meeting hers. "Because anyone who's ever sought it out has either disappeared or been silenced. According to some accounts, the Church itself might have hidden the hymnal centuries ago, deeming it too dangerous to destroy. Vincenzo Malvagio's compositions—his melody—may have been derived from fragments of it."

The implications hung heavy in the air, the onus of the discovery settling over them both. Hana broke the silence. "If these notes are tied to the Black Hymnal, Baumann's ambitions are far more dangerous than we imagined. This is about more than just an insanity-inducing melody. It's about control."

"And the ability to wield that control on a massive scale," Marcus added, gesturing toward the intricate notations. "Look here." He pointed to a cluster of symbols near the bottom of the sheet. "These markings... they're consistent with ones we found in the hidden chamber. Malvagio wasn't working in isolation. His compositions were part of a broader effort, likely tied to the hymnal."

Hana studied the sheet music with a quiet curiosity, her fingers brushing against the parchment. "If Malvagio had access to the hymnal, it's no wonder he hid his work so carefully. He must have known how dangerous it was."

Marcus's expression darkened as he considered her words. "And if Baumann believes the Black Hymnal is real, he won't stop until he finds it. This isn't simply about finishing Malvagio's work—it's about surpassing it. Baumann sees himself as a prophet of some kind, reshaping the world through music. We're not just dealing with a relic—we're dealing with an idea. A weapon."

Hana's fingers drummed against the table as she processed his words. "If Baumann finds it before we do…" She didn't finish the thought, but the burden of it was clear.

Marcus leaned back, exhaling deeply. "We need to figure out what this sheet music is really telling us."

"And quietly," Hana added, her voice firm. "If the wrong people catch wind of this, it won't just be Baumann we're up against. Mind control is the kind of discovery that could spark a war."

The room fell silent as they stared at the sheet music, the cryptic notes and symbols holding secrets they could only begin to grasp. The Black Hymnal was no longer merely a legend. It was real, and its shadow loomed over everything they had fought to protect.

IN A QUIET CORNER of the Archives, Hana and Marcus sat surrounded by stacks of documents, their findings piecing together a chilling revelation. A stifling weight of tension permeated the air as Hana tapped her pen against a notebook, her brow furrowed in thought.

"Baumann's obsession with Malvagio always seemed focused on the melody," she said. "But now it's clear that was just the beginning. The Black Hymnal is what he's really after."

Marcus leaned forward, his elbows resting on the table. "It makes sense. The melody was likely a fragment, a single piece of a much larger puzzle. If the Black Hymnal contains other compositions, they could amplify its effects exponentially." He exhaled deeply, his mind thrumming with urgency. "If Malvagio had the Black Hymnal, he would have hidden it. He knew the dangers of his work. The question is, where?"

Hana picked up one of the sheets of music, her eyes scanning the intricate notations. "Malvagio was more than just a composer. He was a master of symbolism. These notes might be more than music. They could be a map, pointing us to the hymnal's location."

Marcus's eyes widened as the realization struck him. "If that's true, then every note, every symbol, is a clue. We need to analyze this in detail."

SECRETARY OF STATE Cardinal Giovanni Severino's office was as imposing as ever, its high ceilings and dark wood furnishings lending an air of authority that matched the man himself. Seated behind an ornate desk, the cardinal listened intently as Marcus and Hana presented their findings. His expression remained unreadable, but the tension in his posture betrayed his concern.

Severino leaned back in his chair. "If what you're saying is true, then the Black Hymnal poses a threat not only to the Church but to the entire world. This is no ordinary artifact."

"It's more than a threat," Marcus said, his voice firm. "In the wrong hands, it could be catastrophic. Baumann's already shown he's willing to use Malvagio's work to further his agenda. If he gets his hands on the hymnal, there's no telling what he could do."

Severino's gaze shifted to Hana. "And you believe the sheet music holds clues to its location?"

Hana nodded. "Malvagio was deliberate in everything he did. These compositions are more than music. They're a code. If we can decipher it, we might be able to find the Black Hymnal before Adrian Baumann does."

The Cardinal's gaze turned cold, his eyes narrowing. "This must be handled with the utmost discretion. If word of the Black Hymnal's existence were to spread, the panic would be unimaginable. The faithful would lose trust in the Church's ability to safeguard the world's spiritual and historical legacy."

"We understand," Marcus said. "We'll keep this quiet. But we need resources: access to more of the Archives, support from the Swiss Guard… anything that can help us stay ahead of Baumann."

Severino nodded slowly, his demeanor grave. "You'll have what you need. But remember, the Church's reputation is at stake. You must succeed, and you must do so without drawing attention."

Hana met his gaze, her voice steady. "We won't fail."

Severino's eyes lingered on them for a moment before he rose from his chair. "Then go. Time is not on our side."

As Marcus and Hana left the office, the race for the Black Hymnal had just begun, and failure wasn't an option.

CHAPTER
TWENTY-SEVEN

Michael made the sign of the cross and sat back in his side of the confessional, his head resting against the worn, dark oak panel behind him, the screen to his right showing a brief bit of light as the confessor left.

It had been a special request. Michael's functions as a priest had found him taking parishioners' confessions many times in the past, but seldom since his work began in the Secret Archives. But this request had come from a special person, one involved with their current mission: Luciana Mancini. He had nearly forgotten the toll it could take on a priest to listen to confessions. In this case, absorbing the troubled and abusive early history and the later agony and sins of a young woman whose soul had been torn apart by her involvement with Adrian Baumann.

Now he collected himself physically with a heavy sigh, and spiritually with the knowledge that his absolution for her sins and her guilt had helped to soothe her soul.

He left the confessional and found himself face-to-face

with the woman, thin and frail, pale, yet with a look of purpose in her eyes. She offered a hesitant smile and a nod, then spoke softly, "Thank you, Father."

He could only nod in return, having done his duty. He turned to leave her at peace with herself, but she reached out as if to touch him, and he stopped. "Is there something else I can do for you?" he asked.

"No, Father, it is what I can do for you. I still have a friend within Adrian Baumann's group, and I overheard other members in the background when she and I spoke on the phone. It felt... providential, as if... well, I felt it imperative that I let you know."

"Let me know what?" he asked.

"I heard them say Adrian has finished the score for the music box and is on the trail of something else. Something important. There is going to be a special gathering of Adrian's followers. A gala, really, and I believe that the only reason I overheard it was because it needed to be shared with you. Please take this as part of my penance."

THE GRAND BALLROOM of the Viennese mansion was a stunning display of opulence. Gilded chandeliers cast a warm glow over the marble floors, their light dancing off the polished surfaces of ornate mirrors and delicate crystal. Velvet drapes in deep burgundy hung from towering windows, muffling the sounds of the city beyond. The air was charged with the mingling scents of expensive perfume and aged brandy, a fitting atmosphere for the gathering Adrian Baumann had orchestrated.

Baumann stood at the head of the room, his silver-streaked hair and piercing blue eyes giving him an air of authority that commanded attention. He was impeccably dressed in a tailored suit, the dark fabric contrasting sharply with the rich gold accents of the room. Around him, an audience of influential figures—bankers, politicians, and aristocrats—watched with rapt attention. Among them were members of his cult, their loyalty evident in the subtle nods and murmurs of agreement as Baumann spoke.

"We are on the cusp of a new era," he declared, his voice steady and persuasive. "An era where the barriers that divide us—class, nation, belief—will crumble beneath the power of harmony. The Black Hymnal is not just a relic of the past; it was a key to Malvagio's compositions, and it is the key to our future. Its melodies can unite humanity under a single purpose, a shared vision."

A murmur of approval rippled through the room, though not everyone appeared convinced. A portly man in a striped waistcoat leaned toward the woman beside him, whispering something that made her frown. Baumann's gaze flicked to them, and his expression hardened.

"For those who doubt," he continued, his tone taking on an edge, "consider the chaos we face today. War, greed, corruption… these are the products of dissonance. The Black Hymnal can bring order. It can be our salvation."

At the back of the room, a woman in a red dress raised her hand. "But the risks," she said, her voice clear and unwavering. "Music with such power… it could be used for destruction as easily as it could for unity."

Baumann's smile was cold. "And that is why it must be in the right hands. Imagine the alternative—this power falling into the hands of those who would exploit it for their own ends. We must act decisively, or we risk losing everything."

His eyes swept the crowd, his expression one of

absolute conviction. "The monastery in Austria holds the answers we seek. Within its walls lies the final clue to the Black Hymnal's location. With your support, we will uncover it and secure our future."

The applause that followed was hesitant at first but grew steadily louder. Baumann's lips curved into a satisfied smile as he stepped back, allowing his lieutenants to mingle with the patrons and solidify their support.

Marcus Russo adjusted the cuffs of his borrowed tuxedo, the stiff fabric unfamiliar against his suntanned skin. Beside him, Hana Sinclair exuded confidence in a sleek black gown, her hair pinned up to reveal earrings of a single diamond each that glinted in the light. The two blended seamlessly with the crowd as they entered the ballroom, their forged invitations granting them access to Baumann's carefully curated event.

"Stay close," Marcus murmured, his voice barely audible over the hum of conversation. "We're looking for anything that confirms his plans and identifies which Austrian monastery."

Hana nodded, her eyes scanning the room, aware of his fidgeting under the formal attire. "Just act natural," she replied, her tone light. "You look like you belong here."

"I don't," Marcus muttered, but he followed her lead, his movements careful and deliberate as they wove through the crowd.

They positioned themselves near a cluster of attendees who were deep in discussion, their voices low but intense. "The monastery in the Alps," one man said, his German accent thick. "It's been abandoned for, what? Seventy years? Are we certain this information is reliable?"

"Adrian Baumann is never wrong," a woman replied

brusquely. "He's found the threads we need to follow. The hymnal is there, I'm sure of it."

Marcus's ears pricked at the mention of the hymnal. He exchanged a glance with Hana, who inclined her head slightly, urging him to listen further. They edged closer, pretending to admire a nearby painting as the conversation continued.

"But what if the Church intervenes?" another voice interjected. "They won't sit idly by if they discover our plans."

The woman's smile was sly. "Then we make sure they don't. Baumann has accounted for every possibility. We will reach the hymnal before anyone else even knows where to look."

Hana's grip on her clutch tightened, a creeping sense of dread tightening around her thoughts. If Baumann's cult was heading for that Austrian monastery, they would need to act quickly. But before she could whisper a plan to Marcus, a pair of guards near the entrance began scanning the crowd, their eyes searching.

"We've been made," Marcus whispered, his voice taut with urgency. "Time to go."

The tension in the room was taut as party-goers realized the guards were searching among them. Marcus and Hana moved toward the exit, their every step calculated to avoid drawing attention. The guards were methodical, their scrutiny inching closer with every moment. Hana's heart pounded in her chest as she looped her arm through Marcus's, leaning close as if whispering sweet nothings.

"Keep walking," she murmured, her voice steady despite the fear coiling in her gut. "Don't look back."

Marcus nodded, his jaw tight. They were just a few feet

from the door when one of the guards stepped into their path. "Excuse me," the man said, his tone polite but firm. "May I see your invitations again?"

Hana's smile was dazzling as she produced the forged invitation, holding it out with a steady hand. "Of course," she said sweetly. "Is there a problem?"

The guard's stern expression didn't falter as he took the paper, his eyes scanning it with an intensity that made Hana's pulse quicken. He scrutinized the document, his suspicion growing with each passing second. He looked up, his gaze locking onto hers. "This isn't..." he began, his voice laced with doubt.

Before he could finish, Marcus moved forward in a fluid motion, his hand darting out to strike the guard's wrist. The invitation fluttered to the floor as the man staggered, his balance momentarily lost. Marcus grabbed Hana's hand and pulled her toward the door.

"Run," he hissed, his voice low but commanding.

The ballroom erupted into chaos. Shouts echoed off the gilded walls as guards scrambled to respond. Guests gasped and stepped back, their murmurs of confusion adding to the cacophony. Marcus and Hana burst through the grand double doors into the cool night air, their breath visible in the chill as they sprinted across the mansion's manicured gardens.

The sound of pursuit was close behind—boots pounding against the gravel paths, voices barking orders in multiple languages. The intricate hedges and topiary offered some cover, but not enough. Marcus's mind raced as he scanned their surroundings, searching for an escape route.

"This way!" he shouted, veering left toward a wrought iron gate at the edge of the property. The gate loomed ahead, its pointy spikes silhouetted against the moonlit sky. Marcus reached it first, vaulting over with surprising agility. He turned and reached out, helping Hana as she scrambled after him. Her gown caught briefly on the iron, but she tore it free, landing hard on the cobblestone street beyond, her palms scraping against the rough surface. Marcus lifted her quickly, and they rushed off. The guards reached the gate seconds later, their shouts growing fainter as Marcus and Hana disappeared into the maze of narrow Viennese streets. The sound of their own footsteps echoed in the night, adrenaline propelling them forward.

They didn't stop running until they reached a safe house several blocks away, a nondescript apartment building tucked into a quiet corner of the city. They plunged through the outer door, slipped quickly inside the apartment Hana had secured earlier, and locked the door behind them. Inside, Marcus leaned against the wall, his chest heaving as he tried to catch his breath. Hana paced the room, her hands trembling slightly as the consequence of their escape sank in.

"We've got a location," Marcus said finally, his voice steady despite the lingering adrenaline. "Now we just have to beat them to it."

CHAPTER
TWENTY-EIGHT

The journey to the remote Austrian monastery was as daunting as it was breathtaking. With Michael and Karl on duty back at the Vatican, the rest of the team—Marcus, Hana, and Lukas—traveled in Karl's battered Jeep that groaned with every twist and turn of the mountain road. The snow-dusted Alps towered on either side, their jagged peaks piercing the cloudy sky. The thick forest pressed in around them, its dense canopy reducing the sunlight to mere streaks of gold filtering through the branches. The sound of the wind howling through the trees was punctuated only by the crunch of gravel beneath the tires.

"It feels like we're heading straight into a Grimm Brothers' fairy tale," Hana murmured, her eyes scanning the imposing landscape. Her voice held a mix of awe and unease as if the very air carried whispers of long-buried secrets.

Marcus glanced at her, his hands tight on the steering wheel. "Fairy tales usually have monsters, and we're driving straight toward one," he said, his tone grim. His gaze flicked to the rearview mirror, half-expecting to see Baumann's forces tailing them. Once they had heard that Baumann's group planned to gather at an abandoned Austrian alpine monastery, the team had quickly narrowed down the cultists' destination: the Red Messiah Monastery, where Malvagio had stayed while preparing some of his compositions. The monastery had been newly built in Malvagio's time with superb acoustics. For over two centuries, choirs sang their heavenly incantations here that echoed throughout the snowy mountainsides. The monastery had been abandoned to the elements decades ago. It was now just a matter of getting there before the cultists.

Lukas, seated in the back, rested his rifle against the seat beside him. "If Baumann knows we're here, we won't have much time to stake out a plan. We'll need to move quickly and be ready for anything." His voice was low but carried the heft of his military training.

The road narrowed further as they climbed higher, the incline steepening until the Jeep struggled to maintain its grip. The air grew thinner and colder, and snow began to fall in lazy flakes, dusting the windshield and turning the surrounding forest into a monochromatic tapestry.

"There it is," Marcus said, his voice softening with a mix of reverence and apprehension. He pointed ahead to where the trees thinned, revealing the monastery perched on a rocky outcrop. Its ancient stone walls were weathered by centuries of harsh alpine winters, and its steep, red-tiled roof was partially obscured by mist. The bell tower rose like a solitary sentinel against the darkening sky, its silhouette stark and foreboding.

Hana leaned forward, her breath fogging the glass. "It

looks like something time forgot," she said. "You can almost feel the history seeping out of those walls."

Marcus pulled the Jeep to a stop at the base of a narrow staircase carved into the cliffside. The stairs wound upward in sharp, uneven turns, leading to the massive wooden doors of the monastery. "This is as far as we can go by car," he said, cutting the engine. "From here, we're on foot."

The three stepped out into the biting cold, their boots crunching on the frost-covered ground. Marcus grabbed his satchel, double-checking its contents: tools, a flashlight, and a notebook. Lukas slung his rifle over his shoulder, his eyes scanning the treeline for any signs of movement. Hana tightened her scarf, bracing herself against the chill.

The ascent was treacherous. The staircase was slick with ice, and the howling wind threatened to topple them with each step. Hana clung to the railing, her knuckles white as she focused on placing one foot in front of the other. The height became dizzying as they climbed higher, the forest below shrinking into a patchwork of green and white.

"Imagine carrying supplies up here," Hana muttered, glancing back at Marcus. "The monks must have been made of sterner stuff than us."

Marcus chuckled despite the tension. "Monastic life was never about comfort. And considering the records we've found, Malvagio wasn't exactly seeking comfort when he came here."

At last, they reached the top. The towering wooden doors loomed before them, their iron fittings weathered with rust. Intricate carvings adorned the wood, depicting scenes of saints and angels locked in battle with demonic figures. The imagery was unsettling, as if warning any who dared enter of the struggles faced within.

Marcus pushed against the doors, and with a groan, they creaked open, revealing the monastery's shadowy interior. The vast hall was cold and laced with spectral illumination, the faint glow of daylight filtering through narrow stained-glass windows. The air was suffused with the scent of aged wood and lingering incense, as though the echoes of centuries-old prayers still clung to the stones.

"We need to find the library," Marcus said, his voice echoing slightly in the cavernous space. "If Malvagio left anything behind, that's where it will be."

Hana shivered, pulling her coat tighter around her. "This place feels... alive," she said softly, her eyes darting to the shadows that shifted and flickered at the edges of her vision. "Like it's watching us."

Lukas adjusted his rifle, his expression grim. "Then let's make sure we don't give it anything to see."

The trio set off, their footsteps echoing through the silent halls as they began their search. The monastery's secrets waited, hidden in the depths of its ancient walls.

THE MONASTERY LIBRARY was a labyrinth of towering shelves, their contents a mix of ancient tomes and crumbling scrolls. Dust motes danced in the shafts of light streaming through stained-glass windows, casting colorful patterns on the floor. The atmosphere was heavy, as though the room itself guarded its secrets jealously.

Marcus's eyes swept the rows of bound books, his archaeologist's instincts honing in on the details others might overlook. "These records date back centuries," he murmured, running his fingers over the spines of the nearest volumes. "If Malvagio was here, there'll be a trace of him."

Hana pulled a ladder closer and climbed to the upper shelves, the sound of its wooden legs scraping against the stone floor reverberating in the cavernous library. The shelves stretched skyward, crammed with books that exuded the musty aroma of centuries. Her fingers brushed against a leather-bound ledger, its cover embossed with the monastery's seal, worn but still distinct. The magnitude of the volume surprised her, as though it carried the consequence of the secrets it held.

Balancing carefully, Hana opened the ledger, its brittle pages crackling with each turn. The faded ink required her to lean close, squinting in the dim light. "This ledger mentions Malvagio," she called down, her voice carrying a mixture of excitement and disbelief. "It says he sought refuge here in 1783 and... wait, there's a note about him accessing the 'restricted vault.'"

Marcus, who had been combing through a nearby stack of books, froze mid-reach. His head snapped up, and his expression became more acute. "Restricted vault? Where is it?"

Hana flipped the page, her brow furrowing as her eyes scanned the cramped text. "It doesn't say. But it's somewhere within the library."

Marcus nodded, already moving toward the nearest wall of shelves. "Then we'll find it. Lukas, keep watch by the entrance. If anyone's followed us, I want to know before they get the drop on us."

The search resumed in earnest, the tension in the room substantial. Marcus sifted through tomes and scrolls, his movements quick but methodical. Hana moved from one section to another, scanning inscriptions and diagrams for anything resembling a map or clue. Lukas, stationed near the heavy library doors, kept his weapon ready, his eyes darting between the shadows.

It was Lukas who finally spotted it. His voice cut through the quiet. "Over here."

The others hurried to his side, where he pointed to a tapestry depicting a scene of monks in prayer. The fabric's edges were frayed, but its colors remained vivid. Behind it, the faint outline of a door was visible in the stone wall, its edges weathered but intact.

Lukas pulled the tapestry aside, revealing the door—a heavy stone slab inscribed with Latin text that shimmered faintly in the dim light. Marcus leaned in, running his fingers over the words. "'Only the penitent may enter,'" he translated, his tone grave. "Typical of the Church to add a moral riddle."

Hana stepped forward, tilting her head as she studied the carvings. "There's a mechanism here," she said, pointing to a series of levers and dials embedded in the stone. Her voice held a mix of curiosity and caution. "It looks like a puzzle lock."

Marcus crouched beside her, his brow bent in concentration. "Let's hope Malvagio didn't make this too complex. We don't have time to waste."

The two worked in tandem, their movements precise and deliberate. Hana called out patterns and symbols, her neural pathways firing in rapid succession to connect them to the Latin text above. Marcus adjusted the levers and turned the dials, his archaeologist's intuition guiding his hands. Each click of the mechanism echoed like a drumbeat, marking their progress.

Finally, with a deep, resounding thud, the mechanism unlocked. The stone door creaked open, revealing a small chamber. Marcus used his flashlight to peer into the darkness of the small room. The shelves lining the room were filled with scrolls and relics, their contents preserved in the dry, cool air. At the center sat a latched chest, its intricate metalwork glinting like a treasure from legend.

Hana stepped forward, her hands trembling as she opened the chest. Inside were fragments of sheet music, their edges charred as though they had narrowly escaped destruction. Marcus gently lifted one, holding it up to the flashlight. The notes and symbols felt almost alive, their arrangement imbued with a strange, mesmerizing energy.

"These are pieces of the Black Hymnal," he whispered, his voice saturated with awe and dread. "Malvagio's legacy." He quickly opened his reinforced satchel and placed the fragile papers between the covers.

The distant sound of boots on stone shattered the team's moment of triumph. Lukas spun toward the library entrance, his rifle at the ready. "We've got company," he said grimly.

Marcus and Hana exchanged a glance, their expressions darkening. Baumann's cult had found them.

The door to the library burst open, and Adrian Baumann strode in, flanked by a group of armed followers. His presence was as commanding as ever, his piercing blue eyes locking onto Marcus and Hana with a predatory gleam.

"Ah, Marcus," Baumann said smoothly, his voice echoing in the cavernous room. "Always one step ahead. But this time, I'm afraid you've reached a dead end."

Hana stepped forward, her chin held high as she looked out from the once secret room. "You're too late, Baumann. We have all the fragments left of it."

Baumann's smile was cold. "Do you? And how far do

you think you'll get with them?" He raised a hand, and his followers fanned out, blocking the exits.

Marcus's mind raced as he assessed their options. The fragments were too important to lose, but escape seemed impossible. The edge of his flashlight beam caught the image of a narrow spiral staircase at the back of the room, partially hidden by a collapsed shelf.

"Lukas," Marcus said quietly, nodding toward the staircase. "Cover us."

Lukas didn't hesitate. He fired a warning shot into the air, causing Baumann's followers to flinch. Marcus grabbed Hana's arm, pulling her toward the staircase as Lukas provided cover. The narrow passage echoed with the sound of their footsteps as they climbed, the satchel clutched tightly to Marcus's chest.

Baumann's furious shouts echoed below, but the team didn't stop. They burst out onto the monastery's upper level, the cold night air hitting them like a slap. A rope bridge stretched across a chasm to a nearby outcropping, their only route to safety.

"Go," Marcus urged, ushering Hana onto the swaying bridge. Lukas followed, his rifle trained on the library entrance. As Baumann's followers emerged, Lukas fired another shot, forcing them to take cover.

The team reached the other side, breathless and shaken but alive. Below, the monastery loomed in the darkness, its secrets once again sealed away. For now, they had the fragments. But Baumann's pursuit was far from over.

CHAPTER
TWENTY-NINE

The road from the Austrian monastery wound through a landscape cloaked in twilight, the forested hills shrouded with shadows from the fading sun. Marcus sat at the wheel of the Jeep, his grip firm but his knuckles pale. Hana occupied the passenger seat, her laptop balanced precariously on her knees, while Lukas sprawled in the back seat, his rifle resting on the seat beside him. The car's heater hummed softly, battling the alpine chill that seeped through the windows.

"How long until we hit the border?" Lukas asked, his voice low and watchful as his eyes scanned the darkening surroundings.

Marcus glanced at the GPS mounted on the dashboard. "Another two hours, give or take. After that, it's a straight shot to Rome."

Hana sighed, running a hand through her hair as she stared at the illuminated screen of her laptop. "I still can't make sense of this," she muttered, scrolling through digital scans of the fragments they had recovered. "These sequences... they're not just music. There's a layer of mathematical precision here that doesn't belong in conventional composition."

"The Black Hymnal wasn't conventional," Marcus said, his eyes fixed on the winding road ahead. "Its composition wasn't intended to create harmonious notes to raise a worshipful song to the divine or an expression of joy. Everything in it was deliberate, calculated. If these fragments point to something bigger, we need to figure it out." He paused, then finished, "I can only presume these are the sole surviving fragments of the Black Hymnal. And, if so, Baumann will be after them. And us."

The tension in the car was substantial, the heaviness of the fragments in Marcus's satchel serving as a constant reminder of the stakes. The road descended into a valley, the forest thinning to reveal a small village nestled at its center. Lights twinkled in the windows of stone cottages, and smoke curled from chimneys into the crisp evening air.

"We should stop here for fuel and supplies," Marcus said, slowing the car as they approached the village. "It'll be our last chance before the border. I'll call Michael from there and have him inform Cardinal Severino of what we found. We'll need heightened security and as much intel on the cultists' movements as we can get."

The group moved quickly, splitting up to gather what they needed while keeping a low profile. Lukas kept watch near the car, his hand never far from his weapon. Hana disappeared into a general store, returning with a bag of provisions, while Marcus filled the tank at a creaky old pump after making his call. Every moment felt like borrowed time, the fear of being tracked pressing heavily on them.

Once back on the road, the conversation shifted to strategy. "We need to analyze these fragments as soon as we're secure in Rome," Hana said, her determination evident. "There's something here we're not seeing—something vital."

Marcus nodded. "First thing tomorrow, we'll lock ourselves in the research room and start piecing it together. Lukas, you'll coordinate with Michael on the security he's getting from the cardinal. Baumann won't stop, and we need to be ready."

Lukas's eyes met Marcus's in the rearview mirror. "Understood. Let's just hope we're faster than they are."

The rest of the journey passed in tense silence, each of them lost in their own thoughts. When they finally reached Rome, the city's familiar clamor felt like an odd comfort. A Vatican escort met them at the outskirts, whisking them through the narrow streets to the Apostolic Palace. As they entered the secure research room, the importance of their mission settled over them anew. They had the fragments, but the true challenge was just beginning.

The streets of Rome thrummed with their usual chaos. Motorcycles weaved through traffic, tourists snapped photos of ancient ruins, and street vendors called out their wares in a cacophony of voices. But beneath this vibrant surface, a shadowy threat loomed.

Near Piazza Navona, a Vatican courier navigated the narrow alleys with deliberate speed. Clad in a plain black coat, he clutched a leather satchel to his chest. Inside were classified documents—intelligence on Baumann's cult and their operations. His every step was measured, his eyes scanning the crowds for potential threats.

Unbeknownst to him, he was already being followed. Three figures moved through the bustling market, their casual attire blending seamlessly with the tourists. Their eyes never left the courier, their pace matching his as he weaved through the throng.

The courier's path took him through a quieter street, the din of the marketplace fading behind him. It was here that his pursuers made their move. One of them, a wiry man with a scar cutting across his cheek, closed the distance with alarming speed.

The courier heard the faint shuffle of footsteps too late. A hand clamped down on his shoulder, spinning him around as another figure stepped into his path. His grip on the satchel tightened, and his free hand reached instinctively for the small canister of pepper spray in his pocket.

"Don't make this harder than it has to be," the scarred man hissed, his voice low and menacing. "Hand over the bag."

The courier's heart pounded as he assessed his options. He could see no escape route, the alley now boxed in by the other two assailants. Summoning his courage, he stepped back, fumbling for the canister. Before he could deploy it, one of the attackers lunged, striking his wrist and sending the spray clattering to the ground.

"You shouldn't have resisted," the scarred man sneered, wrenching the satchel from the courier's grasp.

The courier stumbled back, his breath ragged. "You don't know what you're dealing with," he managed, his voice shaking.

The man's smirk deepened. "Oh, we know exactly what we're dealing with."

Before the courier could respond, a sharp blow to the

back of his head sent him crumpling to the ground. The attackers melted into the shadows, the satchel in their possession.

Across the city, similar scenes unfolded with precision. Baumann's cult members targeted key figures connected to the Vatican's heightened investigation, sowing fear and disruption. Researchers disappeared from their homes, their notes and files ransacked. Even the basilica's guards found themselves overwhelmed as whispers of betrayal and sabotage spread through their ranks.

In a secure room within the Apostolic Palace, Hana watched the escalating reports on a muted television screen. The news reported these incidents as vandalism or civil unrest, avoiding mention of their relation to either the Church or Baumann's cult. Neither entity needed that kind of notoriety, so the news was filtered through carefully curated facts. But there was no doubt of the targets or the source of the assailants to those who knew what was going on in the shadows of Rome. Her face became unreadable with every update. "They're escalating," she said, her voice tight with frustration. "Baumann's making a statement."

Marcus, seated across from her, looked up from the fragments of the Black Hymnal spread before him. His face was pale, his exhaustion evident. "It's more than that," he said quietly. "He's isolating us. Cutting off our resources, creating chaos. He wants us cornered."

A loud knock interrupted their conversation, and Father Michael Dominic entered the room. His usual calm demeanor was tinted with urgency. "The attacks are growing bolder," he said, his voice low. "Several key researchers have gone missing. We've increased security, but Baumann's network is vast. We need to decode the hymnal before he completes his plans."

Hana met his gaze, her expression resolute. "We're close," she said. "The fragments... they're pointing to something, but we haven't connected all the dots yet."

Michael's gaze softened, and he placed a reassuring hand on her shoulder. "You'll figure it out," he said. "You always do."

She reached up and placed her hand on top of his. "*We* always do."

THE APOSTOLIC PALACE had become a fortress. Swiss Guards patrolled the halls, their halberds gleaming under the chandeliers, while plainclothes security operatives monitored every corner. Michael oversaw the preparations, his every decision weighed against the mounting threats.

The research room, once a place of quiet contemplation, now buzzed with frenetic energy. Maps, notes, and photographs covered every surface, each detail scrutinized for clues. Marcus stood at a central table, the fragments of the Black Hymnal spread before him like pieces of a puzzle. Hana worked beside him, her laptop open as she cross-referenced historical records and astronomical data.

Lukas entered, his expression grim. "The guards are reporting increased activity near the Vatican walls," he said. "We've spotted unfamiliar faces—scouts, most likely. Baumann's preparing for something."

Michael nodded, his expression unreadable. "Our defenses are strong, but they won't hold indefinitely. Marcus, Hana, how close are we?"

Marcus rubbed his temples, his exhaustion evident. "The fragments point to a specific tonal sequence, but it's incomplete. It's like having a lock but no key. Without the full sequence, we can't unlock the hymnal's true purpose."

Michael's gaze hardened. "Then you'll focus on decoding it, and we'll focus on keeping you safe. Baumann's advance ends here."

As the team dispersed to their tasks, the charge of their mission settled over them. The fragments of the Black Hymnal held the key to either salvation or destruction, and the battle to decode them had only just begun.

CHAPTER
THIRTY

The research room was cloaked in an almost reverent silence, pierced only by the soft rustling of paper and the faint tapping of Marcus's pencil against the desk.

"It's more than a melody," Marcus murmured to himself, his voice barely audible. "It's a language... an equation in sound." The fragments of the Black Hymnal were laid out before him, each piece meticulously organized to make sense of the chaotic genius embedded within. A small desk lamp cast a warm glow over his notes, highlighting the intricate notations that had consumed his attention for hours.

Hana, seated across from him, looked up from her laptop. "What do you mean?" she asked, her tone cautious but intrigued.

He gestured to a specific section of the sheet music. "Look here. These notes... they're mathematically precise. The intervals between them aren't random. They align with frequencies corresponding to specific emotional responses in the human brain. The Black Hymnal went beyond simply composing music; it was designed to engineer a response."

Hana leaned closer, her eyes flicking over the page. "You're saying it's designed to manipulate people?"

Marcus nodded, his expression grim. "And not just individuals. This"—he tapped the parchment with a finger—"is meant to affect entire groups, maybe even entire populations. Malvagio wanted to create what he originally called *The Purification Symphony* and later *The Devil's Symphony* for a reason. It's a composition designed to override free will."

The influence of his words settled over them like a shroud. Hana leaned back in her chair, her arms crossed tightly across her chest. "If Baumann finds this and completes Malvagio's score…"

"He'll have the power to control anyone who hears it," Marcus finished. "Governments, armies, entire nations could fall under his influence. This isn't only about power. It's about what comes next—absolute domination."

He stood and began pacing, the tension in his movements mirroring the urgency in his voice. "Malvagio must have known this would happen. He did more here than just create music; he crafted a weapon based on the Black Hymnal. And Baumann… Baumann understands its potential better than anyone. We're racing against someone who's been planning this for years, maybe longer."

Hana's eyes followed him, her own thoughts spiraling. "What if the melody isn't just a weapon? What if it's… contagious? A kind of viral influence that spreads with every performance? Baumann wouldn't need to broadcast it globally. If the right people hear it, they could become vectors, spreading its effects exponentially."

Marcus stopped mid-step, Hana's words striking him like a physical blow. "That would explain why Malvagio so carefully encoded the sequence we discovered in the music box. He was trying to control its spread."

The room grew colder, as though the enormity of their discovery had sapped the air of its warmth. Marcus returned to his seat, his hands trembling slightly as he resumed analyzing the fragments.

"We have to find the sequence," he said, his voice steady despite the tremor in his hands. "But we can't use it. We need to understand it so we can destroy it."

Hana nodded, her resolve hardening. "Then we work through the night if we have to. This has to end here, Marcus."

HANA PACED the length of the room, her thoughts whirring like a machine on overdrive. The fragments of the Black Hymnal were spread out on a long table, their cryptic symbols and notes like an unsolved riddle. She paused, staring at the notations, her mind piecing together the implications of Marcus's findings.

"Marcus," she said suddenly, her voice cutting through the quiet. "If these frequencies can manipulate emotions, what happens when they're amplified?"

Marcus looked up from his notes. "Amplified how?"

Hana gestured to the fragments. "Malvagio's work wasn't just about individual compositions. He was creating something scalable. These notes... they're designed to interact with specific acoustic environments. Cathedrals, for example. Places with natural resonance that could amplify the melody's effects. I mean, you saw how much more powerful the music box's sounds were when played in the basilica."

Marcus's eyes widened as the implications dawned on him. "Malvagio's *Devil's Symphony* could be broadcast—played in a massive venue, maybe even transmitted globally. This is nothing short of forced alignment. A single, unified will imposed by the melody."

A chill crept into the room as his words settled over them. Marcus leaned back in his chair, the weight of the situation pressing down on his mind. "That's why the Vatican suppressed this. They knew. Even back then, they understood what this could do."

"And now Baumann has the same knowledge or will have if he gets these fragments of the Black Hymnal to finish Malvagio's work," Hana said. She ran a hand through her hair, her frustration evident.

Marcus broke the silence, his tone somber but determined. "There's something else we're missing. Malvagio must have built in a fail-safe. Remember, he'd carefully encoded the sequence in the music box in an attempt to control it. I don't doubt he would have also created something to counteract the melody if it ever got out of control. We know he experimented with his other compositions from the numerous instances in his lifetime when he played them, and audiences were affected in some way. Having seen the effects, he surely realized a failsafe was necessary."

Hana's gaze intensified. "A counter-melody?"

"It would make sense," Marcus replied. "If he truly understood the power of what he was creating, he wouldn't have left it unchecked. He would need to control the spread, at the least, even to counteract it, if necessary. We need to look for clues in these fragments... something that hints at a way to neutralize the effects. Similar to how the sound-cancelling tones we used countered the music box melody."

Hana moved to the table, her earlier frustration replaced by a renewed sense of purpose. "Then let's find it. If there's even a chance that Malvagio left us a way out, we have to uncover it."

As they delved back into their work, the room pulsed with the significance of their discovery. The fragments of the Black Hymnal were more than notes on a page. They were the key to humanity's salvation or its downfall, and the clock was ticking.

FATHER MICHAEL ENTERED the room quietly, his presence a steadying force amid the frenetic energy. He paused at the doorway, observing the fragments of the Black Hymnal spread across the table. His gaze lingered on the intricate notations, his expression one of quiet concern.

"You've made progress, I see," he said, his voice breaking the tense silence.

Marcus looked up from his notes, his exhaustion evident but his determination unshaken. "If you can call it that," he said. "We've figured out what Baumann wants to do. We just haven't figured out how to stop him. Theoretically, he can't do anything, now that we have the only fragments of the Black Hymnal as well as the music box. But he has proven himself to be unrelenting."

Michael stepped closer, his eyes scanning the fragments. He reached out, brushing his fingers lightly across one of the sheets as though its dark history might seep into his skin. "What have you learned?"

Hana spoke up, her tone measured but urgent. She

explained their findings, laying out the melody's manipulative power, its resonance with specific environments, and Baumann's likely plans to amplify its effects. She didn't shy away from the worst implications—the potential for global domination and the erasure of free will.

Michael listened without interruption, his hands clasped behind his back. When she finished, he was silent for a long moment. Finally, he spoke, his voice low and steady. "You're playing with something far more dangerous than you realize."

Marcus bristled, his frustration bubbling to the surface. "We don't have a choice. If we don't act, Baumann will find a way to destroy everything."

Michael's gaze remained steady. "I'm not suggesting inaction. But you need to understand what you're dealing with. This melody isn't merely a series of notes and frequencies. It's intent. Power. When you reconstruct it, you're not just unlocking a composition. You're unlocking something far older, something that might not be contained by ink and parchment."

Hana's voice softened, her earlier frustration giving way to concern. "You think it's alive?"

Michael hesitated, choosing his words carefully. "Not alive in the way we understand it. But power like this… it takes on a life of its own. It appears to carry on the intentions of its creator, and those intentions linger long after the creator is gone. If Vincenzo Malvagio infused this melody with the darkness from the Black Hymnal, completing it could unleash that darkness in ways we can't predict."

Marcus stood, his hands planted firmly on the table. "Then what do you suggest we do? Destroy the fragments and hope Baumann doesn't find another way? That's not an option. He's too close."

Michael stepped closer, his expression grave. "I'm suggesting extreme caution. If you complete this melody using the Black Hymnal, as Malvagio did or tried to do, you need to be prepared for what comes next. This is about ensuring that what you unleash doesn't consume you in the process."

The room fell silent. Marcus exchanged a glance with Hana, his resolve unshaken but his heart heavy. The path ahead was clear, but it was fraught with peril, and the consequences of their actions would echo far beyond the confines of the Vatican walls.

CHAPTER
THIRTY-ONE

The Vatican's tranquil evening was shattered by the distant rumble of approaching vehicles. Adrian Baumann's forces moved with military precision, their black SUVs cutting through the cobblestone streets of Rome like shadows. As they neared the heavily fortified entrance, Baumann's operatives executed a well-rehearsed plan. Using forged credentials and insider knowledge, they bypassed the initial security checks with ease. Meanwhile, a small team expertly disabled the main entrance's surveillance system, creating a blind spot in the Vatican's defenses. Within moments, the once peaceful and secure surroundings of the Apostolic Palace were transformed into a potential battlefield: vulnerable, mute, awaiting the war to come. Baumann, standing in the lead vehicle, surveyed the scene with a cold smile, his gloved hand resting lightly on the doorframe.

"Tonight, we claim what is ours," he said, his voice calm yet commanding. The others in the vehicle nodded, their expressions grimly determined. Armed followers poured from the convoy, their movements precise as they surrounded the perimeter with military efficiency. Each carried weapons concealed beneath their coats, moving like phantoms through the Vatican's narrow streets, their entry now secured and their mission underway.

WITHIN THE PALACE WALLS, alarms blared, the sound echoing through the ancient halls. The Swiss Guards mobilized swiftly, their boots striking the marble floors with persistence. Cardinal Severino, visibly shaken, hurried into the secure research room where Marcus, Hana, and Michael were huddled over the fragments of the Black Hymnal. The music box, its score, and Malvagio's diary remained locked in the restricted area.

"Baumann is here," Severino said, his voice trembling as he instinctively clutched a rosary. "He's brought an army. They've already breached the outer gates."

Marcus exchanged a glance with Hana, his jaw tightening. "We need to move the fragments," he said, grabbing his reinforced satchel from beneath the table. "If they get their hands on these, it's over."

"The Archives is the safest place," Michael interjected, his calm demeanor steadying the group. "But we must move quickly."

The lights flickered as the power fluctuated, briefly plunging the room into brief darkness before the emergency generators roared to life. Hana's laptop screen dimmed, its soft glow casting eerie shadows across the walls. Outside, the sharp crack of gunfire shattered the air, followed by shouts and the clash of metal.

• • •

BAUMANN STEPPED out of his vehicle as the attack began, his polished shoes crunching on the cobblestones. He adjusted his coat, his eyes scanning the Vatican walls with an air of detachment. "They think they can hide," he muttered, more to himself than anyone else. "But the symphony calls to me. I *will* have it."

His followers began their assault, scaling walls and disabling security cameras with ruthless precision. Smoke grenades billowed, obscuring the approach as chaos spread through the Vatican's outer defenses, an incursion the likes of which hadn't occurred in centuries

DEEP WITHIN THE BELVEDERE PALACE, the Apostolic Archives became a fortress. Karl and Lukas, seasoned Swiss Guards, led a small team tasked with defending the heart of the Vatican's stored knowledge. The ancient corridors, usually silent and filled with the scent of aged parchment, were now alive with tension and the distant echoes of conflict.

"Seal the secondary entrances," Karl ordered, his voice steady despite the chaos. "If they get in, we'll funnel them through the main hall."

Lukas nodded, his rifle held at the ready. "Understood. What about Marcus and Hana?"

"They're securing the fragments," Karl replied, his expression grim. "We hold the line until they're safe. No exceptions."

The first wave of attackers breached the outer gates, their movements swift and calculated. Smoke grenades filled the hallways, obscuring vision and sowing confusion. Karl's team fired warning shots, their voices rising above the din to direct the defenders.

"Hold your positions!" Karl shouted, his voice carrying authority and resolve. "No one passes this point!"

In the midst of the firefight, Lukas spotted movement in the shadows. He raised his assault rifle, his finger resting lightly on the trigger. "Contact left!" he called out, firing a precise shot that struck an attacker's weapon, disarming them before they could retaliate. Another figure lunged forward, and Lukas swung the butt of his rifle, knocking the intruder to the ground.

Meanwhile, Marcus and Hana raced through the labyrinthine corridors of the Archives, the fragments securely wrapped and clutched in Marcus's hands. The dim lighting and echoing footsteps amplified their urgency. A text message came on Hana's phone, and she stopped to read it. "Michael is guarding the restricted area and wants us to find another safe area."

"We need to get to the hidden vault," Marcus said, his breath coming in short bursts. "It's the only place they won't find."

"How much time do we have?" Hana asked, glancing over her shoulder as shouts and footsteps grew closer.

"Not enough," Marcus replied grimly. He adjusted the satchel, ensuring its precious contents were secure. "Stay close. If we're separated—"

"Don't finish that sentence," Hana snapped, her determination overriding her fear. "We're not splitting up."

The pair reached the vault—a hidden chamber concealed behind a nondescript bookshelf.

Marcus activated the mechanism, a series of levers and dials that required both precision and speed. The door slid open with a low groan, revealing the reinforced interior.

"In, quickly," he urged, ushering Hana inside. As the

door closed behind them, the sound of gunfire and shouts faded, leaving them in tense silence.

THE BATTLE RAGED FOR HOURS, the attackers' persistence met by the unyielding resolve of the Vatican's defending Swiss Guards. and Gendarmerie. Yet Baumann, ever the strategist, had planned for this. As dawn broke, the siege came to an abrupt halt. Smoke lingered in the air, and the once-pristine marble floors bore the scars of the conflict—bullet holes, scorch marks, and scattered debris.

Marcus and Hana emerged from the hidden vault, their expressions weary but resolute. They found Michael in the main hall, his robes dusted with debris but his calm demeanor intact.

"The fragments are secure," Marcus reported. "But Baumann…"

"He escaped," Michael said quietly, his tone heavy with disappointment. "He's retreated for now, but this isn't over."

OUTSIDE THE VATICAN WALLS, Baumann stood amid his retreating forces. Despite the failure to retrieve the fragments of the Black Hymnal, his expression was one of quiet triumph. He turned, addressing his closest followers.

"Let them think they've won," he said, his voice carrying a chilling conviction. "The unleashing of the symphony is inevitable now." He clutched at his shoulder bag, heavy on his arm, a smile of victory spreading like the music he planned to release on an unsuspecting world.

CHAPTER
THIRTY-TWO

The morning sun bathed the Vatican in an eerie quiet, its golden rays illuminating the scars of the night's violence. The Apostolic Palace, usually a beacon of serenity, stood as a battered symbol of resilience. Bullet holes marred the ancient stone walls, shattered glass crunched underfoot, and the acrid stench of smoke lingered in the air. Swiss Guards moved through the scene like ghosts, their once-pristine uniforms now streaked with grime and blood. Every face bore the same expression of exhaustion and grim determination.

Marcus Russo stood at the entrance to the Archives, his eyes scanning the devastation. Several guards sat on makeshift benches nearby, their injuries ranging from minor cuts to more serious wounds hastily bandaged by medics. The steady hum of emergency generators filled the air, an audible reminder of how close they had come to losing everything.

"Status?" Marcus asked a young guard who clutched his arm, a blood-soaked bandage wrapped tightly around it. The guard's face was pale, but his eyes burned with resolve.

"We held them back, sir," he replied, his voice steady despite the pain. "They didn't breach the inner sanctum."

Marcus placed a reassuring hand on the man's shoulder. "You did more than hold them back. You protected something far greater than any of us. Rest now. You've earned it."

Father Dominic approached, his robes streaked with soot and his expression somber. He carried a small notebook, its pages filled with notes taken during the night's chaos.

"The Archives..." He choked on the next words. "Somehow they... got through."

"What do you mean?"

"The restricted area was infiltrated and—"

"The music box?" Marcus asked, his eyes wide.

Michael nodded. "Gone."

"But how? You were stationed there all night."

Michael looked up, his brow wrinkled. "Me? No, Hana messaged me that *she* was there. She asked me to remain with—"

Marcus reached for a nearby table, supporting himself as the realization hit him. "I should have realized it. You would have used the earpiece to tell her. It was a text message. Something anyone could fake."

He explained to Michael the message Hana had received. They now realized the massive onslaught of the night had served as Baumann's distraction. Yes, Baumann wanted the Black Hymnal fragments, but armed with the music box and its score, he still had all he needed to unleash more than enough of the horror he intended.

Michael's gaze lingered on the wounded guards. "We

thought faith and resolve carried us through this night, but we can't rely on those alone. Baumann's forces are relentless, cunning, and the Vatican hasn't been prepared for such an assault for hundreds of years."

As the two men spoke, a faint sound carried through the still air—an impromptu choir of nuns had gathered in a distant chapel, their voices rising in a hauntingly beautiful hymn. For a moment, it seemed to wash over the devastation, a fragile reminder of hope amid the ruins. Marcus closed his eyes briefly, drawing strength from the melody.

"We'll hold, Michael," he said finally. "No matter what Baumann does, we'll find a way to stop him."

THE RESEARCH ROOM felt oppressive in its silence, the toll of the siege still hanging heavily in the air. Marcus sat at the central table, the fragments of the Black Hymnal meticulously arranged before him.

He leaned over one fragment. His fingers traced the elegant, almost hypnotic script. The melody itself was complex, but the annotations—written in Latin and a ciphered alchemical script—hinted at something far darker.

"These instructions," Marcus muttered, breaking the silence, "they're also predictions. Malvagio knew exactly what he was creating."

Hana, seated across from him, looked up from her laptop. Her usually distinct features were softened by exhaustion, but her eyes remained keen. "Predictions?" she echoed, her voice laced with concern.

Marcus pointed to a line of text scrawled in the margin of one fragment. "Here. It mentions 'resonance beyond mortal comprehension' and 'influence that bends the will of nations.' Malvagio was predicting his ability to alter the very fabric of society."

Marcus looked at Hana, his expression grim. "And Baumann understands that. Every note, every sequence, it's all engineered to manipulate emotions and behavior on a massive scale. If he plays this…"

"He won't," Hana said firmly, though her voice carried an undercurrent of fear. "We'll stop him. We have to."

She returned her attention to her laptop, cross-referencing the annotations with historical records. "These symbols," she began, pointing to a series of markings. "They match those found in alchemical texts from the seventeenth century. Remember, Malvagio was known not just for being a composer but also for being an alchemist. This melody is very likely a ritual of alchemy. And every performance of the melody is intended as an invocation. The shadowed beings that arose from the playing of the music box could be bare whispers of the beings that the completed *Devil's Symphony,* using the Black Hymnal's chords, could invoke."

IN THE DIM light of the Vatican's secure interrogation chamber, Hana stood across from the captured cultist. The man's disheveled appearance—his torn clothing, matted hair, and hollow cheeks—belied the fiery conviction in his eyes. Despite his chains, he radiated an unsettling confidence, his lips curled in a faint, mocking smile.

"You think you've won something," he said, his voice calm and even. "But this is just the overture. The symphony is inevitable now."

Hana stood firmly, her expression cold and unyielding.

"Perhaps you'd like to elaborate on that. Or would you prefer to spend the rest of your days in this cell?"

The cultist chuckled, a low, chilling sound. "You don't understand, do you? Baumann is destined to complete what Malvagio started. You can't stop him."

Hana leaned forward, her voice dropping to a dangerous whisper. "Maybe not. But I can make sure Baumann loses everything before he gets the chance. So tell me: where is he going?"

The cultist's smile faltered, his bravado cracking under her piercing gaze. He leaned back, the chains clinking as he shifted uncomfortably. Finally, he spoke. "Prague," he said. "The city of a hundred spires. The stage of the eternal hymn. That's where it all began for Vincenzo Malvagio. And that's where Baumann will finish it."

Hana's mind raced. Prague, with its rich history of alchemy and mysticism, was the perfect setting for Baumann's next move. Her pulse quickened as the pieces fell into place.

She straightened, her resolve hardening. "Thank you," she said, her tone laced with finality. "You've just helped us stop him."

As she turned to leave, the cultist's voice followed her. "You're too late. The symphony's final note has already been written. And now we have all we need to play it to its fullest."

Hana didn't look back. She stepped into the corridor, her thoughts focused on the road ahead. Prague awaited, and with it, the next chapter in their battle to stop the Devil's Symphony.

CHAPTER
THIRTY-THREE

The hum of the Dassault Falcon's engines filled the cabin with a steady rhythm, a reminder of the sleek, purposeful speed with which Hana's private jet cut through the clouds. The Falcon, a symbol of her family's considerable wealth and influence, was both a sanctuary and a command center as it whisked them toward Prague. Inside, the leather seats and polished wood accents exuded understated luxury, but the atmosphere was anything but relaxed.

Hana sat near the window, her laptop perched on a small table, its screen alive with maps, notes, and digital scans of the fragments they had secured. The faint glow illuminated her facial features, which were drawn tight with concentration. She pushed a strand of chestnut brown hair behind her ear as she scrolled through pages of historical records. Beside her, Marcus leaned over a map spread across the table, his finger tracing the winding streets of Prague's Old Town.

"If Malvagio left anything in Prague," Marcus said, his

THE DEVIL'S SYMPHONY

voice low but steady, "it's likely tied to locations with significant acoustic or symbolic resonance. Cathedrals, concert halls, old conservatories... places where sound carries and lingers."

Hana nodded, her eyes scanning the notes. "And Baumann knows that. He'll already be working to narrow down the possibilities. We need to be faster."

Across the cabin, Father Michael sat quietly, a rosary slipping through his fingers as he murmured a prayer. The soft cadence of his voice added an air of solemnity to the space. When he finished, he looked up, his expression calm but resolute. "Prague has always been a city of dualities," he said. "Beauty and darkness, faith and heresy. If Malvagio saw it as a stage, it was likely because he understood the city's spiritual and cultural significance. We must tread carefully."

Hana glanced at him, appreciating his grounded perspective. "Treading carefully hasn't exactly been our strength," she said with a wry smile, though her tone carried an undercurrent of seriousness.

Marcus straightened, his focus clinging to the map. "Then we'll adapt. If Baumann's ahead of us, we can't afford missteps. He's proven he's willing to do whatever it takes."

The jet's interior lights dimmed briefly as the pilot's voice came over the speaker. "We're beginning our descent into Ruzyne Airport, Ms. Sinclair. Estimated arrival in fifteen minutes. Please prepare for landing."

Hana closed her laptop and leaned back in her seat, her mind already racing through their next steps. Baumann's cult had proven its reach, and she knew better than to assume they were safe.

As the jet descended, the sprawling city of Prague came

into view. The red rooftops of the Old Town glowed in the evening light, the Gothic spires of St. Vitus Cathedral reaching toward the sky. The sinuous curve of the Vltava River reflected the setting sun, creating a breathtaking panorama that momentarily stole their breath.

"Prague," Michael murmured, his tone contemplative. "A city steeped in mysticism and history. It's no wonder Malvagio was drawn here."

Hana's lips tightened, betraying her frustration. "Mysticism and history are all well and good," she said, "but we're walking into a battleground. Baumann knows this city's significance as well as we do."

The jet touched down smoothly on the runway, its engines spooling down as it taxied toward a private hangar. A black town car waited for them on the tarmac, arranged by Hana's contacts within her family's extensive network.

Marcus glanced back at the sleek jet they had just left and then ahead at the gleaming town car. "Nice to have a fiancée who can whisk you about Europe as needed, eh, Michael?"

Michael smiled and reached out to take Hana's hand in his own. "I'm blessed in more ways than I can count in this life."

Hana squeezed his hand in return as they approached the car. The driver, a tall man with memorable features and a professional demeanor, opened the doors as they reached it.

"Welcome to Prague, Ms. Sinclair," he said with a slight bow. "The car is ready. Your accommodations and initial contacts have been arranged as per your instructions."

Hana nodded, wasting no time. "Thank you. Let's move quickly. We have a lot of ground to cover."

As they climbed into the car, Marcus pulled out a folder containing their leads. "Our first stop is the Lesser Town district," he said. "There's an ancient conservatory there that was active during Malvagio's time. It's a good place to start."

The drive through Prague's cobblestone streets was both mesmerizing and unsettling. The city's architectural beauty stood in stark contrast to the tension that gripped the group. Tourists wandered through the squares, snapping photos and laughing, oblivious to the undercurrent of danger that followed Marcus, Hana, and Michael.

Hana watched the streets pass by, her mind replaying the cultist's words from the interrogation room. "Prague... the stage of the eternal hymn." She shivered involuntarily, the phrase carrying an almost tangible weight.

"Keep in mind," Marcus cautioned, as though reading her thoughts, "we're chasing a man who believes he can rewrite history. If Baumann plays the symphony, he'll do more than reshape the world. He'll enslave it."

Michael's voice was steady as he spoke. "Then we must ensure he doesn't succeed. Faith, determination, and vigilance will be our tools. Let us use them wisely."

The car came to a halt outside the conservatory, its Baroque façade a testament to centuries of musical excellence. The team stepped out, their resolve steeled by the task ahead. The streets around them buzzed with anticipation, as though the city itself understood the prospect of what was to come.

THE CONSERVATORY WAS a relic of Prague's Baroque era, its grand façade adorned with intricate carvings of angels and musicians. Inside, the room held the scent of aged wood and the faint echo of forgotten melodies. The corridors were lined with display cases showcasing antique instruments and manuscripts, a testament to the city's rich musical heritage.

The team was greeted by a curator, an elderly man with wire-rimmed glasses and a cautious demeanor. "You're looking for something specific?" he asked, his Czech accent thick but his English fluent.

"Historical records tied to Vincenzo Malvagio," Marcus replied, his tone firm but respectful. "He spent time in Prague during the late eighteenth century."

The curator's expression grew heavy with emotion. "Malvagio... that is a name we do not speak lightly. He was a controversial figure, even in his time. Some of his work... it is said to be cursed."

"We understand the risks," Michael interjected. "But this is a matter of great importance."

Reluctantly, the curator led them to a private archive room, its walls lined with shelves groaning under the weight of centuries-old volumes. "Whatever you find here," he said, "I hope it brings you the answers you seek. But be careful. Malvagio's shadow still lingers."

Hours passed as they sifted through dusty ledgers and faded manuscripts. It was Hana who uncovered a letter, its edges brittle with age, tucked inside a leather-bound journal. She read it aloud, her voice steady despite the growing unease in the room.

"'Prague is the stage of the eternal hymn,'" she translated. "'Here, the melody finds its resonance. The city itself is an instrument, and I am merely its player.'"

Marcus frowned, memories and fears tangling in his brain. "He saw Prague as more than a city. To him, it was a conduit, a place where his music could achieve its full power."

A shadow crossed Michael's face. "If Baumann believes this too, he'll stop at nothing to harness it."

Hana photographed the letter and inserted its address into her GPS: their next destination.

As they stepped out of the conservatory into the cool evening air, the city's vibrant life felt almost surreal. Street performers played violins on the Charles Bridge, their melodies weaving through the chatter of tourists. Yet amid the picturesque scene, Hana felt a prickle of unease.

"We're being watched," she murmured, her voice low but urgent.

Marcus followed her gaze, his eyes scanning the crowd. Three figures loitered at the edge of the square, their attention fixed on the team. One of them spoke into a phone, his lips moving rapidly.

"Cult operatives," Marcus said under his breath. "They must have followed us from the airport."

Hana's mind raced. "We need to split up. Draw them away from the conservatory."

Marcus hesitated but nodded. "I'll take the lead. Michael, stay close to Hana."

"I plan to," the priest said, glancing at his fiancée.

The group moved quickly, weaving through the labyrinthine streets of the Old Town. The cultists pursued them, their pace quickening as they realized their targets were aware of their presence. Hana broke away, darting down a narrow alley lined with crumbling facades. The sound of footsteps echoed behind her, growing louder with each passing second.

Her breath came in bursts as she reached the end of the alley, only to find her path blocked by a high iron gate. She turned, her heart pounding, as the cultists closed in. But before they could reach her, Michael appeared from the shadows, wielding a heavy piece of wood he had grabbed from a nearby construction site.

With precise, powerful swings, he forced the attackers back, his movements fluid and unrelenting. "*Go!*" he shouted to Hana, who scrambled over the gate as Michael held the figures at bay.

Once on the other side, Hana turned to see the priest vault over the gate with unerring agility. Together, they disappeared into the twisting streets, their pursuers losing track of them in the maze-like alleys.

They regrouped with Marcus near the Astronomical Clock, their breaths ragged but their determination unwavering.

"They know we're here," Hana said, her voice steady despite the adrenaline coursing through her. "We'll have to move fast."

Marcus nodded, his expression resolute. "Prague isn't merely a backdrop for Baumann. It's a battleground. And we're not leaving until we've won this war."

CHAPTER
THIRTY-FOUR

The air beneath the conservatory was damp and heavy, carrying with it the scent of mildew and decay. Marcus and Hana descended a narrow stone staircase, their flashlights cutting through the oppressive darkness. The flickering beams illuminated walls adorned with faded frescoes depicting celestial symbols and intricate musical notations, the colors long since dulled by time. The oppressive atmosphere pressed against them, making each step feel heavier than the last.

"This place feels alive," Hana murmured, her voice low but filled with awe. She ran her fingers lightly over the frescoes, tracing the faded outlines of a lyre surrounded by a halo of light.

"It's a repository of knowledge," Marcus replied, his voice hushed. "Whoever built this vault wanted to preserve something… or keep it hidden."

The staircase spiraled downward, the stone steps uneven and slick with moisture. Their footsteps echoed faintly, a haunting counterpoint to the steady drip of water somewhere in the distance. At the bottom, they reached a massive wooden door reinforced with iron bands, its surface etched with elaborate Latin inscriptions. Marcus held his flashlight steady as he leaned in to read.

"'Only those who carry the harmony within may pass,'" he translated, his tone grave. "A warning… or perhaps a test."

Hana's expression hardened. "Let's hope it's not both."

Marcus's attention shifted to the door's mechanism, an ornate puzzle lock embedded with musical symbols. Each lever and dial appeared designed to replicate the notes of a melody, though the sequence wasn't immediately clear.

"It's a melody," Marcus realized, his fingers tracing the intricate patterns. "The sequence matches the notations we recovered from the fragments."

"Can you solve it?"

Marcus nodded, though his brow furrowed in concentration. Humming the notes softly, he worked through the intervals, adjusting the levers in rhythm with his memory of the fragments. The mechanism clicked faintly, the sound almost swallowed by the stillness of the chamber. Finally, with a deep groan, the door creaked open, revealing a vast subterranean chamber.

The air inside was colder, carrying a metallic tang that Marcus couldn't quite place. They turned on their flashlights and found shelves lined all the walls, laden with crumbling scrolls and bound volumes coated in a thin layer of dust, broken up by only a dark side passageway that opened to one side. In the center of the room stood a stone pedestal, and atop it rested a manuscript bound in cracked leather, its surface emblazoned with arcane symbols that seemed to shimmer faintly in the flashlight beams.

THE DEVIL'S SYMPHONY

"This is it," Marcus whispered, his voice reverent as he approached the pedestal, setting his satchel on the ground. Though brittle with age, the manuscript's pages were filled with elegant notations and cryptic annotations. Marcus's fingers trembled slightly as he turned the first page, the ink appearing as vivid as the day it was written.

Hana joined him, her eyes scanning the pages. "It's incomplete," she observed, her tone revealing frustration. "Entire sections are missing."

"But it's a start," Marcus replied. "If we can decode this, we might find the counter-melody we've been searching for."

Their brief moment of triumph was interrupted by the faint sound of footsteps echoing down the staircase. Marcus froze, his senses sharpening. He closed the manuscript and slipped it into an inside pocket of his jacket, then picked up his satchel.

"We're not alone," he said tersely.

Adrian Baumann's voice preceded him, smooth and confident, as he descended the staircase flanked by armed cultists. "I must commend you," he said, his tone almost mocking. "Finding this place... that was no small feat. But surely you didn't think you could keep its secrets from me."

Marcus and Hana stood their ground, the pedestal between them and Baumann's group.

Marcus's hand clutched at his satchel, his body tense but his mind calculating.

"We're not giving you anything," he said evenly. "Whatever you're planning, it ends here."

Baumann chuckled, stepping closer. "You misunderstand me, Marcus. This isn't about taking; it's about sharing. Imagine the world we could create with this knowledge. No more chaos, no more uncertainty... only harmony."

"Harmony at the cost of free will," Hana snapped. "You're not a savior, Baumann. You're a tyrant."

Baumann's smile faltered, his eyes narrowing. "And you're a journalist playing at heroism. But tell me, Ms. Sinclair, have you considered the alternative? Chaos. Division. War. The symphony can bring order to a fractured world. Why resist destiny?"

"Because it's not destiny," Marcus said, his voice cold. "It's a perversion of everything music is supposed to represent."

A quiet intensity settled over Baumann, dark and unyielding, and he gestured to his cultists. "Enough of this. Hand over the manuscript, or we'll take it by force."

Marcus raised his hands in mock surrender, his mind racing. "Fine. You win," he said, reaching into his satchel. "But before I give you this, answer me one question."

Baumann hesitated, curiosity flickering in his eyes. "And what question is that?"

"Why Prague?" he asked. "Why did Malvagio choose this city as the stage for his final work?"

Baumann's lips curved into a sly smile. "Because Prague is more than a city. It's a resonance point, a place where the barriers between worlds grow thin. Today, they may be called vortex sites, but Malvagio recognized this. And so do I."

The revelation struck Marcus like a lightning bolt, but he kept his expression neutral. With a sudden motion, he hurled the empty satchel toward Baumann. The cult leader caught it instinctively, his attention momentarily diverted.

"*Run!*" Marcus shouted, grabbing Hana's hand. They sprinted toward the side passage he had noticed earlier, the sound of Baumann's enraged orders echoing behind them.

THE PASSAGE WAS narrow and uneven, its walls slick with moisture and streaked with years of grime. Marcus and Hana stumbled through the darkness, their flashlights casting erratic beams that barely illuminated the path ahead. The air was heavy with dampness, and the sound of their labored breaths echoed off the stone walls.

Behind them, the cultists' pursuit was relentless. The sound of heavy boots striking the ground reverberated like a sinister drumbeat. Hana glanced over her shoulder, her heart pounding as she caught glimpses of shadows closing in.

"They're gaining on us," she gasped, her voice strained with necessity.

"Keep moving," Marcus urged, his tone steady. He had no idea if there was an exit ahead; he just knew they had to keep moving.

The passage widened abruptly into a small chamber, where a rusted iron grate blocked their path. Marcus knelt, his hands fumbling with the mechanism as the cultists' shouts grew louder. "It's stuck," he muttered, frustration creeping into his voice.

"Let me help," Hana said, dropping to her knees beside him. Together, they forced the grate open, the screech of metal on metal sending a jolt through their nerves.

"Go!" Marcus commanded, shoving Hana through the opening before scrambling after her.

They emerged into a narrow alley behind the conservatory, the cool night air hitting them like a wave. The sounds of Prague's bustling nightlife were a stark contrast to the chaos they had just escaped. Marcus pulled Hana into the shadows, their breaths ragged as they listened for any sign of pursuit.

Baumann's voice echoed faintly from the passage. "You can run, Marcus, but you can't hide. The symphony is inevitable."

Hana's jaw tightened, her resolve hardening. "He won't stop," she said. "But neither will we."

Marcus nodded, his expression grim but determined. "We have the manuscript," he said, tapping his jacket pocket. "And now we may have the key to stopping him."

CHAPTER
THIRTY-FIVE

Hana sat at the desk in the Prague safe house Marcus had arranged, the partial manuscript spread before her under the glow of a single lamp.

Rain beat a frantic staccato against the windowpane, the narrow street below slick and glistening under the orange haze of gas lamps. The safe house was nestled in Prague's Old Town, its ancient stone facade blending seamlessly with the surrounding buildings that leaned in like conspirators. Despite the late hour, faint echoes of laughter and music spilled from a nearby tavern, mixing with the sound of footsteps on cobblestones as night wanderers navigated the labyrinthine alleys. The juxtaposition of vitality outside and tension within only heightened Hana's sense of urgency. She glanced at the half-drawn curtain, feeling watched despite knowing that Marcus had secured the location. Even here, safe houses had been compromised before.

Her gaze returned to the manuscripts on the table. Each

brittle piece felt alive beneath her fingers, vibrating with potential as she carefully arranged them in an attempt to fill in the blanks of the symphony. The hurried scrawl of annotations blurred into a dizzying array of symbols and notes that hinted at Malvagio's dark brilliance.

Marcus entered the room quietly, carrying steaming cups that filled the air with a mix of coffee and hope. He handed one to Michael, placed one beside Hana, and stood over her shoulder, peering at their puzzle with a furrowed brow.

Hana's fingers moved delicately over the parchment, tracing the looping script and intricate musical notations. "This script... it's in Latin," she murmured, more to herself than to the others. "But there are symbols here I've only seen referenced in the margins of alchemical texts. It seems Malvagio was creating a blueprint."

Marcus leaned over her shoulder, his face illuminated by the warm glow of the lamp as he scanned the pages. "A blueprint for what?" he asked, his voice low but insistent.

Hana tapped a particular set of notations. "This sequence here... it matches references to the Prague Codex. Have you heard of it?"

Marcus straightened, his expression darkening. "The Prague Codex is supposed to be a myth," he said, his tone cautious. "A text from the late sixteenth century, rumored to contain instructions for rituals and compositions capable of manipulating the human soul. Historians dismissed it as legend because no one's ever found it."

"Well, it appears Malvagio believed in it," Hana replied, her fingers brushing over the notes as though to extract their secrets. "These annotations reference harmonic structures that only make sense if you're trying to amplify something...

something beyond music. If the Prague Codex is real, it's the missing piece to activating the Black Hymnal's full power. Those two, combined, became the structure on which Malvagio composed his Devil's Symphony."

Michael, seated quietly in the corner, finally spoke. His voice was calm, but the depth of his concern was clear. "And Baumann would know this as well," he said. "If he's aware of the codex, he'll be hunting for it."

Hana nodded grimly, her mind already racing ahead. "Which means we have to find it first."

She turned back to the manuscript, her trained eyes taking in the intricate symbols and annotations. The words began to blur together as she pieced fragments of meaning from the encoded text. "These notes are instructions for playing the melody," she said, her voice flushed with disbelief. "But they're also coordinates… locations tied to key resonances. The Prague Codex must contain a map of these places."

Marcus's breath hitched, and he crouched beside her. "A map?" he repeated, his voice hushed. "Malvagio was planning something global. If these resonances align, the melody could—"

Hana's voice interrupted his thought. "…affect entire populations. This is a weapon… a framework for total manipulation. But it's incomplete," she added, her frustration evident as she gestured to the missing sections. "We can't decipher the full picture without the rest of the codex."

Michael stood, crossing the room to join them. His presence was steady, grounding in the storm of uncertainty. "Perhaps that's a blessing," he said. "If the codex holds such power, even seeking it could be dangerous. Knowledge of this magnitude has a way of corrupting those who pursue it."

"And yet Baumann's already looking for it," Marcus countered. "If we sit back and do nothing, he'll find it first. You've seen what he's capable of. We can't let that happen."

Hana looked up at the two men, her expression resolute. "This is bigger than just stopping Baumann anymore. If the codex is real, we need to understand it. Not to use it, but to ensure it can never be used again by anyone like Malvagio or Baumann."

Michael's gaze lingered on her, his eyes filled with a quiet sadness. "There's a fine line, Hana," he said softly, "between understanding and obsession. Promise me you won't cross it."

"I promise," she replied, though the words felt heavier than she expected.

As the room fell into a tense silence, the lamp flickered briefly, its light casting eerie patterns over the manuscript. Michael placed a comforting hand on Hana's shoulder.

THE FOLLOWING MORNING, the team gathered around Marcus's laptop, its display illuminating their tired faces. On the screen was an article from an obscure academic journal, the title reading: *"The Prague Codex: Myth or Misplaced Masterpiece?"* The author was Dr. Emil Károly, a reclusive Hungarian historian renowned for his eccentric theories and vast private collection of rare texts.

Marcus scrolled through the article as Hana and Michael read over his shoulder. The writing was dense, full of technical jargon and references to forgotten symbology. But buried within the labyrinth of words was a crucial clue.

"Károly claims to have studied the Prague Codex," Marcus said, his tone laced with skepticism. "But he's notorious for his paranoia. According to this, he's turned away everyone from academics to journalists. If he has the Codex, getting access won't be easy."

Hana leaned closer to the screen, her eyes narrowing as she scanned the text. "He mentions Prague's alchemical traditions in connection to the codex. That's a good sign. But... Budapest?"

Michael crossed his arms. "He must have taken the codex there for safekeeping. If Károly's as paranoid as his reputation suggests, he wouldn't trust it to a public institution."

"And if we know this," Hana added, her voice dropping, "so does Baumann. He'll be watching."

Marcus clicked to another page in the journal, an image of Károly's sprawling estate filling the screen. It was a fortress-like mansion on the outskirts of Budapest, surrounded by dense forests and a high stone wall.

"Even if we get to Károly," Marcus muttered, "there's no guarantee he'll let us in. And if Baumann's people are already there, it could turn into a trap."

Hana's jaw tightened. "Then we go prepared. If Károly truly has the codex, we need to secure it before Baumann makes his move."

Michael's expression remained stoic, but a shadow passed over his face. "This isn't just a matter of planning. Károly's been a recluse for decades. Convincing him to trust us will require more than a good story."

Hana nodded. "We need to appeal to his academic side. Show him we're not just after the codex for personal gain."

Marcus leaned back, rubbing his temples. "Fine. But we go together. No one splits off, and we assume Baumann's already got eyes on the estate."

Michael's gaze lingered on Marcus, his tone firm. "If we're going to do this, we can't let our desperation blind us. The Prague Codex is dangerous. More dangerous than any of us can truly comprehend. We need to be ready for whatever we find."

As the team gathered their equipment and maps, the tension in the room was tangible. Budapest loomed ahead, a city of hidden dangers and unanswered questions. But if the Prague Codex was the key to unraveling the Black Hymnal's mysteries, they had no choice but to find it first.

CHAPTER
THIRTY-SIX

The imposing silhouette of Dr. Emil Károly's mansion loomed against the night sky, its high stone walls and wrought iron gates casting jagged shadows on the cobblestone driveway. Nestled in the outskirts of Budapest, the estate exuded an aura of impenetrability, its exterior as much a fortress as a home. Floodlights illuminated the perimeter, and the periodic distant hum of surveillance drones hinted at the advanced security measures in place.

Hana adjusted her tailored jacket, a polished yet professional look befitting her guise as a visiting academic. Marcus stood beside her, clutching a leather-bound folder stuffed with forged documents. Father Michael, dressed in his simple black priest's cassock, completed their ensemble, lending an air of gravity to their otherwise fabricated credentials.

"Remember the plan," Marcus whispered as they approached the gate. "We're researchers from the Pontifical Academy of Sciences, interested in Károly's work on historical manuscripts. Keep it casual, don't oversell."

Hana smiled smugly. "Relax, Marcus. I've conned tougher crowds than this."

A guard emerged from the security booth, his steely gaze sweeping over the trio. "Name and purpose of visit?" he barked in English, his Hungarian accent brisk and clipped.

Hana stepped forward, her practiced smile disarming. "Dr. Hana Sinclair, accompanied by Dr. Marcus Russo and Father Michael Dominic. We're here to discuss rare manuscripts with Dr. Károly. He should be expecting us."

The guard's eyes narrowed as he scrutinized the invitation Hana produced, a carefully forged document embossed with the insignia of the Vatican. After an agonizing pause, he nodded and gestured to another guard inside the gatehouse.

"Wait here," he said curtly before disappearing into the booth to confirm their credentials.

Michael murmured a quiet prayer. Marcus shifted uneasily, his eyes scanning the grounds for potential exits. The tension was palpable, every second stretching unbearably long. Finally, the gate creaked open, and the guard returned with a curt nod.

"Dr. Károly will see you," he said. "Follow the path to the main entrance. Someone will escort you from there."

The trio exchanged brief, relieved glances before proceeding up the gravel path. As they approached the mansion's grand doors, Marcus couldn't shake the suspicion that they were walking straight into a trap.

· · ·

THE DEVIL'S SYMPHONY

THE MANSION'S interior was as grand as its exterior, with vaulted ceilings, ornate chandeliers, and an air of Old World opulence. A butler led them through a labyrinth of hallways, each lined with paintings of stern-faced ancestors and shelves brimming with antique books. Their footsteps echoed ominously in the vast, empty space.

"Dr. Károly is in the study," the butler announced as they reached a heavy oak door. He opened it with a flourish, revealing a room that was equal parts library and laboratory. At the center of the chaos stood Emil Károly himself, a wiry man with graying hair and piercing eyes that seemed to see straight through them.

"Ah, Vatican emissaries," Károly said, his voice curiously dripping with sarcasm. "What an unexpected honor. What brings you to my humble home?"

Hana stepped forward, her tone warm and respectful. "Dr. Károly, we've long admired your work on European manuscripts. We were hoping to discuss some of your findings, particularly those related to alchemical texts."

Károly's gaze flicked between them, his lips curling into a faint smirk. "Alchemical texts, you say? And would these interests happen to include the Prague Codex?"

Marcus tensed, his brain humming with adrenaline. "The codex is one of many subjects we're researching," he said cautiously. "Its historical significance cannot be overstated."

Károly chuckled, the sound brittle and mocking. "You're not very good liars, are you? Save your pleasantries. I know why you're here."

Before they could respond, Károly snapped his fingers, and an armed guard stepped into the room, his weapon trained on the team. "Adrian warned me you might come," he said, his smirk widening. "He's very persuasive, you know. Promised me protection in exchange for my... cooperation."

Hana's heart pounded, but her expression remained calm. "You don't have to do this," she said evenly. "Baumann's goals aren't about preservation or knowledge. He'll destroy everything in his path, including you."

Károly's eyes narrowed, but he hesitated, a flicker of doubt crossing his face. Michael seized the moment, stepping forward with a deliberate priestly calm. "Let us see the codex," he said. "At least then we'll know if we're wrong about what it contains. Then we'll leave and you lose nothing. But if we're right, we can explain what is at stake, giving you options that Baumann couldn't or wouldn't offer."

For a long moment, the room was silent, the tension so thick it felt like a physical weight. Finally, Károly gestured toward a section of the wall lined with bookshelves. "The codex is there," he said curtly. "But if you make one wrong move, my guards won't hesitate."

Hana and Marcus exchanged a glance before approaching the wall as Michael remained near Károly.

Hana's eyes scanned the bookshelf. At its center rested the Prague Codex, its dark leather binding etched with golden symbols that shimmered faintly in the dim light. Next to it was a box, clearly a preservation box used by the venerable Charles University in Prague. Marcus had also noticed it and intentionally nudged the box as he reached for the codex. As they both suspected, it was empty and the perfect size for the codex next to it. Obviously, this priceless historical document had been taken from Charles University.

Marcus glanced at nearby books, recognizing other volumes that had been reported as lost or stolen by other institutions. He realized this reclusive collector had been quietly buying manuscripts and books on the black market, stolen from the authentic owners, for decades.

"We've got it," Marcus whispered, his hands steady as he lifted the Prague Codex. The air around them seemed to grow heavier, the presence of the artifact's significance palpable.

Before Marcus could slip the codex into his bag, the guard stepped closer, his weapon unwavering. "I wouldn't do that," he warned. "You're leaving empty-handed."

Hana's fingers tensed around the taser concealed in her jacket. She took a slow, measured breath, shifting slightly to draw the guard's focus. "You don't have to work for them," she said, her voice smooth but laced with steel. "You know what Baumann is. What he's capable of."

The guard didn't waver more than half a second, but that was enough. In a flash, Hana lunged forward, whipping the taser from her jacket and jamming it against his ribs. A sharp crack filled the air as a high-voltage jolt surged through his body. His eyes widened in shock, his grip faltering as the electrical charge locked his muscles. He stumbled back, his weapon clattering to the floor.

Károly's expression turned to rage, and he reached for something at his waist, but Michael grabbed his arm, stopping him, as Marcus rushed toward them. With a burst of speed, Marcus pivoted and drove his fist straight into Károly's jaw. The impact sent the Hungarian reeling, slamming into the bookshelf behind him. Books toppled around him as he slumped to the floor, dazed.

Hana kicked the fallen guard's weapon away and turned to Marcus. "We need to move—now!"

Marcus, already securing the codex in his bag, nodded. They sprinted for the door, leaping over Károly's prone form. Footsteps echoed from the hallway—more guards coming.

"Back exit," Hana hissed, grabbing Marcus's sleeve.

The trio bolted from the study, the Codex secured in Marcus's satchel. They navigated the mansion's labyrinthine halls, their footsteps muffled by the thick carpets.

As they reached the main hall, Károly's voice rang out behind them. "You can't escape! Adrian will find you no matter where you run!"

Hana glanced back, her eyes blazing with defiance. "Let him try," she muttered.

They burst through the front doors into the cool night air, their breaths forming clouds in the chill. The gates loomed ahead, groaning as Michael opened them, and the trio slipped through just as guards emerged onto the driveway.

Outside, their black SUV roared to life. Marcus, behind the wheel, floored the accelerator, and the tires screeched as they sped away from the mansion. Hana and Michael sat in tense silence, their gazes fixed on the rearview mirror as the mansion receded into the distance.

"That was too close," Marcus muttered, his knuckles white on the steering wheel.

Hana exhaled slowly. "But we have it. And now, Baumann's one step behind."

CHAPTER
THIRTY-SEVEN

Having made their way back to Rome, they found the Vatican Library was silent, its vaulted ceilings and endless rows of ancient books casting a sacred stillness over the room. Marcus and Hana sat at a long oaken table, the Prague Codex spread open before them. A soft golden light from an ornate desk lamp illuminated the text, while the faint aroma of aged parchment filled the air. The room's silence was dissolved only by the whispered rustle of pages as Hana turned them, her movements careful and deliberate.

"This codex is unlike anything I've ever seen," she murmured, her voice tinged with awe.

The manuscript's pages were densely packed with cryptic symbols, musical staves, and annotations written in a mixture of Latin and an unrecognizable cipher. Each page carried its own weight, the ink's precision belying the centuries that had passed since it was written. Much of it echoed what they had found in Malvagio's partial manuscript under the conservatory, proving that the man had used the Prague Codex in his compositions. Using the codex now might help them complete what Malvagio had started.

"It's more than just a guide," Marcus replied, his voice heavy with awe. "It's a masterwork of layered knowledge. It embedded philosophy, alchemy, and theology into every note. No wonder Malvagio sought it as well as the Black Hymnal. Between the two of them, he would have their combined power to embed within his *Devil's Symphony*, which was the pinnacle of his obsession."

Hana nodded, her fingers tracing a line of text. "This passage here… it's describing the 'melodic resonance' required to unlock the composition's full potential. It mentions specific frequencies tied to…" She paused, her brow furrowing as she leaned in closer to the script. "An object. A 'conductor'."

"A conductor?" Marcus echoed, leaning closer.

"Not in the musical sense," Hana clarified. "This is referring to an artifact. Something capable of amplifying the melody's reach." She quickly pulled up a file on her laptop. "Here. Malvagio called it his 'baton.' Before, I thought it was just a prop. Now I realize it was an essential element, something he learned about in the codex."

Marcus's eyes widened, his pulse quickening. "His baton? As in a physical object?"

"Exactly," Hana said, her voice tinged with excitement. She flipped to another page, her finger pointing to a detailed sketch. It depicted a slender rod adorned with intricate carvings and an orb at its tip, radiating lines that resembled musical waves. "According to this, it was forged in Malvagio's time, using methods tied to both alchemical and spiritual practices. I would assume it was forged by Malvagio himself after his discovery of the Prague Codex."

Marcus leaned back, his mind on overdrive, analyzing every angle. "If Baumann gets his hands on that…"

"He won't," Hana said firmly, her gaze locking with his. "Because we're going to find it first."

She flipped back to another page, scanning quickly before her expression darkened. "That baton was a symbol of control. Malvagio's followers revered it as a sacred artifact. He may have hidden it to prevent its misuse."

Marcus exhaled, his shoulders heavy with tension. "That means it's not just dangerous. It's something people would kill to possess. We need more than a plan; we must be ready for whatever Baumann throws at us."

The Prague Codex's revelations were staggering, and as the hours passed, Marcus and Hana pieced together fragments of its secrets. The baton, as described in the text, was a keystone to the music's power, capable of focusing the melody's resonance and projecting its effects over vast distances.

Michael entered the room, his presence grounding. He had been in prayer, seeking guidance, but the concern etched on his face revealed that the spiritual toll of their mission was mounting.

"What have you learned?" he asked, his voice steady.

Hana pushed the codex toward him, pointing to the sketch of the baton. "This is what Baumann's after. The baton is the missing piece. If he gets it, he can control and unleash the melody's full power."

Michael studied the sketch, his lips tightening. "Where is it now?"

"Malvagio's diary doesn't say explicitly," Marcus admitted. "But it gives clues..." He leaned forward, his hands steepled. "The codex mentions a monastery in central France. It aligns with what we know of Malvagio's movements in his later years. I'm guessing that his followers might have kept it there. That might be our starting point. If the baton is anywhere, it's likely there."

"And what about Baumann?" Michael asked. "He's not going to sit idly by while we search."

"That's why we need to move now," Marcus said, his voice firm. "The codex has given us a lead. We can't waste it."

Cardinal Severino's office starkly contrasted with the dim confines of the library. Sunlight streamed through tall windows, casting golden patterns on the marble floor. The cardinal sat behind a massive oak desk, his hands steepled as he listened to Marcus and Hana's findings.

"A conductor's baton forged in Malvagio's time," Severino said, his voice measured. "And you believe it still exists?"

"The Prague Codex points to a French monastery once associated with Malvagio's followers," Marcus replied. "We think it's hidden there. If we find it, we can stop Baumann from conducting the music that could cause dire consequences."

Severino leaned back, his expression grave. "You realize the risks involved in this mission? Not just to yourselves, but to the Church. If word of this leaks—"

"We understand," Hana interrupted, her tone firm. "But the alternative is worse. If Baumann gets to the baton first, everything we've fought to prevent will come to pass."

The cardinal's gaze lingered on her for a moment before shifting to Michael. "And you, Father Dominic? Do you support this course of action?"

Michael's voice was calm but resolute. "I do. If there's even a chance to stop Adrian Baumann, we have to take it. But we must proceed with caution. This baton is too great a temptation... for anyone who wields it."

Severino's lips pressed into a thin line, but he nodded. "All right. You have my authorization. But understand this: failure is not an option. If you don't retrieve the baton, Baumann very well might. And if that happens, the consequences will be most distressing."

Hana stood, her resolve unshaken. "We won't fail, Your Eminence."

Marcus followed suit, the accountability of the mission settling on his shoulders. As they left the office, the enormity of their task loomed larger than ever. Somewhere, Baumann was closing in, and the race to secure the baton had begun.

CHAPTER
THIRTY-EIGHT

The rolling hills of rural France stretched endlessly before them as Marcus, Hana, and Michael made their way toward a small, unassuming chapel nestled in a quiet valley. The stone structure, covered in creeping ivy, looked as though it had been forgotten by time. According to Malvagio's diary, this chapel was likely the final hiding place of his baton, secreted away during the chaos of the French Revolution in 1792.

Stepping out of their Range Rover, Marcus adjusted his coat, feeling the shadows of history pressing down upon him. "This place doesn't look like much," he murmured, glancing at Hana and Michael.

"The best hiding places never do," Hana replied, taking in the worn stone walls and the ancient wooden doors. "If we're right, though, this is where we'll find the baton."

Michael nodded solemnly. "We must be cautious. If Baumann's followers have intercepted any of our movements, they'll also be looking for this place."

Pushing the heavy doors open, the trio entered the

chapel cloaked in flickering half-light. Dust motes floated in the shafts of light coming through stained-glass windows, casting muted colors across the stone floor. The scent of old parchment and incense still lingered in the air, a remnant of centuries of worship.

Marcus ran his fingers over the wooden pews, his stare locked on the altar ahead. "The baton was hidden in 1792. If it's still here, it's not going to be out in the open."

Hana pulled out her notes. "The last recorded mention said it was entrusted to a priest who served here. He was determined to keep it safe from looters during the Revolution."

Michael stepped forward, his eyes on the altar. "Then we should start with what remains of his legacy."

The chapel was small but full of history. Faded paintings of saints lined the walls, their colors muted by time. An old, rusted candelabrum stood beside the altar, its wax-covered base hinting at the long-forgotten prayers offered here. Marcus's eyes swept the room, searching for anything that stood out.

"Look at the carvings on the altar," Hana whispered, running her fingers over the smooth, weathered stone. "These symbols... they match those in the Prague Codex."

Michael nodded, tracing the engravings with reverence. "It's a message... perhaps even a guide to the baton's true resting place."

Marcus approached the stained-glass windows, studying the vibrant images depicting saints, angels, and biblical stories. The craftsmanship was stunning, but something about them seemed off.

"These windows don't match the era of the chapel," he said, running his fingers along the lead framework. "They were installed later... maybe as a way to conceal something."

Michael took a deep breath, stepping up to the first panel, which depicted a robed figure holding a staff. "That's not just any staff," he murmured. "It has the same markings described in the codex."

Marcus's fingers traced the edges of the glass, looking for any imperfections. Then, with an audible click, his thumb pressed into a barely noticeable indentation. A hidden mechanism activated, and the section of the window shifted slightly, revealing an inscription in Latin carved into the stone frame.

"'Beneath the altar, where the righteous pray, the relic rests beyond the light of day,'" Marcus translated.

Hana grinned. "A crypt. It has to be beneath the altar."

Michael exhaled deeply. "Then we must move quickly. We don't know how much time we have before we're discovered."

The trio moved toward the altar, pushing aside the heavy wooden lectern to reveal an aged stone slab. Faint markings lined its edges, similar to those in the codex. Marcus pulled out a small crowbar from his bag and wedged it into the seam. With a grunt of effort, he pried the slab open, revealing a dark staircase leading below.

The air that wafted up was thick with dust and the scent of damp earth. "This is it," Marcus whispered. "The baton has got to be down there."

Carefully, they descended into the crypt. The air grew colder as they moved deeper, their footsteps echoing in the confined space. The walls were lined with ancient coffins, their inscriptions barely legible. At the far end of the crypt, an ornately carved pedestal stood, and resting upon it, gleaming faintly in the dim torchlight, was the baton.

Before Marcus could step forward, a loud crash echoed from above. Shouts followed, and heavy footsteps descended the chapel steps.

"Baumann's men!" Michael hissed. "We've been followed."

Marcus grabbed the baton and secured it in his satchel. "We need to get out of here. Now."

Hana drew a pistol from her bag as shadows appeared at the crypt's entrance. The first cultist lunged forward, swinging a blade. Marcus ducked, countering with a forceful blow that sent the man sprawling. Michael, using an old iron crucifix from the wall, deflected another attacker's strike.

Hana fired a warning shot, which reverberated through the crypt. The remaining cultists hesitated, but Baumann's voice rang out from above.

"Take them down! The baton belongs to us!"

Marcus turned to Hana. "Cover me!" Without waiting for a response, he sprinted toward the crypt's side passage, searching for another exit.

A cultist lunged at him, but Marcus dodged, slamming the attacker against the wall. Pain shot through his side as another landed a punch, but he retaliated swiftly, driving an elbow into the man's ribs.

Hana and Michael held their ground, fending off the cultists as best they could. Michael struck one across the temple with the iron cross while Hana disarmed another with a swift kick.

Marcus found what he was looking for—a crumbling section of the crypt wall. He grabbed a nearby candelabrum and drove its base against the weak stone. The wall gave way, revealing an old tunnel.

"This way!" he called, clutching the baton tightly.

Hana and Michael fought their way toward him, narrowly dodging another attack. As they squeezed through the opening, Marcus pulled a support beam loose, causing the entrance to collapse behind them.

Gasping for breath, they hurried down the tunnel. "That won't hold them for long," Hana warned.

Marcus gritted his teeth. "Then we keep moving."

As they emerged into the moonlit ruins behind the chapel, Marcus glanced down at the baton in his hands. They had won this battle, but the war was far from over. Baumann wouldn't stop until he had what he wanted.

And Marcus knew the real fight had only just begun.

CHAPTER
THIRTY-NINE

The Vatican Library had been transformed into a war room, its quiet sanctity replaced by the hum of urgent activity. Marcus, Hana, and Michael gathered around the long oak table where the Prague Codex and the newly recovered baton rested, their presence an almost magnetic force in the room. Maps, notes, and ancient texts were spread across the table, their edges weighted down by artifacts and paperweights. The heft of what they were attempting to do—neutralize the Black Hymnal's power—pressed down on them like a physical burden.

"This baton isn't just an amplifier," Marcus began, gesturing to the intricately carved rod. "It's the keystone. Without it, the hymn's power is erratic. But if the codex is correct, even using it to neutralize the hymn's effects carries enormous risks."

Hana leaned over the codex, her fingers skimming its brittle pages. As she spoke, the faint, papery scent of aged parchment drifted through the air, like a whisper from the past. "The text suggests the effects of the hymn can't simply be destroyed. It has to be countered, its resonance neutralized by completing the melody with an opposing harmonic structure. Which makes sense—that is basically what we did to neutralize the symphony when we played the final chords simultaneously with the noise-cancelling notes. Only"—she paused, looking at the others with a frown—"we had residual effects. We didn't understand the full extent of what we'd needed to do." She pursed her lips, her brow furrowing. "According to this, to do it properly, we need to reconstruct the symphony in its entirety. Basically, a whole new symphony."

Michael's voice was calm but laced with apprehension. "You're talking about writing a symphony and hoping our new melody is exactly right? Do you understand what that might unleash if it isn't 'just right'?"

Marcus nodded grimly. "That's why we have to control every aspect of this. The codex provides the framework, and the baton ensures the melody remains stable. But even then, it's a gamble."

Hana's gaze met his. "It's a gamble we have to take. Baumann isn't going to stop, and every moment we delay gives him more time to act."

Michael sighed. "Then we move forward. But we do so with caution and prayer."

The group continued their preparations late into the night. Hana cross-referenced the Prague Codex with historical accounts, piecing together the intricate notations that outlined the melody's opposing harmonic counterpoint. Marcus pored over diagrams detailing the baton's purpose, its symbols glowing faintly under the library's warm light.

"This melody isn't just a counterpoint," Hana said,

breaking the silence. "It's a safeguard. Malvagio must have realized the hymn's potential for destruction and built this into its framework as a failsafe. But activating it requires everything to be perfectly aligned... and the baton is the linchpin."

Michael observed them quietly, his thoughts heavy. Finally, he spoke. "If we are to do this, we must also prepare for failure. We need contingencies."

"Agreed," Marcus said, though his tone betrayed his uncertainty. "But right now, our best contingency is making sure we succeed."

As THE NIGHT DEEPENED, Marcus and Hana pored over the codex, its densely packed pages revealing layer after layer of hidden knowledge. The intricate notations and cryptic commentary seemed to come alive under the warm light of the desk lamp.

"This section here," said Marcus, pointing to a passage written in a blend of Latin and ciphered symbols, "mentions a 'sanctified ground' where the melody must reach its crescendo. The phrasing is vague, but it's tied to Malvagio's final days."

Hana frowned, tapping her pen against the edge of the table. "Malvagio fled to Switzerland after his excommunication. He had followers there, a group of alchemists and mystics who protected his work. If the baton and the codex were designed to work together, it makes sense that the final piece of the puzzle is tied to that region."

Marcus flipped through a stack of maps, his fingers settling on one that outlined the Swiss Alps. "There's a reference here to a place called the *'Sanctum Sonata.'* It's described as a natural amphitheater... something about the acoustics aligning with the melody's frequencies."

"An amphitheater carved by nature," Hana murmured, her nerves buzzing with restless energy. "If the melody requires specific resonances to manifest its power, that kind of location would amplify its effects exponentially."

"And Baumann must know this," Marcus said, his voice heavy with certainty. "He's been a step ahead of us before. We have to assume he's already heading there."

Hana leaned back, her pen tapping faster. "Then we need to beat him to it. The codex gives us the knowledge, but the baton is what will give us control. If we can compose a counterpoint symphony before Baumann completes his ritual of playing *The Devil's Symphony*, we might have a chance."

Marcus's expression was grim as he stared at the map. "A chance is all we need. The trouble is... he has the music box, the only instrument capable of playing either one."

As preparations continued, Michael retreated to the small chapel adjacent to the library. The flickering light of a single candle illuminated his face as he knelt in prayer, the shadows dancing across the stone walls. The enormity of what they were attempting weighed heavily on him, and for the first time in years, he felt truly uncertain.

The sound of footsteps drew his attention, and he turned to see Marcus entering the chapel. The archaeologist's usual confidence was tempered by the somberness of the moment.

"I thought I'd find you here," Marcus said, his voice quiet. "You've been distant since we recovered the baton."

Michael rose slowly, his gaze fixed on the flickering flame. "I've been reflecting. Praying. What we're about to do... it's unprecedented. The risks are incalculable."

Marcus nodded, stepping closer. "I understand your hesitation. But if we don't act, Baumann will complete Malvagio's symphony using the Black Hymnal. The consequences of that—"

"I know," Michael interrupted, his tone sharper than he intended. He took a deep breath, softening his voice. "But I also know the Church's history. There have been moments when good intentions led to disaster. Playing this new symphony we come up with, even with the noble intention of avoiding the incantations of evil from Baumann's version… we could be opening a door we can never close."

Marcus placed a reassuring hand on Michael's shoulder. "You once told me that faith is about taking the leap even when you can't see the ground. That's what we're doing. We have to trust that we can control this."

Michael met his gaze, the doubt in his eyes slowly giving way to determination. "Then we must be vigilant. Every step forward must be measured. If there's even the slightest sign that we're losing control… we stop. Agreed?"

"Agreed," Marcus said firmly.

The two men stood in silence for a moment, the substance of their mission settling over them. As they left the chapel, Michael glanced back at the flickering candle, its light a fragile but enduring symbol of hope in the face of darkness.

In his heart, Michael carried a quiet prayer: that their faith would be enough to overcome the shadows they faced, and that the melody they sought to neutralize would not consume them all.

CHAPTER
FORTY

The team's vehicle wound its way up the narrow mountain road, its tires crunching over frost-laden gravel. The Swiss Alps loomed around them, their jagged peaks shrouded in a dense, swirling fog that clung to the landscape like a ghostly veil. The scent of damp earth and pine suffused the air, mingling with the distant echoes of unseen creatures stirring in the shadows of the towering peaks.

As they neared their destination, the skeletal ruins of an ancient abbey emerged through the mist, its crumbling stone walls barely visible in the pale moonlight. Ivy had overtaken much of the exterior, weaving through the shattered masonry like nature's attempt to reclaim what time had abandoned. The gaping maw of the abbey's entrance stood before them, dark and foreboding, as though it hungered for intruders.

Hana adjusted the strap of her satchel, glancing toward Marcus, whose eyes were fixed on the ruins ahead. "This is it," she murmured. "The *Sanctum Sonata*."

Michael's voice was scarcely more than a whisper. "This place has seen centuries of darkness. I can feel it."

The three of them set their earpieces in place as they scanned the desolate structure. Marcus exhaled. "Malvagio's last refuge. And, if Baumann has his way, the birthplace of something much worse."

The abbey had long been abandoned, its history whispered in hushed tones by the locals. Legends spoke of its halls being used for clandestine rituals, its ruins echoing with melodies no human should have played. The thick fog swirled at their feet as they crossed the threshold, the scent of damp stone and decay pressing in around them.

Inside, the air was eerily still. Flickering candlelight lined the crumbling archways, casting shifting shadows along the walls. The remains of old wooden pews were scattered, their surfaces splintered and rotting. Dust particles danced in the limited light, disturbed by the team's cautious movements. Every step echoed, each sound swallowed by the oppressive silence of the ancient structure.

Hana ran a hand along the faded carvings on the wall, their meaning obscured by time. "These symbols... they're musical notations," she said, her breath visible in the frigid air. "More than worshipping happened here. They were preparing for something."

Marcus nodded grimly. "And Baumann intends to finish what they started."

A sudden crash of a door echoed through the ruins, followed by the rhythmic chant of voices rising in unison. The cult had arrived.

Baumann's followers emerged from the shadows, robed figures moving with unsettling coordination. They entered as if in a rehearsed ceremonial formation and barely glanced at the trio, as if they either had anticipated their arrival or were unwilling to break their momentum. Their voices wove together in a hypnotic and ominous harmony, a fragment of Malvagio's unfinished symphony. The sound pulsed through the air, reverberating through the abbey's stone walls, vibrating the very ground beneath them.

"Get to the main chamber," Marcus shouted. "We have to disrupt the ritual before they complete the melody!"

Hana reached for her gun, but Michael placed a hand on her wrist. "No. Not yet. We must stop them another way."

As they sprinted toward the altar chamber, the cultists advanced, their formation tightening, voices rising. The flickering candlelight reflected in their hollow eyes, their expressions vacant yet determined. One of them lunged at Marcus, a jagged dagger flashing in the dim light. He sidestepped just in time, using the momentum to knock the attacker's wrist away and send the blade clattering to the floor. Another cultist rushed at Hana, but she swung her satchel with full force, sending the figure reeling into a crumbling pillar.

Michael, his fingers clenched around his crucifix, began to recite an exorcism incantation. His voice was steady despite the growing chaos, Latin syllables ringing through the cavernous hall, momentarily halting the cultists' advance. Their chant wavered, but Baumann's voice rose above it, powerful and commanding.

"It's too late!" he declared, his arms outstretched as he arose behind the altar, apparently where he had been awaiting his cultists' ceremonial approach. "The final note will be played, and the world will hear Vincenzo Malvagio's greatest work!"

The massive stone altar before him was adorned with ritual objects alongside the music box—ancient scrolls, obsidian chalices, one cradling thick red fluid, and a massive tome that Marcus knew could only be the Black Hymnal. He realized that Baumann must have discovered the main body of the volume somewhere else in the abandoned monastery in the Alps after the trio had escaped with fragments of it. And, with it, he had completed Malvagio's symphony. The pages fluttered as an unseen force moved through the abbey, the air thickening with a detectable energy.

Marcus exchanged a look with Hana. They had to act fast.

Marcus wove through the crumbling pillars toward Baumann. His mind worked rapidly, recalling every historical text he had studied, every architectural clue he had deciphered. This place—this abbey—held more than just history. Surely, it held secrets Baumann hadn't uncovered.

"You don't even understand what you're playing," Marcus called out, his voice carrying through the chamber. "Malvagio didn't just compose a symphony. He created a key—one that unlocks something no one can control."

Baumann turned, his finger dipping into the filled chalice, emerging with blood dripping from it. "You're too late, Russo." He lifted his finger, pressed it to his lips—symbolic of the sacrifice the world would suffer from his act—and stood poised to conduct the final sequence.

Marcus took a calculated step forward. "You think Malvagio wanted this completed? Look around you. The walls—see the inscriptions? This isn't a temple to his music. It's a warning. Even with the baton, he knew the symphony was dangerous. And without the baton to control it? You will be unleashing untold, uncontrollable powers."

For the first time, Baumann hesitated. His eyes darted to the crumbling frescoes along the walls—scenes of figures covering their ears, faces twisted in agony.

"That's why he destroyed the ending," Marcus pressed. "Because he knew what it would do. And he wasn't ready—but I am."

Adrian Baumann moved his hand to the key on the music box. "I will finish what he started. Begin the cleansing of this vile world." At the first turn of the key, a solitary mournful note brought chills to everyone present.

Marcus had mere seconds. His gaze flickered to the marble relief just behind Baumann—an old architectural trick: the keystone. The anchoring point of an arch. If he could trigger a collapse...

With a sudden lunge, Marcus grabbed a nearby broken beam and swung it against the anchoring element of the already weakened archway. The impact sent a deep crack snaking through the stone. Dust rained down as the structure groaned under its own weight.

Baumann stumbled backward as a section of the ceiling gave way, the force of the collapse knocking the music box from the altar. The sound of the first notes faltered, their harmonic thread unraveling.

Marcus dove forward, snatching the music box from the rubble.

Suddenly, another of the precarious stones from the half-collapsed archway gave way, and a tumble of massive stone blocks brought down more of the ceiling. The remaining cultists, fearing a total collapse, fled as the abbey walls trembled.

Hana and Michael turned away from the crushing

debris and suffocating dust cloud but didn't run, unwilling to leave Marcus behind. When the stones settled, Michael and Hana rushed to Marcus's last position, found him on the ground choking on the dust, and helped him stand. He nodded to them—he was unscathed. The trio looked toward where Baumann had stood.

"It's over," Hana breathed, looking down, seeing only a pile of massive boulders.

Michael exhaled deeply, gripping his pectoral cross. "Not yet."

CHAPTER
FORTY-ONE

The abbey lay in ruin, its once-mighty walls now sagging under the influences of time and recent devastation. The air was dense with the scent of scorched stone and damp earth, the lingering remnants of the hymn still seeming to linger in the vast emptiness. Marcus, Hana, and Michael stood in the center of what remained of the ritual chamber, their breaths visible in the cold of the early morning air.

The silence was profound. Not a whisper of Baumann's remaining followers, no sign of lingering resistance. The battle had ended, and yet the toll of its consequences pressed heavily upon them.

Hana wrapped her arms around Michael, glancing warily at the archways now cast in pale dawn light. "They're gone," she murmured. "But it doesn't feel over."

Michael exhaled deeply. "Evil doesn't just disappear. It recedes, waits." His eyes scanned the rubble covering the altar where Marcus and Baumann had struggled over the music box, his expression grim. "And sometimes, it finds new voices."

Marcus adjusted the strap of his satchel, his eyes scanning the broken floor, spying where the Black Hymnal had been whirled off by the impact. He couldn't allow himself to relax just yet. His instincts, honed over years of unearthing hidden histories, told him there were still secrets left untold within these walls.

The chamber, once suffused with the malevolent energy of the hymn, now felt strangely hollow. The walls, scarred by centuries of ritual and ruin, bore faded frescoes of saints and sinners locked in eternal struggle. Marcus's gaze lingered on one particular image: a figure cloaked in shadow, its outstretched hand touching the strings of a harp while chaos erupted around it.

"This place," he said, his voice low, "has always been a battleground. Baumann's fight was just the latest in a never-ending line. Malvagio began the battle long before him. Before even Malvagio came the Prague Codex and its instructions for the baton. Before then, the Black Hymnal. And before that...? Evil has woven itself throughout human history, seeking to enter the fabric of our lives through whatever means."

Hana nodded, her fingers brushing over the cracks in the floor. "And it's not finished. We stopped this ritual, but who knows how many others Baumann set in motion?"

Michael's expression was one of quiet determination. "Then we must ensure this is the last time such darkness rises from these ruins."

Marcus looked down at the music box still in his grasp. "We need to secure this. It can't fall into the wrong hands again."

Michael nodded. "The Vatican will ensure its safety. We

also need to secure anything else that poses a potential danger."

Moving carefully through the debris, Marcus knelt beside the remnants of the Black Hymnal. Where once the tome had pulsed with an unnatural energy, now only torn scraps of parchment and broken bindings remained. He reached forward, gingerly lifting what was left of its cover. The markings were barely legible, the once-formidable text reduced to nothing more than a whisper of its former self.

"We can't leave even a trace of it behind," Marcus said, his voice resolute. He retrieved a sealed container from his pack, gently placing the largest fragments inside. "If someone is desperate enough, they'll try to piece it together."

Hana crouched beside him, handing him a set of forceps to lift the more delicate pieces. "It should be locked away where no one can find it. Not in the Vatican. Not in any archive."

Michael nodded. "It should be buried."

Marcus hesitated, then gave a solemn nod. "Destroyed, if we can. But if destruction isn't an option, we ensure that no one can ever use it again." He snapped the lid shut on the container and fastened the clasps tightly.

For the first time since the night began, he allowed himself to breathe. This chapter was ending, but the responsibility of what they had unearthed would follow them for the rest of their lives.

Nearby, Hana found another piece of the hymnal, a fragment barely larger than her palm, scorched at the edges but still intact. Its notes, though incomplete, thrummed faintly under her touch, as though resisting its fate. She handed it to Marcus without a word, her eyes filled with a mix of wonder and fear.

THE DEVIL'S SYMPHONY

"It's strange, isn't it?" she said softly. "That something so small could hold so much power."

Marcus reopened the container and placed the fragment inside, his movements deliberate. "Power always comes with a price. And it's always heavier than it seems."

As the last pieces were secured, the three of them stood in silence, the impact of their actions pressing down on them. They had won, but the victory felt fragile, as if it could crumble under the wrong step.

As the team began their final survey of the abbey, Hana's fingers brushed over an unusual groove in the stonework near the shattered altar. The markings were subtle, buried beneath layers of soot and grime, but as she cleared away the dust, her breath caught in her throat.

"Marcus, look at this," she called, tracing the barely visible symbols. The script was ancient, older even than the abbey itself. Marcus joined her, running his hands over the markings as he deciphered the text.

"'The true melody lies beyond the veil.'" His voice was hushed, hesitant.

"What does it mean?" Michael asked.

Marcus's pulse quickened as he examined the inscription more closely. The symbols surrounding the text weren't just decorative. They were coordinates, or at least something resembling them. The arrangement suggested a location, though deciphering it would take time and resources. He pulled out his phone to take photos of it.

"Maybe Malvagio wasn't working alone," Marcus said slowly. "Or he didn't just create a single composition. He created a system, a network. This inscription... it's a map to something bigger."

A flicker of surprise crossed Michael's features. "Are you saying there is more music like this? More ways to unleash that kind of power?"

Hana's gaze remained fixed on the inscription, her mind sifting through options. "It's possible. Malvagio might have hidden his work across Europe, maybe even beyond. If Baumann's cult knew about this site, they might already be searching for the others."

The realization settled over them like a cold shadow. The battle they had fought, the sacrifices they had made, were just the beginning of a much larger conflict.

Marcus straightened, his resolve hardening. "We've stopped one melody. Now we find the rest. And this time, we end it all."

As the morning light crept farther into the abbey, casting long shadows over the broken altar, the team gathered their belongings. The inscription remained, a silent warning etched in stone. Beyond the veil lay truths they could scarcely imagine, but one thing was certain: their fight was far from over.

CHAPTER
FORTY-TWO

The echoes of St. Peter's Basilica seemed to carry a solemn weight as Marcus, Hana, and Michael followed a Swiss Guard through the mazelike halls of the Vatican. The grandeur of the corridors, adorned with centuries-old tapestries and golden fixtures, were incongruous with the heavy burden they carried. Each step toward Cardinal Severino's chamber felt slower, weighted with the gravity of their mission and its aftermath.

The guard stopped before a set of towering double doors carved with intricate depictions of saints and martyrs. With a firm knock, he announced their arrival and pushed the doors open. Inside, the chamber was a testament to the Church's opulence and history. High ceilings adorned with frescoes depicted scenes of divine triumph, while the long mahogany table at the center seemed almost insignificant by comparison. A grand chandelier cast a soft golden glow, illuminating the solemn faces of the trio as they entered.

Cardinal Severino rose from his seat at the head of the table, his crimson robes billowing slightly as he gestured for them to sit. His face, usually composed and unyielding, bore the marks of recent sleepless nights. Lines etched deeper into his brow, and his piercing gaze carried an unusual softness, as if he too grappled with the strain of what had transpired.

"Please, sit," Severino said, his voice steady but lacking its usual authority. As they settled into their chairs, he took his own seat and folded his hands before him. The silence that followed was oppressive, dimmed only by the faint crackle of the fireplace at the far end of the room.

"You've done what few could even comprehend, let alone achieve," Severino began, his tone measured. "The retrieval of the music box and the remains of the Black Hymnal is a triumph, but it has left us with questions—and burdens—that we must now address."

Michael leaned forward, his expression solemn. "Your Eminence, the music's power was unparalleled. But the residual effects of even the few notes played recently still carry a dangerous resonance. We must ensure they are destroyed, and such music can never be used again."

Severino nodded slowly, his eyes narrowing in thought. "Precisely why this meeting is so crucial. The Church has long safeguarded relics of both divine and dark origin. This, however, is a challenge unlike any we've faced. What we decide here will shape how we confront threats like this in the future."

Hana glanced at Marcus, her brow furrowing. "The music box and baton—their very existence means others will come looking. Baumann's cult might be scattered, but their ambition hasn't abated."

Severino's lips thinned as he processed her words.

"Which is why we must act decisively. The fragments, the Prague Codex, the music box, and the baton must be secured where no one can access them. Not even the Secret Archives should be considered entirely safe."

The depth of his declaration hung in the air. Marcus shifted uncomfortably in his chair, his instinct as an archaeologist conflicting with the necessity of burying knowledge. Yet, even he couldn't deny the danger posed by these remnants of Malvagio's dark discoveries and inventions.

Severino's gaze softened as he addressed the room. "You three have risked everything to bring this to light. Now, I ask you to trust the Church to ensure it remains hidden in the darkness."

LATER THAT DAY, the team descended into the deepest vault of the Vatican Secret Archives known as the Riserva. The air grew colder with each step, the dim light from torches casting long, flickering shadows on the stone walls. These were the Archive' most secure chambers, a place few ever knew existed and even fewer were permitted to enter. It was a sanctum of secrets, its shelves lined with relics and artifacts whose stories had been deliberately forgotten.

Severino led the procession, carrying a small, ornate chest containing the fragments of the Black Hymnal. Beside him, Marcus held the Prague Codex, its ancient pages wrapped in protective cloth. Michael followed closely, clutching the music box and Hana the baton, their expressions tense as they descended deeper into the labyrinthine passages.

The vault door loomed before them, a massive structure of reinforced steel and intricate carvings. The engravings depicted scenes of divine protection: angels shielding humanity from dark forces, swords clashing against unseen evils. It was a reminder of the Church's role as a guardian, a bulwark against the darkness.

Severino paused before the door, his fingers brushing over a hidden panel. He pressed his hand against it, the faint glow of a biometric scanner illuminating his face. With a series of soft clicks and a hiss of air, the door began to open, revealing a chamber that appeared more as a fortress than an archive.

Inside, the room was lined with glass cases, each containing relics of immense power and danger. Some were simple in appearance—a vial of darkened liquid, a rusted blade—while others radiated an almost palpable energy. In the center of the room stood an empty case, its reinforced glass glowing faintly from the protective wards embedded within.

"Place the items here," Severino instructed, his voice firm. "This vault has been blessed and warded. It will hold them until a more permanent solution can be arranged."

They each stepped forward, their movements deliberate, as they placed the artifacts inside the case. Each piece was arranged carefully on a velvet-lined tray.

As the glass lid sealed shut, a faint hum filled the room, the wards activating to encase the artifacts in an impenetrable barrier. Marcus exhaled deeply, stepping back to join the others. For the first time in what felt like weeks, he allowed himself to breathe freely.

Michael crossed himself, his whispered prayer breaking the silence. "May these remnants remain dormant, never to harm another soul."

Hana glanced at Severino, her expression resolute. "This is a temporary solution. If someone—even within the

Church—decides to exploit these artifacts, we're right back where we started."

Severino met her gaze, his tone unwavering. "We'll ensure that doesn't happen. The Church's duty is to protect, even from within."

As the vault door closed behind them, the hum of the wards faded into silence. The team exchanged a final glance, each of them grappling with the knowledge that, while the hymn had been silenced, its echoes might still find ways to resurface.

THE MEETING RESUMED in Severino's private chambers, the tension detectable by all. The conversation shifted to the question of what to do with the knowledge they had gained.

Marcus broke the silence. "The symphony's effects... they're unlike anything we've encountered. If we can study the copies of the scores and manuscripts we made and the interpretations they revealed—understand how they work—we can develop defenses against anything similar in the future."

Michael's expression hardened. "You're suggesting we tinker with forces we barely comprehend. That's precisely what led to this mess. Knowledge like this corrupts, Marcus. It's safer buried."

Hana interjected, her voice calm but firm. "Michael, Marcus isn't saying we use it. He's saying we prepare. Baumann's cult isn't the only group out there. If another faction finds something similar, we'll be defenseless without understanding what we're up against."

Severino held up a hand, silencing the debate. "Both points are valid. The Church has always walked the line between preserving dangerous knowledge and ensuring it does not fall into the wrong hands. But this situation... it demands unprecedented caution."

Michael's gaze remained fixed on Marcus. "Once you open the door to studying it, you risk letting the wrong people through. How do you plan to control that?"

Marcus hesitated, then spoke with quiet conviction. "By ensuring the right people are the ones studying it. People who understand the stakes. People who won't exploit it."

Severino leaned back in his chair, his expression contemplative. "We'll form a commission, a select group of trusted scholars and clergy, overseen by the Vatican's highest authorities. The study will be strictly controlled and monitored."

Michael's frown deepened, but he said nothing more. The room fell into a heavy silence, each of them weighing the essence of their choices.

Finally, Severino stood. "This is the path we've chosen. May God guide us in navigating it wisely."

As they left the chamber, Marcus glanced at the ancient walls of the Vatican, their shadows stretching long in the dim light. The decision had been made, but the quiet aftermath of the questions it raised would linger far longer than any of them cared to admit.

CHAPTER
FORTY-THREE

The quiet village of Murcote perched high in the Swiss Alps had long been a place where the forgotten sought refuge. Tucked between high cliffs and dense, whispering forests, it was a settlement seemingly untouched by time. Its cobblestone streets wound through clusters of aged stone houses, their ivy-covered walls standing resilient against the encroaching years. Few travelers passed through, and the villagers were content to remain unnoticed by the world beyond the mountains.

It was here, in the shadows of a crumbling chapel, that Baumann lay, barely clinging to life. His once-commanding presence had been reduced to that of a broken man—his body battered, his influence shattered. Deep lacerations marred his arms and shoulders, his ribs ached from the force of his last encounter at the abbey, and every breath felt like dragging shards of glass into his lungs. Had he not jumped back and crouched into the alcove at the base of the wall behind the altar, the massive archway's stones would have crushed him entirely. He had survived, but at what cost?

When he had regained consciousness, he had only barely been able to crawl out of the old abbey. A kindly old woman named Muer Elizabeta, who had spent her years tending to the sick and weary, had found him collapsed near the chapel steps. A handful of villagers had taken him in, unaware of the darkness that clung to him like a persistent shadow. Elizabeta had assumed he was another lost soul seeking redemption, injured in the crumbling structure as he had been in prayer. If she had known the truth, she might have left him there to die.

Now, from his resting place in her home, Baumann could imagine his followers' whispers, rumors of the destruction at the abbey, of how the hymn had been silenced forever. He clenched his jaw. They were wrong. The melody hadn't died; its echoes still lingered, waiting for the right moment to rise again. He had failed, yes—but he hadn't been defeated.

His fingers twitched, seeking the strength to move, but the pain anchored him in place. His thoughts were clouded, his mind a fractured maze of anger and desperation. The scent of burning wood from the hearth filled his nostrils, its warmth doing little to chase away the cold in his bones.

A knock at the door startled him. Muer Elizabeta peered in from the adjacent room, her voice rough with age. "You have a visitor."

Baumann's eyes narrowed. He doubted any of his former followers had returned. Who else would seek him out in his exile?

Hana Sinclair slipped into the dimly lit room, her every step careful, her presence quiet but unmistakable. Dressed in neutral tones, her brown hair tucked under a scarf, she hardly resembled the investigative journalist who had played a key role in dismantling Baumann's plans. But her eyes, sharp and unyielding, gave her away.

Baumann exhaled a slow breath, his lips curling into a faint, bitter smile. "I should have known you'd come." His voice was hoarse, stripped of its former power.

Hana took the seat across from him, pulling a small recorder from her coat pocket. "No theatrics, Adrian. No grand declarations. Just the truth."

He let out a hoarse chuckle. "Truth? You mean the version of events the Vatican will allow to exist?"

She leaned forward, her elbows resting on her knees. "You lost, Adrian. Your people deserted you. The music box and the Black Hymnal are with us. But you and I both know this wasn't just about a single artifact. What else were you looking for?"

A flicker of something—pride? Resentment?—passed over Baumann's face. He coughed, wincing from the effort. "You think you know everything about Malvagio's work? The symphony was only one movement. He created more. Hidden compositions, waiting to be found."

Hana's heartbeat quickened, though she kept her expression neutral. "Where?"

Baumann smiled faintly, shaking his head. "No. You'll have to figure that out on your own. But I will tell you this —Malvagio never worked alone."

She frowned, pressing him. "Who else?"

Baumann's eyelids grew heavy, exhaustion threatening to pull him under. "Look beyond the Vatican's records. The Church isn't the only one hiding things."

Hana studied him for a long moment, weighing his words carefully. He was weak, barely clinging to life, but his mind was still dangerous. The Baumann she had known—ruthless, manipulative—was still in there, even if his body was failing him.

She stood, pocketing the recorder. "If you're lying, I'll be back."

Baumann managed another weak chuckle. "If I were lying, you wouldn't have come in the first place."

THE SOUND of church bells echoed through the Vatican Gardens as Marcus sat on a stone bench, turning Baumann's words over in his mind. The interview had left Hana shaken—though she had tried to hide it when she told Marcus about the meeting, he had seen the unease in her eyes.

Malvagio never worked alone.

That single phrase had unraveled everything Marcus thought he knew. If Baumann's words were true, then the danger hadn't ended with the securing of the several artifacts involved. There were other compositions, other artifacts still out there, waiting to be discovered. Waiting to be played.

A part of him wanted to ignore it, to let the Vatican lock away what remained and move forward. But another part of him—the part that had spent years chasing buried truths—knew that leaving these secrets hidden would not make them disappear. Someone else would find them. Someone less equipped to stop them.

Michael approached, his presence grounding, his expression expectant. "You've been quiet since Hana's report."

Marcus exhaled. "Baumann gave her just enough

information to make us doubt that we've seen the last of this."

Michael frowned. "You think we should pursue it?"

The archaeologist hesitated. "I don't know. But I do know that if Malvagio's work isn't truly gone, we need to be the ones to find it before someone else does."

Michael nodded slowly, crossing his arms. "Then we make sure we're prepared. No more surprises."

Marcus stood, his hands in his coat pockets, staring at the towering walls of the Vatican beyond the garden. "There's more to this than we thought. If Malvagio's reach extended beyond what we knew, then we've only just begun to understand the true scale of this."

The priest placed a hand on his shoulder. "Then let's make sure we finish it."

The two men stood in silence for a long moment, visions of the future pressing down on them. The battle had ended, but the war for history's darkest melodies had only just begun.

CHAPTER
FORTY-FOUR

It began as whispers on the wind, scattered reports trickling in from across the globe. A violinist in Vienna played an unfamiliar tune in his sleep, his bow moving across the strings with uncanny precision—when he woke, he swore he had never heard the melody before. In a cathedral in Prague, an organ played a chord progression of its own volition, though no one had touched the keys. In an isolated monastery in Peru, monks recorded a strange harmonic vibration reverberating through their chapel walls, though no earthly source could be found.

At first, these incidents were dismissed as oddities, curious footnotes in local news reports. But as they became more frequent, those who understood the dangers of Vincenzo Malvagio's work grew uneasy. The deep, rolling echoes of the lost melody—the very sounds that had nearly consumed the Vatican—weren't fading as they had hoped. Instead, they seemed to be taking root elsewhere, waiting to be found.

In a Parisian conservatory, a promising young pianist was found unconscious at the foot of his grand piano, his hands still resting on the keys. The doctor who examined him claimed he had suffered some kind of seizure, but the recording device in the room had captured something chilling—a fragment of music, played with eerie precision, that didn't match any known composition. The young man, once revived, could recall nothing except the sensation of something—someone—guiding his hands.

Elsewhere, in Kyoto, a centuries-old koto—a traditional Japanese string instrument—was found vibrating on its own inside a sealed display case in a museum. Security footage captured the moment it resonated with an unseen force, playing a note that sent shivers down the spines of the staff. The museum curator, a man deeply familiar with historical artifacts, reported it to a friend in the Vatican.

In Buenos Aires, a group of street musicians performing in a public square suddenly stopped mid-performance, their instruments emitting discordant tones. One violinist collapsed, clutching his head, while a guitarist's fingers locked into a trance-like movement, strumming an eerie, hypnotic progression. Bystanders watched in stunned silence before someone began filming, capturing the unease and confusion. The footage, which quickly went viral, showed a woman in the crowd whispering, "That song... I've heard it in my dreams."

In an underground jazz club in New Orleans, a trumpeter found himself improvising a melody he had never played before, his fingers moving as if compelled. The audience, entranced, listened with growing unease as the song took on a haunting, almost suffocating quality. When the final note rang out, the club's power surged and cut off, plunging the room into darkness.

By the time word of these incidents reached Marcus and Hana's attention, it was undeniable. The hymn hadn't died—it had merely scattered, fragmented into new forms, waiting for someone to piece it back together.

HANA SAT at her desk in Rome, her laptop screen flickering as she compiled reports from across the world. The Vatican's secure network had been flooded with messages from scholars, musicians, and clergy who had encountered inexplicable musical phenomena. Each report alone might have been dismissed, but together, they formed a pattern—a deeply unsettling one.

Marcus leaned over her shoulder, skimming the reports with a furrowed brow. "This isn't coincidence," he murmured. "It's as if the melody left behind fragments of itself, attaching to instruments, locations, even people. As it did in the basilica when we'd attempted to counter the final chords of it. It's still out there."

Hana nodded, her expression tight with concern. "And the people experiencing these events don't even realize what they're playing. They think they're improvising, discovering new compositions—but the melody is guiding them. It's finding new ways to be heard."

She clicked on a video sent by a researcher in Vienna. The grainy footage showed the unconscious violinist, his fingers moving across the strings in sleep. The music was haunting, discordant, yet mesmerizing.

"That's a piece of the symphony," Marcus said, his voice barely above a whisper. "Altered, but unmistakable."

Hana rubbed her temples, frustration evident in her posture. "We've secured the music box and the remnants of the Black Hymnal. The Prague Codex is sealed. The baton is locked away. So how is this happening?"

Marcus exhaled, leaning against the table. "Maybe the music was never just ink on paper. Maybe it existed in ways we didn't fully understand—an imprint, a resonance that lingers in the world, looking for vessels to play it."

She pulled up another report, this one from a monastery in Spain. A recording had captured a group of monks chanting, their voices gradually shifting into a sequence of notes none of them recognized. The audio was unsettling—somehow layered, as if multiple voices were overlapping in an unnatural harmony. The monks claimed they had felt an overwhelming compulsion to continue singing, their voices growing heavier, until one of them collapsed from exhaustion.

Marcus exchanged a glance with Hana. "If this is happening worldwide, then the music never truly ended. It's adapting."

MICHAEL PACED the softly lit study of the Vatican Archives, his arms crossed tightly against his chest. The air was thick with the scent of aged parchment and candle wax, but the usual comfort he found in this sacred space eluded him. He turned abruptly to face Marcus and Hana, who sat across from him, their faces drawn and weary.

"We should let this go," he said finally, his voice quiet but firm. "We did what we set out to do. We ended Baumann's movement, and prevented a catastrophe. This —whatever is happening now—is dangerous. If we keep digging, we risk bringing it all back."

Marcus met his gaze, his expression unreadable.

"Ignoring it won't make it disappear. If the hymn is resurfacing, we need to understand how—and why."

Michael shook his head. "That's exactly how Baumann thought. He wanted to understand. He wanted to control it. And look where that led him."

Hana sighed, rubbing the bridge of her nose. "Michael, I get it. Believe me, I do. But this isn't over. If we don't act, someone else will. And if the wrong people find these fragments, it's possible they won't hesitate to complete what Malvagio finally realized was too dangerous and what Baumann restarted. There is always someone greedy enough for power to take risks the world shouldn't face."

Michael was silent for a long moment, his fingers tightening around the silver cross he wore around his neck.

Marcus gave a nod, though the weight in his chest remained. He knew the road ahead was uncertain, but there was one truth he couldn't ignore:

The music was far from finished.

CHAPTER
FORTY-FIVE

The Vatican Secret Archives were silent, the only sound the soft scratch of Marcus's pen against paper as he transcribed the fragile Latin script before him. The room was awash in a golden haze, the flickering light from the antique chandelier casting elongated shade across the towering bookshelves. For weeks, the archaeologist had combed through restricted sections, cross-referencing Malvagio's compositions with any texts that might suggest a counterbalance to his work. A permanent answer had always felt just beyond reach—until now.

Tucked inside a centuries-old folio, wedged between theological treatises and forgotten compositions, Marcus found a weathered parchment unlike the others. The ink, though faded, carried the unmistakable distinction of deliberate notation. His breath caught as he translated the first line: ***Symphonia Divina—A Harmony Against the Abyss.***

His heart pounded as he read further. Malvagio hadn't

only composed the *Devil's Symphony*—he had foreseen the need for its counterforce. This wasn't a fragment of a lost work; it was a full composition, hidden away to keep it safe from those who would distort its purpose. The *Divine Symphony of Creation*, as the text called it, was meant to suppress and dissolve the distant memories of the darker melody.

But what stunned Marcus the most were the annotations written in the margins—notes from a long-dead scholar who had studied the piece two centuries ago. The scholar warned that the *Divine Symphony of Creation* wasn't simply meant to be played—it had to be enacted under precise conditions, ones that required not only technical mastery but spiritual purity. It was more than just a melody; it was an invocation of balance, one that required absolute harmony between participants and purpose.

Marcus exhaled slowly, his mind reeling. If this was authentic, they had found their solution. But there was something else—a warning scribbled at the bottom of the manuscript in a hurried, almost frantic hand:

Only the purest intent may summon harmony. Should corruption take hold, discord will reign once more.

The implication chilled him. This was no ordinary countermeasure—it was a razor's edge. Played correctly, it could neutralize the lingering influence of Malvagio's work with the Black Hymnal. Played improperly, it could unleash something even worse.

HANA SAT across from Marcus in his private study, the document spread between them. The candlelight cast a golden hue over the parchment, illuminating the dense notation that had been preserved for centuries. Her eyes scanned the text, taking in the precise symbols and annotations, each one more intricate than the last.

"This isn't just music," she murmured, her fingers tracing the delicate markings. "Like the *Devil's Symphony*, it's an incantation, woven into the melody. Malvagio didn't just compose a song; he created a formula for balance. This one is for the good, if we can believe what we've read about it."

Marcus nodded. "Which means we're not just dealing with sound. This is harmonic mathematics, theological resonance—he used his earlier understanding about harmonic creation and imbued it in this final work as well. All of which goes beyond what we know."

Hana tapped a section near the bottom of the page. "Here—this passage. It describes this as a completely new symphony that counteracts the effects of the *Devil's Symphony*. If we can reconstruct this and play it correctly, it should be able to neutralize whatever lingering echoes remain." She then flipped to notes beside her. "See here? I've been trying to create a counter symphony and making some progress, but not much. But what I have determined to be the right chords exactly matches parts of the *Divine Symphony*." She looked up at them. "We were on the right track. But now we have the exact and fully completed counter symphony from Malvagio's own hand."

Marcus leaned in closer, his expression thoughtful. "But there's a risk. If even one note is wrong, the effect could be unpredictable."

Hana sighed. "That's why we have to get it right. The world can't afford another mistake like the one Baumann made."

She glanced at another section of the document, her

brow furrowing as she translated the Latin text. "There's something else. This melody—this counterforce—it's not just something anyone can play. The manuscript states that the participants must be attuned to its purpose. If their intent is anything less than pure, the melody itself could shift, distorting instead of neutralizing."

Marcus exhaled, rubbing the back of his neck. "That makes sense, given the warning at the bottom I'd seen earlier. Malvagio must have realized that the symphony could be used as both a shield and a weapon. If someone unworthy tries to wield it—"

"It could cause even greater chaos," Hana finished grimly. "Which means we can't just find someone to play it. We need to ensure whoever does—whether it's one of us or someone we trust—knows exactly what they're doing."

They sat thoughtfully for a moment before Hana stated what they both wondered. "Why would Malvagio create this Divine Symphony and not play it?" They looked at each other. Finally, she answered for them both. "Because he feared that his past endeavors made him unworthy, not of a pure enough heart, to play it himself."

Marcus leaned back in his chair, staring at the manuscript. The heft of what they had found settled over him like a heavy cloak. They had the answer, but using it would demand only the right person—and who would that be?

MICHAEL SAT in his office in the Archives, the heavy wooden crucifix on the wall behind him a prominent fixture in the room. His fingers drummed lightly against the armrest of his chair as he listened to Marcus and Hana outline their discovery. His expression remained impassive, though his eyes betrayed the storm of emotions raging beneath the surface.

"You want to play a melody designed to counteract the most dangerous composition in history," Michael said at last. "And you think this will simply erase the harm Malvagio's earlier composition has caused?"

Marcus met his gaze. "Not erase—contain. Dissolve the residual energy before it can be weaponized again."

Michael sighed, rubbing his temples. "And what if you're wrong? What if playing this counter-melody only amplifies the echoes instead?"

Hana folded her arms. "If we do nothing, the melody's influence will keep spreading. We've already seen what's happening across the world. If there's even a chance that we can stop it, don't we have to try?"

Michael was silent for a long moment, staring into the flickering candlelight. Finally, he exhaled and nodded slowly. "Fine. But this plan stays guarded. If the wrong people even suspect that another symphony exists, they will try to exploit it. We cannot allow that to happen."

Marcus gave a resolute nod. "Then we do this in secrecy. And we do it right."

Michael steepled his fingers, his voice quieter now. "There's one more thing: if Malvagio designed this as a true counterforce, it means that the same warning we'd read before applies to this symphony—it requires a 'participant to offer up their connection to the divine.' It implies it is an irreversible exchange. A person's soul becomes bound to the melody, like a vessel of the music."

The room fell into silence, each of them absorbing the reality of what lay ahead. The final movement had begun —but whether it would end in harmony or discord was still uncertain.

CHAPTER
FORTY-SIX

The air inside the Sistine Chapel was thick with anticipation, a charged stillness that made every breath feel heavier. The vaulted ceiling, adorned with Michelangelo's divine frescoes, loomed above the assembled group, its celestial figures seeming to observe the moment with an eerie awareness. The scent of ancient wood and incense lingered in the air, mingling with the faint metallic tang of candle smoke.

Marcus stood at the center of the chapel, his hands tightening around the leather-bound folder that contained the meticulously reconstructed fragments of the Black Hymnal. The magnitude of history—of power, of danger—pressed down on him like a physical force. He glanced at Hana, who stood beside him, her expression unreadable but her posture tense. Michael was just behind her, clad in his priestly robes, his face a careful mask of neutrality.

A handful of Vatican officials stood in the pews, their presence a reminder that this endeavor, while secretive, wasn't entirely unsanctioned. Among them were archivists, scholars, and a select few participants who had been chosen for their skill, piety, and absolute discretion. Swiss Guards Karl and Lukas, already instrumental in defending this mission, stood to the back, ready—again—to defend against any unforeseen intruders. In front of them, Luciana Mancini, without whose help they would have never discovered the location of the Black Hymnal, knelt, rosary in hand, as she silently prayed. They had all sworn oaths of silence, understanding that what they were about to witness could never be spoken of beyond these walls.

The musicians stood ready, their instruments gleaming in the candlelight. The strings had been tuned, the keys had been tested, and every note had been rehearsed under the strictest conditions. This wasn't merely a performance; it was an act of restoration, a correction to a long-standing distortion in the fabric of existence.

Michael cleared his throat. "When we do this," he said to his two companions, his voice steady but low, "there can be no mistakes. We cannot afford an error."

Marcus exhaled and gave a single nod. He reached into the folder, pulling out the roll of music they had meticulously crafted based on the score they had found of the Divine Symphony, his fingers trembling slightly. He had studied this composition for days, analyzing its structure, its intended harmonics, the delicate balance between its light and dark elements. It was a key, a force crafted to counteract the destructive melody that had haunted them all.

He opened the drawer of the music box, stationed on a pedestal before him. He inserted the roll onto the spindle and closed the drawer. The room tensed. Then, with a single precise movement, he picked up the baton lying beside the music box with one hand and turned the onyx key with the other, winding it fully. Lifting both hands now, baton held high, he took a deep breath as the first note of the *Divine Symphony* floated into the hush of the air.

The first notes drifted into the cavernous chamber, soft and deliberate. The gems and crystals vibrated to reflect the notes on the spindle, creating ethereal sounds reminiscent of worldly instruments but with the aching beauty of a heavenly source. A sound like violins led, quivering with an otherworldly resonance that sent chills down Marcus's spine. A deeper sound like woodwinds joined, weaving its delicate timbre into the fabric of the piece. Then, slowly, deeper bass tones swelled beneath them, grounding the composition like the foundation of a cathedral.

Marcus allowed the sounds to pull his arm, the baton flowing across the air gently joining the melody on its own, then dipping, then nearly flying as the music poured over and through the tip of it. The music expanded, filling the sacred space, wrapping itself around the towering columns and intricate frescoes. The air itself seemed to change, becoming charged with an electric energy. The candle flames flickered, though there was no breeze, and the very stones of the Vatican vibrated in response to the counter-melody.

Outside, the effects began to spread. Within the corridors of the Vatican, the echoing remnants of Malvagio's work, which had once whispered through empty halls and hidden chambers, began to dissolve. Priests walking near the Archives felt a sudden, inexplicable lightness in their chests, as if a pressure they had never noticed had finally lifted. In St. Peter's Square, tourists paused mid-stride, their conversations faltering as an inexplicable calm washed over them, craning their heads as if to hear some sounds beyond their hearing.

Beyond the Vatican, the melody rippled as unheard waves outward. In Paris, a conservatory pianist who had been unknowingly replicating Malvagio's influence on his compositions suddenly froze at his piano, his fingers released from the achingly painful force that caused him to play the eerie sequence that had haunted him for days. In Kyoto, the koto that had played by itself inside a museum display case fell silent. In Vienna, the violinist who had woken from his sleep-playing episodes found his instrument oddly still in his hands, its strings resonating no longer.

And only 1.4 kilometers away, the fractured and cracked tile floor of St. Peter's Basilica shivered and sealed itself, reuniting the sanctity and wholeness where Michael had conducted their first attempt at completing Malvagio's original symphony.

Marcus could feel it working, feel the negative energy dissipating as the melody carried its cleansing force across unseen vibrations throughout the world. But with every note, the weight upon his shoulders grew heavier. His vision blurred slightly, his body swaying, the baton swooping in currents of spiritual passion in his right hand. He suddenly gripped the conductor's stand tightly with his left hand, forcing himself to stay upright under the power of it all.

The music built toward its climax, a crescendo that threatened to break something unseen. And then—

The world around Marcus flickered. The Sistine Chapel blurred, its colors bleeding together, and suddenly, he wasn't in the present anymore.

All sound ceased.

The chapel full of people—gone.

He was somewhere else. *Somewhen else.*

Vincenzo Malvagio sat before him, hunched over a massive wooden desk cluttered with parchment. Candles burned low, flickering dancing shadows over his gaunt face, his eyes hollowed by sleepless nights and obsessive study. The air in the chamber was thick with ink, dust, and the faint scent of burning wax. Outside, the wind howled through the narrow streets of eighteenth-century Venice, rattling the wooden shutters of his secluded study.

Marcus watched as Malvagio traced trembling fingers over his composition of the *Devil's Symphony*. His breath came ragged, his body tensed with an almost frantic energy. He muttered in Latin, his voice rising and falling in near-prayer, near-despair.

"This is not what I intended," Malvagio murmured, his eyes reflecting the wavering candlelight. "It was meant to elevate, not destroy. It was meant to bring harmony, purity... and yet, I have woven discord and evil."

In one hand, he clutched the torn ending to the score for the Devil's Symphony. His fingers curled around the bit of parchment; he pressed both fists to his temples as though the pressure of his own creation had become unbearable. The *Devil's Symphony* had taken on a life of its own; he had witnessed it that very day as his followers had succumbed to its power. And he knew he had lost control. He had tried to create perfection, but in doing so, he had birthed something far more dangerous.

Slowly, he opened his fist and he held the final chords of his masterpiece of music to the candle in front of him. A parchment corner curled away from the flame as if refusing to be destroyed by his bout of guilt. He pushed the fragment closer, and even the flicker of flame bent away from it. Gritting his teeth, he forced the parchment to the core of the wick, and in a sudden burst of flame, the fire of his determination caught. The parchment became no more than a blackened single sheet of ash. He let it fall to the table, the flame subsiding, the remnants now no more than the blackened ash of history. He rubbed it into the table, blackening the heel of his hand in the process. He rubbed the ash on his trousers.

"I must counter it," Malvagio whispered, his ink-stained fingers trembling as he reached for a blank parchment. "I must correct my mistake." He dipped his pen in his ink well, hesitating as he glanced to the side at the music box. He pondered the ornate object, the instrument that could bridge worlds, his whispers barely audible. "And once countered... this cannot remain..." His voice trailed off as he frantically began writing notes for his *Divine Symphony of Creation*.

Marcus gasped as the vision swirled, breaking apart. He felt himself being thrust back, the sound of the Sistine Chapel's music crashing over him like a wave. His legs buckled, and he barely caught himself against the podium. He trembled, drenched in sweat, his breath coming in short gasps as the last of the symphony's notes slowly dissipated through the air. The baton's orb light extinguished, as the last chord vibrated its fervor for life throughout those present.

Hana was beside him instantly. "Marcus! What happened?"

He looked at her, his mind still reeling from what he had seen. "Malvagio... he never meant for any of this. He knew it was wrong. He tried to fix it before it got out of his hands."

Michael stepped up to them, his expression grim. "But he failed."

Marcus swallowed, nodding slowly. "Yes. And no. He meant for someone to play his *Divine Symphony* to counter what he'd already released because he knew he couldn't. But then he planned—"

Suddenly, as the final vibration of the counter-melody faded into silence, a deep peace settled over the chapel. And in that instant, the music box before them shuddered, the image of it blurred and shifted in their sight. The threesome stepped back from the pedestal as the box cracked, then fragmented, and then it disintegrated into no more than a pile of glittering dust, its gold and gems and entire structure a heap of powder so fine, so soft that the very breath of the air caught bits of it, carrying it away.

Marcus looked at Michael's wide eyes and Hana's open mouth. "A self-destruct. I heard him in my vision, and now I understand. He wanted someone to play the *Divine Symphony* to counter any remnants of what he had inadvertently released. But the temptation to use it otherwise would be too strong for our world. He crafted a self-destruct once the final note of his *Divine Symphony* was played."

Hana nodded, her eyes rimmed with tears at both the power of what one man could achieve and the agony he must have felt at realizing what he had done.

Michael crossed himself, grateful that divine grace could bring a change of heart to a man who had once meant great harm, but who, when he turned to God's forgiveness, had acted on it. In the end, Malvagio had sacrificed his lifelong efforts and personal ambition for the greater good.

The participants in the audience had been captivated

by the joyful and healing restrains of the melody and many still sat transfixed in rapt ecstasy over the power of the goodness, the divine blessing, they had beheld, if only for the time the symphony had played. Slowly, they began to rise, most crossing themselves, some bowing in a final prayer, then quietly leaving this most holy of chapels, their lives forever changed.

The world outside remained unchanged to those unaware, but to Marcus, Hana, and Michael, something had shifted—something profound and irreversible.

Marcus sat on the edge of the altar, the baton resting across his knees. His hands trembled as he stared at the object, its surface now dull and lifeless. The substance of what they had done—what they had risked—pressed heavily on his shoulders.

Hana approached, her expression a mixture of relief that Marcus hadn't been "sacrificed," at least not in body, as Malvagio had predicted was necessary. She placed a hand on his shoulder, her touch grounding him. "It's over, Marcus. We did it. You did it."

He looked up at her, his eyes clouded with doubt. "Did we? Or did we just bury something that will resurface in another century?"

Michael joined them, his presence calm and steady. "What you did here today wasn't destruction. It was preservation. You've ensured that this music will never harm anyone again."

Marcus shook his head slowly. "But at what cost? The symphony was history. Dark history, yes, but history nonetheless. I can't help but wonder if I've crossed a line I swore never to breach."

Hana knelt beside him, her gaze unwavering. "You didn't destroy history, Marcus. You saved the future.

Sometimes, preservation means making the hard choice to protect what's ahead, not just what's behind. Surely, as an archaeologist, you must see that."

The three of them sat in silence for a moment, the consequence of their journey settling over them.

Only one other person remained in the chapel: Luciana Mancini, still kneeling, rosary in hand, but her head uplifted, eyes wide open, a beatific smile on her lips.

Outside, the sun rose higher, its light cutting through the lingering mist and casting the abbey in a golden glow. It was a symbol of renewal, a reminder that hope could emerge even in the wake of destruction.

The *Divine Symphony of Creation* had silenced the echoes of the Devil's Symphony. But the cost of that silence would stay with them forever.

CHAPTER
FORTY-SEVEN

The candlelight in the Vatican Archives flickered gently as Marcus, Hana, and Michael sat in quiet contemplation. The events of the past months had left them physically exhausted and mentally drained, yet a profound sense of fulfillment settled over them. The echoes of Malvagio's original symphony had been silenced, and for the first time in what felt like ages, a rare peace filled the air.

Marcus exhaled slowly, glancing between Hana and Michael. "I don't think I could have done this without you two," he admitted, his voice heavy with sincerity. "This entire ordeal… it tested us in ways I never imagined."

Hana offered a small smile, leaning back against the wooden chair. "That's what partners do, Marcus. We watch each other's backs. And despite everything, we made it through."

Michael nodded, clasping his hands together. "The work isn't over, but for now, we should allow ourselves to acknowledge what we've accomplished. This signified more than just a musical composition. It was about preserving something far greater—our ability to resist forces that seek to corrupt history and disrupt the future."

Marcus let those words settle. The duty of responsibility hadn't lifted, but it had shifted into something more manageable, something with purpose. He turned his gaze toward the bookshelves lining the dimly lit room, their spines bearing the weight of centuries of history. Each of those volumes held knowledge, power, and secrets. Some had shaped civilizations, while others had nearly destroyed them.

He let out a quiet chuckle. "It's strange, isn't it? We spend our lives uncovering the past, believing that knowledge is always a force for good. But this... this was different."

Hana's expression softened. "Because this transcended mere knowledge. It was power. And power, when misunderstood or misused, can become a weapon."

Michael leaned forward. "And yet, despite everything, we prevailed. I keep thinking about the night in the Sistine Chapel, when the counter-melody resonated through the Vatican. That was the moment I realized we weren't just fighting an idea—we were fighting history itself, the remnants of something that had refused to die."

Marcus nodded slowly. "It was as if the past was still trying to shape the present, still demanding to be heard. But we didn't let it. We gave it resolution."

For a long moment, none of them spoke. The silence was no longer oppressive, but reverent—a testament to what they had overcome. This journey had changed each of them. Michael had seen firsthand how dangerous history could be when left unchecked. Hana had reaffirmed her belief that knowledge must be wielded with wisdom. And Marcus, ever the skeptic, had been forced to confront the reality that faith and history were intertwined in ways even he hadn't fully understood.

Marcus ran a hand through his hair and let out a deep breath. "I suppose the real question is... what do we do now?"

Hana smirked. "You're not seriously considering retirement, are you?"

He laughed, shaking his head. "Not a chance. But I think our purpose has changed. We can't just be historians anymore. We have to be guardians. Not just of artifacts, but of the truth itself."

Michael's expression grew thoughtful. "And that truth must be protected—not hidden, not destroyed, but safeguarded against those who would use it for the wrong reasons."

Hana tapped her fingers against the wooden table. "Then we move forward. With caution, with wisdom, and with the understanding that history is never truly buried. It lingers, waiting for the right—or the wrong—person to find it."

Marcus nodded. "Then we make sure it's always in the right hands."

The three of them sat in silent agreement, the consequences of their decision settling into place. The journey they had embarked upon had changed them forever. And though this chapter had come to an end, they knew, with certainty, that their work was far from over.

· · ·

Later that evening, the team was summoned to a private audience with Vatican Secretary of State Cardinal Severino. The grand chamber was lit by a faint, amber glow, throwing shadows that flickered along the high stone walls. Severino sat behind his ornate desk, his hands folded, his expression unreadable.

"You have done the Church a great service," he began, his voice carrying the authority of centuries of tradition. "The threat that lingered for so long has finally been laid to rest. Malvagio's legacy will not return to haunt us."

Marcus inclined his head respectfully. "It was a privilege to assist in preserving history, Your Eminence."

Severino's eyes sharpened. "History, yes. But let me be clear—this victory does not mean we are safe. There will always be those who seek out dangerous knowledge, who believe they can control forces beyond their understanding. The Church has fought such battles for centuries, and it will continue to do so long after we are gone."

Hana's face inclined toward the cardinal. "Are you saying we should expect more like Malvagio?"

Severino sighed, rubbing his temple. "Not necessarily like him. But others, yes. Those who believe in power without consequence. The preservation of knowledge is a noble pursuit, but it is also a dangerous one. We must remain vigilant."

Michael exchanged a glance with Marcus before speaking. "Then let us be the ones who stand guard over these truths. If history has shown us anything, it is that leaving dangerous knowledge buried only invites others to dig it up."

Severino regarded them for a long moment before nodding. "Then you must tread carefully."

. . .

As the first light of dawn crept through the windows of the Archives, Marcus stood alone among the rows of ancient texts and forgotten manuscripts. His fingers brushed over the spine of a worn tome, its pages filled with the secrets of the past.

He had spent his life uncovering history, bringing hidden truths to light. But now, he understood that some things were better left protected, not exposed.

Hana and Michael approached, their footsteps light against the stone floor. "You're thinking about what's next, aren't you?" Hana asked.

Marcus turned to them with a slight nod. "I can't ignore what we've learned from all of this. Malvagio's symphony was a warning, not just about music but the power hidden in history. If we don't take responsibility for these artifacts, someone else will."

Hana crossed her arms, a knowing smile on her lips. Michael, too, smiled, realizing what she was about to ask their friend. He put his arm around her waist, giving his fiancée a small but loving squeeze before releasing her. "So what's the plan?"

Marcus exhaled, his decision crystallizing. "I want to dedicate my work to uncovering and safeguarding historical artifacts that pose similar dangers. We can't erase the past, but we can ensure it doesn't repeat itself."

Michael nodded. "Then it seems our journey isn't over. We've seen what happens when history is left unchecked. If we can prevent another Malvagio coming to light, we must."

Marcus smiled, feeling the resonance of the decision

settle comfortably over him. "Then we start now. No more shadows. Only truth—protected."

As the morning light filled the Archives, the three stood together, ready for whatever lay ahead. They had closed one chapter, but a new one was just beginning.

EPILOGUE

The early autumn light had faded long before Marcus found himself again in that familiar study, a quiet closure settling over him like the dusk outside Rome's timeworn streets. In the aftermath of years consumed by unspeakable truths and relentless investigations—of Vatican intrigues, forbidden manuscripts, and the maledictions left behind by Malvagio—the routine of daily correspondence had become both an anchor and a reminder of battles fought in shadow. Academic inquiries, research journals, and even the occasional cryptic missive had all melded into a tapestry of normalcy that belied the chaos of his past.

That morning, however, as he methodically sorted through letters and documents, his fingers stilled at the sight of a mysterious letter. It bore no return address—only his name, Marcus Russo. A ripple of unease stirred him, a sensation not unfamiliar after the revelations of recent months.

Inside, he found a brief letter, addressing him formally

as "Mr. Russo." It thanked him for releasing her from the pain of guilt that had threatened to overwhelm her. She explained that her life now held purpose, and how the music he had conducted had swept through her soul, exchanging a life of desperation to purify an unclean world against its will into one of self-sacrifice to improve the world. She had joined Mother Teresa's Missionaries of Charity to actively serve in the poorest of the world's slums. She said the melody he had released resonated deep in her soul, and she knew it would remain with her throughout life as she continued on the path revealed to her during the symphony.

Marcus sat back, the letter now resting on his desk as a living testament to the sacrifice of one's history in order to reclaim one's future. Was that what Malvagio had meant about a sacrifice? Or could he even have known what the world of spirit would exact as a price for tampering with the heavens?

Marcus recalled each step of his own arduous journey: the discovery of the eerie music box, the unveiling of the Black Hymnal's accursed melodies, the cryptic warnings from allies, like Hana and Michael and the cardinal, and the ceaseless pull of a destiny entwined with darkness and light.

In that moment, as the study's fire cast shifting patterns on the walls and the distant toll of church bells mingled with the soft murmurs of Rome's streets, Marcus felt the weight of the sounds that had haunted his steps, and this final note brought clarity: the journey wasn't yet complete. The letter was an epilogue that transcended endings—a call to understand that every discovery, every effort, would always embody lingering sorrow and the promise of renewal.

Thus, in the waning light of that autumn day, as the harmonies of a long-forgotten melody whispered on, Marcus Russo stepped forward. Not as a man resigned to unfinished business, but as one ready to embrace the next movement—a deliberate cadence that would, at long last, bring cohesion to a story of darkness, discovery, and, ultimately, redemption.

FICTION, FACT, OR FUSION?

Many readers have asked me to distinguish fact from fiction in my books. Generally, I like to take factual events and historical figures and build on them in creative ways, but much of what I write is historically accurate. In this book, I'll review some of the chapters where questions may arise, hoping it may help those wondering where reality meets creative writing.

PROLOGUE:
Vincent Malvagio is fictitious. His personality and interest in the effects of sound reflect an interest in a century where many prodigious and productive composers (Mozart, Beethoven, Bach, and many others) filled European concert halls and cathedrals with their music, affecting audiences both then and now.

CHAPTER 7

Franz Mesmer (1734–1815) began his studies at the Jesuit-run University of Dillingen in 1754. He became deeply intrigued by the idea that external forces could influence the body's internal "misbehaving fluids"—a concept rooted in the prevailing medical theories of his time. This fascination led him to develop a therapeutic method he called **animal magnetism**, which he believed could realign the body's energies to restore health. Initially, he used magnets to channel this force, but later relied on the movement of his hands, intense eye contact, and even the ethereal tones of the glass harmonica to induce healing. His techniques gave rise to the term "mesmerizing," and he is often credited as a forerunner of modern hypnotism. Though celebrated by some as an innovator, Mesmer's work was also the subject of intense skepticism and criticism during his lifetime.

Cardinal Antonio Bellari is a fictional character.

CHAPTER 8:

Benjamin Franklin did, in fact, invent the **glass armonica** in 1761—a remarkable instrument born of his fascination with music and science. Inspired by the popular parlor trick of rubbing the rims of water-filled wine glasses to produce musical tones, Franklin reimagined the concept into a more elegant and playable form. He mounted a series of glass bowls, graduated in size and nested along a horizontal spindle, which could be spun by a foot pedal. As the performer touched the spinning glasses with moistened fingers, the armonica emitted haunting, ethereal tones unlike anything previously heard. It quickly gained popularity among composers and audiences alike, praised not only for its novelty but for the otherworldly quality of its sound. Even Mozart and Beethoven composed for it. Though its popularity waned by the nineteenth century, the glass armonica remains one of Franklin's most curious and enchanting inventions—equal parts entertainment and alchemy.

CHAPTER 13:

Santa Lucia Monastery is an architectural complex in the town of Adrano, in the Province of Catania, in the region of Sicily, Italy. The former Benedictine monastery currently serves as an elementary school, alongside the Giovanni Verga High School.

CHAPTER 16:

San Lorenzo Monastery is fictional, although San Lorenzo is a large district outside of Rome.

CHAPTER 24:

The Black Hymnal is fictional.

CHAPTER 26 AND 27:

The Red Messiah Church, perched high in the remote Austrian Alps, was constructed in the mid-eighteenth century during a period of intense religious revival across Central Europe. Commissioned by a breakaway sect of millenarian monks, the church was named in honor of a prophesied redeemer figure—the Red Messiah—believed by its founders to herald the end of days through blood and revelation. Built of crimson-hued stone quarried from the surrounding mountains, the church stood as both sanctuary and warning, its frescoes depicting apocalyptic visions and veiled saints whose eyes seemed to follow the penitent.

For generations, it drew the devout, the desperate, and the dangerously obsessed. But as its teachings drifted further from orthodoxy and local rumors of occult rites spread, the church fell under suspicion. Eventually, during the late nineteenth century, it was abandoned—left to crumble beneath snow and silence.

This long-forgotten mountaintop sanctuary became the historical basis for the fictional Red Messiah Monastery featured in these chapters, reimagined as a hidden refuge cloaked in ancient heresies and prophetic mystery.

CHAPTER 35:
The Prague Codex is fictional.

CHAPTER 36:
Charles University was founded in Prague in 1348 by the Holy Roman Emperor Charles IV. At the time, it was the only institution of higher education in Europe north of the Alps and east of France. Today, it is known as one of the world's oldest universities and is still active.

CHAPTER 43:
There are several small villages nestled in the Swiss Alps. My fictional village of Murcote is a fusion of Murren (population 450) and Morcote (population 750), two

picturesque, but challenging to travel to, villages high in the Alps.

Author's Notes

Dealing with issues of theology, religious beliefs, and the fictional treatment of historical biblical events can be a daunting affair.

I would ask all readers to view this story for what it is —a work of pure fiction, adapted from the seeds of many oral traditions and the historical record, at least as we know it today.

Apart from telling an engaging story, I have no agenda here, and respect those of all beliefs, from Agnosticism to Zoroastrianism and everything in between.

∼

THANK you for reading *The Devil's Symphony*. I hope you enjoyed it and, if you haven't already, suggest you pick up the story in the earlier books of *The Magdalene Chronicles* series, and look forward to forthcoming books featuring the same characters and a few new ones in the continuing *Vatican Secret Archives Thriller* series, and this new *Vatican Archaeology Thriller* series.

WHEN YOU HAVE A MOMENT, **may I ask that you leave a review on Amazon**, Goodreads, Facebook and perhaps elsewhere you find convenient? Reviews are crucial to a book's success, and I hope for all my novel series' to have long and entertaining lives.

· · ·

GARY MCAVOY

IF YOU WOULD LIKE to reach out for any reason, you can email me at gary@garymcavoy.com. If you'd like to learn more about me and my other books, visit my website at garymcavoy.com, where you can also sign up for my private mailing list.

WITH KIND REGARDS,

Gary McAvoy

AUTHOR'S NOTES

Dealing with issues of theology, religious beliefs, and the fictional treatment of historical biblical events can be a daunting affair.

I would ask all readers to view this story for what it is —a work of pure fiction, adapted from the seeds of many oral traditions and the historical record, at least as we know it today.

Apart from telling an engaging story, I have no agenda here, and respect those of all beliefs, from Agnosticism to Zoroastrianism and everything in between.

∾

Thank you for reading *The Devil's Symphony*. I hope you enjoyed it and, if you haven't already, suggest you pick up the story in the earlier books of The Magdalene Chronicles series, and look forward to forthcoming books featuring the same characters and a few new ones in the continuing

AUTHOR'S NOTES

Vatican Secret Archives Thriller series, and this new Vatican Archaeology Thriller series.

When you have a moment, **may I ask that you leave a review on Amazon**, Goodreads, Facebook and perhaps elsewhere you find convenient? Reviews are crucial to a book's success, and I hope for all my novel series' to have long and entertaining lives.

If you would like to reach out for any reason, you can email me at gary@garymcavoy.com. If you'd like to learn more about me and my other books, visit my website at garymcavoy.com, where you can also sign up for my private mailing list.

With kind regards,

Printed in Great Britain
by Amazon